THE BEAUTY SERIES
BOOK THREE

GEORGIA CATES

GEORGIA CATES BOOKS, LLC

Published by Georgia Cates Books, LLC

Copyright © 2014 Georgia Cates

All rights reserved.

This is a work of fiction. Names, characters, places, brands, media and incidents are either the product of the author's imagination or are used fictitiously. The author acknowledges the trademarked status and trademark owners of various products referenced in this work of fiction, which have been used without permission. The publication/use of these trademarks is not authorized, associated with, or sponsored by the trademark owners.

Sign-up for Georgia's newsletter at www.georgiacates.com. Get the latest news, first look at teasers, and giveaways just for subscribers.

Interior Formatting by Indie Formatting Services

Editing Services provided by Jennifer Sommersby Young

Photograph by Brett Jackman, Polar Impressions Photography

ISBN-13: 978-1496177070 (CreateSpace-Assigned)

ISBN-10: 149617707X

*For Grandma Dale, the inspiration behind Margaret McLachlan.
I miss you.*

"Soul meets soul on lovers lips."

—Percy Bysshe Shelley

CHAPTER ONE
LAURELYN MCLACHLAN

THIS IS AN UNPRECEDENTED MOMENT. I'M AWAKE BEFORE JACK HENRY, studying his sleeping figure—it's a fine one—but that's not what makes this morning a new experience. I'm waking next to him as my husband.

Wow. I did it. I married a man who propositioned me a year ago, asking me to be his companion for three months. His idea of our pairing deciphered into something much different back then—an offer of noncommittal sex in exchange for the time of my life. Translation? I agreed to be his whore. There, I admit it, and it was the best decision I've ever made regardless of what kind of label we place upon it. Now he's my husband—forever mine—and I couldn't be happier.

No number fourteen for him. Ever.

We began as strangers—as most couples do—but our beginning was so much more complicated. That simple word makes me giggle each time I hear or say it now. There's never a time I don't recall the freakish control my husband displayed when he told me he was a man who didn't do complicated. Damn, was he ever wrong. I turned his world on its head. To know I hold that power over him makes me feel invincible. And adored.

Some would consider our inception into this whirlwind a perverted one. Even I did in the beginning, but then we became so much more than either of us intended. Now we're Mr. and Mrs. Jack Henry McLachlan and this is the beginning of the rest of our lives. We're setting out into the world to write our own story—in stone, never sand.

I look at my husband's face and see his eyes flutter beneath his lids, a clear indication he's dreaming, and I wonder what a man like him sees when he's in the deepest of sleep. Whatever it is, I don't want to disrupt it so I slide to the edge of the bed in slow motion and place my feet on the floor of the plane's bedroom suite. I look over my shoulder to make sure I haven't disturbed his slumber—and he's unmoving—so I ease from the bed with the agility of a thief in the night.

When I'm finished in the bathroom, I return to bed and repeat the same motion in reverse. I'm so pleased with myself because I've managed to slip into bed next to Jack Henry without waking him. But then I realize I'm basking in my accomplishment prematurely. He suddenly rises, pinning me beneath him, a huge grin wide across his face.

"Mornin'." He lowers his mouth to mine and kisses me as his grin grows larger, a sweet kiss just on the surface of my lips. "My wife." He places his forehead against mine. "You know… I think I like the sound of that."

"You better love the sound of it."

"Hmm. Maybe it'll grow on me with a little time."

I push against Jack Henry's chest and we roll so I'm on top. "And maybe you'll grow on me." I lower my mouth to his as close as possible without our lips touching. "If I try really, really hard."

I move my knees on each side of his hips and slowly grind against him. His hands creep up my thighs until they're on my waist. "I think something may already be growing on you. Really, really hard."

"You and that mouth of yours, Mr. McLachlan."

"You love this mouth of mine, Mrs. McLachlan, along with everything it does to you." He's told me that before.

He slides his hands up the sides of my bare body and then quickly turns us so I'm on my back again. His mouth begins a journey at my neck and leaves a trail of wet kisses on its way down until reaching my belly button. "And this tongue of mine. Don't forget how much you love what it does to you as well."

He dips it inside my navel and I lace my fingers through his hair before dragging my nails across his scalp. "I could never forget about your highly talented tongue. Or how good it made me feel last night."

He looks up at me and beams. "Our wedding night was everything you hoped it would be?"

I can't believe he thinks he has to ask. "It was perfect—everything I dreamed plus a whole lot more I couldn't have possibly imagined. I didn't know I could be so happy."

"Last night exceeded my every expectation." He laces his fingers together and places them on my belly before propping his chin on top. "It was the same physical act we've shared countless times but I never imagined it feeling so different as husband and wife." I run my fingers through his hair again but I'm speechless. I think he's waiting for me to respond but I can't because my heart feels like it might explode from the love I have for this man. "Come on, L. You're making me feel pretty damn sappy since you aren't saying anything."

I beckon for him to come closer and caress his cheeks once we're eye to eye. "You're right. It was a level of intimacy we've never shared and I couldn't feel more connected to you."

He tucks each side of my hair behind my ears before pressing his forehead to mine. "You are my world and I'll do anything to make you happy."

"You. That's all it takes to make me smile."

He nuzzles against my neck and I feel the freshly grown scruff on his chin. "Your face was smooth at the wedding yesterday. I can't believe you already have this much growth."

He reaches up and strokes his chin with his hand. "Is it too rough for you?"

"No. I like you with stubble. It's sexy. I wouldn't mind you growing it a little."

"But just a very light beard, right? Nothing heavy like I had several months ago?"

I've never seen him with heavy growth. "I didn't know you grew a beard."

"I fell into a depression and sort of let myself go for a while when a certain unnamed young lady left me without a word."

He isn't the only one who was in a bad place. "I was depressed too but I didn't grow a beard. I took the highlights out of my hair—the lighter streaks didn't seem to go with the darkness I felt."

"When my beard grew out, I found highlights." He points to his temples. "And several here on each side."

I grab his face and turn it to the side for a better look. "Really?"

"Yeah. Gray ones," he laughs. "Are you really oblivious to the fact that you just married an old man?"

I turn his face back so he's looking at me. "You're thirty. That's not old. Got it?"

He playfully rubs his nose against mine, giving me an Eskimo kiss. "Your disappearance put me through hell so I blame you for giving me my first gray hairs."

He rubs his nose up the length of my neck. "Does that mean you won't get any more since I'm never leaving again? Even if you toss me out on my keister?"

"Sorry. I'm afraid it's inevitable. I got my hair from Dad and he was mostly salt with little pepper by forty-five. That doesn't leave you many years with a youthful-looking husband."

I'm imagining Jack Henry with gray hair in place of his near black. I'm certain he's going to be like Richard Gere and only get better looking with age. "So when people see us together ten years from now, they'll think I'm some sweet young thing on the arm of my sugar daddy?"

He's laughing. "No, they'll see our swarm of mini-Laurelyns buzzing around us and know I was smart enough to make you mine while I was still young and had a chance with you."

"Exactly how many children are in a swarm?"

His lips next to my ear, he whispers, "Several."

I won't be distracted by the stir his nearness causes in my groin. "'Several' is a number that may vary quite a bit depending on who you're talking to."

His fingers lace through the nape of my hair and his thumb rubs that spot below my ear. "You once told me you saw yourself with three."

"Three is a few—which isn't several."

"I know but I'd like to talk you into more." He runs his nose down the length of my neck again and I feel his warm breath on my skin. He knows how much that turns me on. "And I'd like to persuade you into starting on the first one right now."

He didn't want a wife or children when we met. Somewhere in the theory of my future, I wanted a husband—which I now have—but I'd like to wait on the children. I want to enjoy us before a baby is added to the mix. "Why are you so anxious? We haven't been married a full day yet. Don't you want time for the two of us?" He rolls onto his back and stares at the ceiling. "What's going on with you and this rush to start having babies right away?"

He sighs and turns onto his side so we're facing one another. "Dad's side of the family has a significant history of heart disease and heart attacks. He's fifty-five and has already had his first episode. His brother wasn't fifty when he had his first heart attack. I'm afraid that'll be me in twenty years, so I feel like waiting to start our family is wasting time I could be spending with our children while I'm still young and healthy."

This is the reason he hoped I was pregnant. He's afraid of dying young. I had no idea he had this fear bottled inside him. "You don't know that you'll have those kinds of problems."

"You don't know that I won't." He reaches for the back of my neck and pulls my face to his. "Promise me you'll think about it."

This beautiful man wants to create a life with me—little people that look like us. Isn't that what he once told me he saw when he imagined his future with me? I want him to have everything his heart desires—and this is something only I can give him—so how can I not consider it? "I'll think about it. Promise."

"Thank you." He kisses my mouth so lovingly. It isn't urgent as many of our kisses are. It's sweet, and he makes me feel so beloved. "I love you so much, L."

"And I love you but I need you to promise me you'll share these fears and concerns. I'm your wife and I want to know everything. Your hopes. Your dreams. And especially your fears." He needs to see he shouldn't keep these things from me.

He touches his finger to the tip of my nose. "You. You're what my hopes and dreams are made of."

I pull him back on top of me. "You know exactly what to say to get into a girl's panties."

He runs his hands over each of my bare hips. "I think you'd need to be wearing knickers in order for me to get into them but you're not, Mrs. McLachlan."

"Oops." I cover my mouth with my fingers. "You're right. Mr. McLachlan took them off hours ago."

"You never put them back on and now you're under me, completely naked."

I bring my legs up and squeeze him closer. "For good reason. Easier access."

He rubs the back of my thighs, squeezing them. "Easier access. I like that. You should go without knickers all the time."

"Maybe I will."

Jack Henry possesses my mouth as I lower my hands down his back until I have two handfuls of his perfect ass. "I love your… bum."

He moves from my mouth to the side of my face and then on to that special place below my ear. "My bum, huh?" His voice is a breathy whisper. "Is my Yank wife turning Aussie so soon?"

"Maybe." His mouth creeps down my neck. "Probably. I see no reason to fight it since I'm here to stay."

I feel a sudden drop in the plane's altitude. Jack Henry lifts his face to look at me but he doesn't appear alarmed. "I think we're descending." He leans over to take his phone from the bedside table. "Dammit. The flight is right on time."

A pilot's voice comes over the overhead speaker. "We're beginning our descent into Maui so our flight will be landing as scheduled in approximately fifteen minutes. It's been a pleasure serving you, Mr. and Mrs. McLachlan. Looks like you'll be having beautiful weather for the duration of your honeymoon. Maui is currently seventy degrees and sunny with a high of eighty-three later today."

I make my pouty face. "Only fifteen minutes."

"I know. It's not enough time for me to do what I want to you. And we still have to get dressed and be in our seats for the landing." He gives me one last kiss. "We'll have plenty of time to do everything we want once we're on the ground. We're here as long as we want to be."

He kisses me chastely and gets up. He's naked, his back to me as he stands, searching through the suitcase for a change of clothes. I take a few seconds to admire his physique. He's so beautiful. And all mine.

I get up and walk over to grab something to wear. I opt for the first outfit I find since the clock is ticking. A strappy floral sundress with a fuchsia cardigan packed right on the top. It should look lovely with the lei I'll be given when we land.

We're dressed with clean faces and freshly brushed teeth when we buckle into our seats. We have maybe one whole minute to spare, but I plan on indulging in a long, hot bath—hopefully with Jack Henry joining me—once we arrive at our hotel. I hope our suite has a huge shower to accommodate both of us because I have lots of naughty things I want to do to him.

He holds my hand as the plane touches down and I'm immediately relieved. I grew a little more accustomed to flying while touring with Southern Ophelia but I'm still happier when my feet are on solid ground. "Have you visited Hawaii often?"

"Yes. Quite a few times." He brings my hand to his lips and kisses my knuckles. "I'm glad your first time is with me."

I wonder what brought him to Hawaii. A family trip, perhaps? Maybe business. Or possibly pleasure with a companion. A pang of jealousy strikes within. I wish I wasn't on my honeymoon thinking of such things but I'm curious by nature. "How many times have you visited?"

He answers immediately, "A lot. I couldn't even take a guess at a number. Dad spent the year working like crazy but he'd take off for two weeks after harvest season so we could come here. It's my mum's favorite getaway so she'd bring us even when Dad was too busy to come. We always stayed at the same house—it felt like my second childhood home."

"So you were always with your family?"

"No. I came once without them."

"You came alone or with a friend?" I shouldn't ask since I might get an answer I won't like.

"Friends." Plural. What does that mean? Friends, like the ones everyone has or the kind of friends only he has? I mean had.

He's laughing but I'm not. "Friends?"

"Well, I guess drunken college buddies is probably a more accurate description of the company I kept the time I came without my family."

Oh—that I can handle. "You and your pals came here to party?"

"Yeah, but only once during break. The guys wrecked the place and the owner was furious. The damage wasn't minimal. Mum paid for it but threatened to beat me within an inch of my life if it ever happened again." He's grinning. "I knew she wasn't kidding so I never brought them back."

"I bet Margaret wanted to beat your ass."

"There was definitely some smacking with a purse. She loves to do that. She knows it doesn't hurt but it sounds like it does so she enjoys it. And it's dramatic. She did that to me in front of my mates. God, I was humiliated. But of course, that's why she did it." I'm laughing as I imagine my mother-in-law clobbering her college-age son with her handbag in front of his friends. "Have you seen her in action? She should've been a professional boxer. She can get at least three good licks in before your brain has time to register that you're being smacked."

I love Margaret so much. She's going to be the best mother-in-law I could ever wish for. I could stand to learn a thing or two from her. "I'm going to have her teach me her moves."

"Baby, please don't. I can't take any more unnecessary roughness. Unless you want to get unruly with me in the bedroom." He leans over to kiss the side of my neck and my skin instantly prickles while something stirs deep within my belly. He loves doing that to me.

"Down, boy. We're not at the hotel yet." He leans back and I can tell he's fighting a grin. "What? Are you up to something, Mr. McLachlan?"

"Maybe, but it's a surprise, Mrs. McLachlan. One I can't wait to show you."

❦

THE CAR STOPS ONLY MOMENTS BEFORE JACK HENRY'S WARM HAND SQUEEZES mine gently. I recognize the sound of an opening car door. I'm guessing the driver is probably waiting for us to get out. "Can you see anything through your blindfold?"

That's right. My husband has blindfolded me in the car, not the bedroom.

"No. Not a thing." And I can't. All I see is total blackness and it's disorienting. But not as much as what we're doing now. It's becoming more and more evident that we aren't at a hotel. This is something entirely different.

I feel him slide across the seat away from me as he tugs on my hand. "This way, love."

I step out of the car and hear waves in the distance as I breathe in the salty air. We're at the beach and I'm confused. I don't understand why he'd bring me here directly from the airport instead of checking into our room so we could take a hot shower after our long flight. It's too early to swim. And I'm in a sundress, not a swimsuit.

These are the thoughts of a nagging wife so I hastily put them away. What do I have to complain about? I'm married to the man of my dreams and he treats me like a queen. I could do much, much worse.

"Walk this way." I take a few baby steps in the direction he's pulling me. I can't see but it feels like he's walking backward as he holds both of my hands. "Don't be afraid, L. I won't let you fall. Ever."

I don't doubt him for a moment. "I trust that you won't, but I have an innate instinct telling me I will so it's hard to ignore."

"Not much further."

It's not sand I'm walking on. It feels firm, like concrete or asphalt, but I take about twenty more steps before we stop. "I'm taking your blindfold off but I want you to keep your eyes closed until I tell you to open them."

"Okay."

He removes my blinder and the sun shines directly on my face. I feel its warmth against my skin and see its brightness on the other side of my closed lids. "You can open them."

The breeze from the ocean blows a strand of hair into my face and lodges itself in the slit of one my eyes. I shake my head to make my hair fall over one shoulder. When I straighten, I look before me and see a magnificent beachfront home.

I wait for him to say something—give me an idea about what we're doing here—but he doesn't. "Is this where we're staying?"

"Yes." He's beaming, appearing so proud of himself. Maybe he's pleased he has pulled one over on me because he has. I completely expected a honeymoon suite in one of Maui's finest hotels but this is so much better. "Do you like it?"

Now I'm the one grinning like the Cheshire cat because I know this means we don't have to be quiet. We can lose control without the fear of being heard by others. "Are you kidding me? It's breathtaking. Who wouldn't love it?" I wrap my arms around him and squeeze his middle. "This is going to be so much better than a hotel."

"This is it—the house I was telling you about. My vacation home as a child."

Oh my. I can't believe he brought me to the place he thought of as his second home while growing up. "Oh, Jack Henry."

"It wasn't possible for me to come to Maui with my bride and not stay here."

He would've been so limited on time when planning our honeymoon. I can't believe a place like this would have a vacancy. "Then we're incredibly lucky it was available for rent on such short notice."

He beams before turning me so I'm facing the house. Behind me, he snakes his arms around my waist and pulls me tight against him, his mouth next to my ear. "I own it, L. I bought it for you. It's your wedding gift." I turn my face toward him and his stubble grazes me. "I want to spend the rest of our lives making happy memories here with you and our children."

Omigod. Best. Husband. Ever.

CHAPTER TWO
JACK MCLACHLAN

I ONCE THOUGHT I DIDN'T WANT A WIFE AND KIDS BUT IT WAS BECAUSE I hadn't met the right person. Everything is different now—I'm married to the perfect woman and I can't wait until she becomes the mother of my children.

I'm glad L asked me why I was anxious to begin our family. I'm not sure I would've ever been brave enough to volunteer that information. Fear. It's not something a man likes to admit but that's the beauty of my relationship with L. I can tell her anything.

She turns in my arms and kisses me between words. "You. Are. Amazing."

"I'm glad you think so since it seems you're stuck with me for the rest of our lives."

"Happily stuck by choice. There's a difference."

I watch the sun dance on her face as the palm tree leaves above move in the breeze. A shorter strand of hair at her temple has escaped her grasp and I tuck it behind her ear. "Are you truly happy?"

"It isn't possible for me to be happier than I am in this moment."

I grasp her face and look into her golden-brown eyes. I see her sincerity and know her words are true. She didn't marry me for any reason other than her love for me, so Laurelyn Paige Prescott McLachlan is a woman to be treasured. "Nor could I."

I lean down to scoop her from the ground and she squeals. "I think it's time I carried my bride across the threshold. I want you to see the rest of the house."

I turn the knob and gently push the door open with my foot. L is like a wide-eyed child. I return her to her feet and her head oscillates slowly as she takes it all in.

The floor plan is open so she's able to see the living room along with the kitchen and dining room. She says nothing and I can't tell if she likes it or not. "What are you thinking?"

"How much I love you," she says, propelling herself into my arms for a kiss. "You take care of me," she says against my mouth. "No one's ever done that before."

It's a shame. She should've been cared for by loving parents. But she wasn't, and it's shaped her into the person she is today. I don't know how she's not utterly damaged but she's the complete opposite—the strongest person I know. I wonder who she would've been if they'd treated her the way they should have.

I give her a quick kiss and take her hand. "Come. I want to show you the rest."

I begin with the five smaller bedrooms and work our way toward the master suite. I ask her to close her eyes. I cover them with one hand and use the other to lead her into the center of the room. I like this grown-up game of peekaboo. "No peeping."

"I'm not. And I don't have X-ray vision so I can't see through flesh and bone."

"True." I take my hand away once she's facing the bed. "Okay. Open your eyes."

She softly gasps as she scans the room—our newly remodeled master suite. "I was only able to have this room and one other remodeled since the purchase was so rushed. Do you like it?"

"I love it. I couldn't have chosen anything more perfect." She turns in my arms and slides her hands up to my shoulders. "Or sexier."

This is my first time seeing it as well and I'm pleased with the results, although it's very different from our bedroom at Avalon. This is a lot girlier, yet not emasculating.

It's lighter. The walls are pale beige, almost white. It's going to reflect the morning sun even with the drapes pulled, so I doubt there'll be much sleeping late in here. I don't mind because I'm an early riser, but it could be a problem for L. She loves her sleep.

There's fabric and upholstery everywhere. Coordinated shades of pale blue, beige, and cream dominate; plenty of candles wait to be lit. It smells heavenly—much like the red currant L loves so much. I don't have to work hard to imagine what this bedroom suite will look like lit up tonight or how beautiful L will look illuminated by candlelight.

I'm so glad she approves. "I think the designer did a great job. I gave her full control. The only requirement was that she make it romantic."

"Mission accomplished." L walks toward the bed and runs her hand down the post. I wonder if she thinks I made a special request for that. I didn't, but I admit it's a very nice surprise. "This is absolutely amazing. Makes me want to stay in bed all day—with you."

"Then I believe I owe Miss Rutledge a bonus for a job well done." I take her hand and lead her toward the small sitting room currently occupied by a chaise with a side table. It's not a huge area but it'll suffice for what I have in mind. "I was thinking this would make a perfect nursery. It isn't big but I think it'll hold a crib and changing table. Maybe a rocking chair in the corner."

She's quiet as she looks around the room and I fear I may have pushed her too hard, too soon. That's not my intention at all. I don't mean to press her. It's only been an hour since our conversation—and she told me she'd think about trying to have a baby—so I need to back off before I anger her.

"I'm sorry. I didn't think of how that sounded until I heard myself saying it." I pull her into my arms and kiss the top of her head. "I'm sure I've bombarded you with the baby-making talk but I promise I'm not ignoring your need to think it over."

"It's okay. You're being honest with me about what you want and the reason why. I could never be upset with you about yearning to start a family with me." She twists in my arms so we're facing one another.

"The baby-making part doesn't scare me. We've had a lot of fun practicing, but I worry about the after part. We've had so little time together."

An hour isn't even close to long enough. She needs way more time to sort this out. "I think it's a good idea to put the baby talk on the back burner for now."

"Agreed."

I kiss the side of her face. "I have something else to show you."

We walk the hall toward the other remodeled room. "This is a vacation home and it often houses two families, so it has two master suites."

"Another romantic getaway?"

I laugh inwardly. "Not exactly." I grasp the knob. "Close your eyes."

"This is becoming a habit for you." She does as I tell her so I open the door and lead her into the second master suite. "You can open your eyes now."

Her eyes are wide as she assesses her surroundings. Mirrored walls. Overhead lights. A stage. A pole.

She's grinning so I take that as a good sign. She walks up the steps onto the stage and runs her hand up the golden brass. "Wow. This room is a little presumptuous on your part, Mr. McLachlan. One might assume you have an obsession with pole dancers."

She has no idea.

I join her on the stage and place my hands on her hips, pushing her backward until she's pressed against the brass extending from floor to ceiling. "I have an obsession with one."

She reaches for the button of my jeans and pulls it free. She looks down—and so do I—to watch her skillful fingers push the zipper of my pants down. Then her hands are inside the waistband of my boxer briefs, shoving them down. "I may have my own obsession." And like a scene worthy of any man's sexual fantasy, L drops to her knees before me.

Oh God. My wife is so smokin' hot. How did I get so lucky?

She looks up at me from her knees, the same way she's done countless times before, and it couldn't be sexier. Until I see her tongue stroke me from base to tip. I want to close my eyes and become totally lost but I can't stop watching her mouth on me. It's too fucking hot.

She goes through a series of motions. Fast. Slow. Soft. Hard. I can't predict what's coming next and I fucking love it.

She's at it no more than a minute and I'm almost ready to come because she's too damn good at this, but her mouth isn't where I want to come. I tap the top of her head. "Stop, L."

She does and I help my wife to her feet. My hands go fishing beneath her dress where I grasp her almost nonexistent knickers and drag them down her legs. She steps out one foot at a time and kicks the two white lacy triangles aside. She sheds her cardigan and pulls her dress over her head before chucking it across the stage. She's left wearing only her bra and heels, though not for long. The bra is going, but not the heels. Those stay.

I step back and behold the lovely sight of my bride. Laurelyn is absolutely the most beautiful woman I've ever seen. I can't believe I get to call her mine forever. I'm a fortunate man.

She gives me a come-hither motion with her finger and I obey. I have no choice because I'm hers to do with as she pleases. This woman owns me completely. "Inside me. Now."

She reaches over her head and grasps the pole tightly. She lifts her lower body to wrap her legs around me and I understand the position she has in mind. My girl is strong. Most women don't possess the physical strength it takes to do the things she's capable of on a pole. "This is new. I like it."

She frees one hand and pulls my face to hers for an urgent kiss, and I'm again made aware of the physical power she possesses. "Wrong. You're gonna love it," she whispers as she sinks down, pushing me deep inside her.

I groan with pleasure and grasp her bum so I can move with her in perfect rhythm. I thrust hard and she matches me evenly. My girl does me fucking proud but it doesn't last near as long as I'd like. She brought me close to the edge using her mouth so I'm ahead of her. I know I am. She gave me a huge head start so I slow down—I'm not crossing the finish line without her.

I bring my fingers around to her most sensitive spot. I rub it in no particular order, the way she did when she went down on me. Fast. Slow. Soft. Hard. And I know when her breathing picks up that she's close. And then it's over for me as I explode inside her. "I. Love. You. L."

I'm buried deep inside her and she has no reply for me, but I know why. I feel the ripple of her body tightening around my cock and know she's too preoccupied with her own climax to respond.

When it's over for her, she lets go of the pole and wraps both arms around my shoulders. "I love you too," she says, kissing my mouth. She holds on tightly, trembling. I'm guessing it's overuse of her muscles since she hasn't had a workout like that in a while. "I think I'm a wee bit out of practice. I'll be feeling the results of that little trick all week."

I don't want her sore on our honeymoon. There's way too much I want to do with her.

"You should take a soak in the tub. It'll help relax your muscles and then I'll give you a massage when you're out."

She looks up at me so adoringly and stretches on her toes to nuzzle my nose. She isn't tall enough so I lean down and meet her halfway. "Mmm. I was right. You're definitely the best husband ever."

"I'm just getting started, babe. You haven't seen anything yet."

I carry her to the bath—not because I don't trust her legs—but because I want to. I set her down and make her sit on the vanity stool. She laughs and says I'm being ridiculous but I don't care. I can never overdo it when it comes to her comfort.

I turn on the water and the room quickly becomes a sauna. "Check the water to be sure it's not too hot for you."

She gets up and walks over to the tub to dip her fingers under the stream. "Perfect." She slips off her heels, which managed to stay on during the transport here, and she's instantly at least three inches shorter. "Will you soak with me? I wasn't the only one exerting my body."

I had planned on checking in at the vineyards while she soaked but how could I possibly decline an invitation like that? "Absolutely, but let me get your body wash and shampoo first."

I return with her bath supplies and shed my pants, which somehow didn't manage to get removed during our sexual escapade. We step into the tub together. I sit first, per our routine, and then L lowers herself gracefully as ever into her usual spot between my legs so she can lean back against my chest. I revel in the simple feel of my beloved's skin against mine.

This is how life should be. No more emptiness in three-month affairs with women I don't care to know. I can't believe I once found—whatever the right word is—in what I used to do. It certainly wasn't happiness or fulfillment. I don't have a label for it. L is my everything and there's no going back. I wouldn't have it any other way.

I run my hands along her hips, massaging them under the water. I feel something stuck to one of them. It feels like a sticker and the corner pulls up more and more as I rub so I give it a yank.

She gasps and I immediately know I've done wrong. "Jack Henry!"

Oh hell. I think I'm in trouble. "Should I have not done that?"

"No. You shouldn't have."

"I'm sorry, L." I hold up the flesh-colored square and she goes pale. "I thought it was some kind of sticker accidentally stuck on your bum. What is this?"

"It was my birth control patch."

"Oh." She's going to think I took it off on purpose because of the baby talk. She's probably going to be pissed off at me the rest of our honeymoon—or cut me off so she won't get pregnant. Shit. "I didn't know. I swear. Do you have another one to put on?" I move to get out of the tub. "I'll get it for you right now."

She stops me by grabbing my hand. "I have one left but it's for next week. I'll be short one week of hormones so that's probably as good as not wearing one at all."

"Please don't be mad. It was a stupid move but I didn't know."

She relaxes against me again and I breathe a sigh of relief. "It's okay. I told you I started new birth control so I'm sure you assumed it was the pill. I guess I should've told you what kind so we'd be on the same page."

I didn't know the ramifications of my actions but it doesn't stop me from feeling as though I've wronged her. "I told you I refused to wear condoms on our honeymoon but I will. I deserve that for being stupid enough to yank off that patch without asking what it was first."

"Baby, it's okay. You don't have to do that. Rubbers aren't fun for you or me. I used a spermicide as backup last night. We'll just use that the next couple of weeks and I'll restart the patch next month. I hadn't been on it long anyway."

I'm lucky. She could seriously be giving me shit right now. "Thank you for not being angry with me."

"There's nothing to be angry about, McLachlan."

"You say that now but what will your feelings be if you end up with a bun in the oven because I ripped that thing off your arse?"

She leans her head back and tilts her face to kiss my chin. "I would think it takes two to tango and it's meant to be."

CHAPTER THREE
LAURELYN MCLACHLAN

I'M CONFUSED. I'VE ALWAYS ASSOCIATED DARK SAND WITH UNATTRACTIVENESS but this isn't. It's… breathtaking. "Black sand." I hear the surprise in my own voice. "This isn't at all what I expected to see on a Hawaiian beach."

Jack Henry laughs at me, apparently entertained by my astonishment. "It's another reason I love this place so much. It's different from the beach at my Auckland house. Polar opposites."

I rake my toes through it. "Had I known it was black, I wouldn't have expected much so I'm glad you didn't mention it."

He prepares my lounger, spreading a towel across the cushion. "The lava of an erupting volcano rushes into the ocean and it cools when it hits the water. The waves force it back onto the beach and that's why the sand is black."

I sit on the chair. "My husband, the environmental scientist. Who knew?"

Jack Henry repeats the same process on the second lounger and then joins me. He's wearing my favorite sunglasses and I can see my reflection when he looks my way. "So this little piece of heaven is your private beach?"

"It's our private beach, Laurelyn. Everything of mine is now yours. You're going to need to get used to that."

I unfasten the back of my bikini top and allow it to drop. "Then it's okay for me to do this?"

"Damn, L," he laughs while scanning the property for prying eyes. "It's ours, and it's private, but that doesn't stop the occasional beachgoer from stumbling across here."

"Well, I guess they'll think they've happened upon a topless beach." I toss my bright red top over and it lands on Jack Henry's chest. "Because I'm not putting it back on."

"Damn rebel."

"Damn right."

I lie on the lounger, basking in the sun. I love the outdoors; it's still the only place where I feel completely free. As a child, going outside was my only escape from her. My mom was always hungover—except when she was high—so the house was forever dark, dreary, and cold. I wasn't allowed to open the curtains for sunlight. The brightness hurt her eyes and prevented her from sleeping all day so she could party all night. Lifting a window for fresh air was out of the question since it allowed her precious, frigid air conditioning to escape.

Those were bad days. Bad years. I don't want to think about those times and ruin this perfect moment. The weather is beautiful and I'm soaking in the sunshine. I have my man by my side; therefore, I want for nothing. Everything in the world is right.

"You're doing some serious thinking over there."

How can he possibly tell? I turn to look at him. "How do you know?"

He points toward my thigh. "You're tracing the infinity symbol on your leg with your fingertip. It gives you away every time."

I didn't realize I was doing that, but he did. He always does.

"What's on your mind, babe?"

Do I brush the thoughts of my childhood away, keeping it to myself so I don't ruin this perfection? Or do I put it out there so Jack Henry can know a little more about the wretched past that makes me who I am today?

He already dislikes my mom. I'm certain this will only add fuel to his contempt—but he's straight up asking, so it doesn't feel right to keep it from him. "When I was a kid, the outdoors was one of my only escapes from my mom when she was high or hungover. I feel my freest when I'm in the sun." He doesn't reply and I'm pretty sure it's because he's fuming. "I'm sorry. I shouldn't have said anything. I've ruined this beautiful moment."

Our loungers are side by side, close enough that my hand is within his reach. "You haven't ruined anything." He strokes his thumb across the top of my hand and it finds its way to my wedding ring. "I'm your husband so I want to know everything. The good and the bad."

Most of the good has happened since I met him but what about the ugly? Is he really ready to hear that stuff?

"I want to ask you a question about the wedding."

Sounds like he's preparing me for something bad. He never tells me he's going to ask a question. "Okay."

"Why did you let your dad walk you down the aisle? He's never been a father to you so I don't understand how you felt like he deserved that honor." His voice is oozing with contempt for the sperm donor.

I didn't wimp out, if that's what Jack Henry thinks. I'm done with flaking. There's only one reason I allowed Jake to do it. Irony. "Think about it. He claims me as his daughter and his first official act as my father is to give me over to you—a strong, honorable man who will always take care of me. I thought it was quite fitting."

"Huh," he says. "I was worried your mother guilted you into doing it but I should've known better. That's not who you are."

"She thinks she convinced me. I choose to let her believe that but I have the pleasure of knowing otherwise."

"My wife, the satirist. I'll know better than to ever cross you."

"You will if you know what's good for you."

"I'm not mistaken about what's good for me. It's you, L. Always you."

Oh, sheez. Hearing him say that almost makes my bikini bottom melt away.

I get up and take his hands. "You think I'm good for you, huh?" I pull so he knows I want him to slide to the foot of the lounger.

"I know so. No doubts."

I grin as I push my thumbs inside the band of my swimsuit and shimmy out of it. "I know something else that's good for you."

I kick out of the red fabric at my ankles and step closer to Jack Henry.

He grabs my ass and I squeal as he pulls me closer. He watches my face as he slides his hand between my legs. "And I also know what's good for you."

He rubs his hand up and down, back and forth, in an exquisite torture, before gliding his fingers through my slick center. Yet I know what he's doing when he avoids my most sensitive area, the spot where I crave his touch most. It's purposeful on his part because he wants to feel me ride his hand. And I give in because I have no choice.

I grab his wrist and guide his hand upward while rocking my hips against it. I'm worse than any petted cat. And I'm pretty sure he loves it. "More," I plead.

He crooks his thumb and rewards me by stroking my clit. "My girl is greedy."

He has no idea.

My head is spinning because I want him so much. "I want you inside me when I come," I tell him while reaching for his swim trunks. He makes no haste in helping me get them down and then I crawl over him. I sink down hard so he's deep inside me and he returns his hand to its previous task. "Is this what you want?"

He knows it is. "Yes!"

I move up and down, sliding him in and out, gaining unrestrained pleasure as his hand rubs my clit. I arch my back and thrust my breasts forward as I hold his shoulders. "I want to feel you come all around me, L."

And I do.

I feel those familiar quivers squeezing Jack Henry while he's inside me. Seconds later, I recognize the telltale rhythmic quivering and know he's met his undoing before I ever hear him groan my name.

Nothing beats both of us coming at the same time.

He grabs my face and kisses me hard. When he finishes, he presses his forehead against mine. I think he loves doing that. I know I do because it makes me feel so adored. "You and I are going to have an amazing life together. I'm going to make certain of it."

"I know." And I do. There's not a bit of doubt in my mind. "Wanna go skinny-dippin'?"

boys and a toddler girl—fill our table to capacity. I have spent much less time around children than Jack Henry but even I know this is going to be entertaining.

His eyes immediately hone in on this picture-perfect family and he slips his arm around me. He gives my arm a slight squeeze and I'm pretty sure I can accurately guess what he's thinking—that'll be us one day. And it will be. It's not a question of if, but when.

"Hello," the couple says in unison as they assist their children into their seats.

"Hello." We mimic their greeting.

The wife settles the baby girl into a high chair. "We didn't realize we'd be seated with anyone but we'll try to keep the circus to a minimum. Won't we, boys?"

The boys do a fair job of ignoring their mother so I take that as a bad sign and a likely indicator of the free show to come.

"It's okay. We're used to kids." Jack Henry looks at me and shrugs. It's a half-truth because he's very used to children. Me... not so much.

"You must have left yours at home?" the husband asks.

"No. We don't have children yet. We're here on our honeymoon."

"Then congratulations are in order."

"Thank you."

We continue the small talk with the couple briefly before the server brings our first round of mai tais. "Wow. That's beautiful." It's a tall, stemmed glass curved in the center, the dark rum collecting in the bottom. Each is garnished with a tiny umbrella, pineapple slices, and cherries with a lovely purple orchid next to a sprig of mint leaf. I can smell the liquor as soon as it's placed in front of me. I'll need to show restraint so I don't get wasted.

"I must admit I don't feel very masculine with such a pretty drink in my hand." Jack Henry holds his glass toward mine for a toast. "Here's to us and a very long and happy life together."

I touch my glass to his. "Thank you for making me your wife." I lean over and a place a kiss against his lips.

"Yuck! That's so gross. I may throw up." I hear gagging noises from one of the boys across the table, followed by a chastisement and apology from his mother.

I silently pray this isn't what we have to look forward to during the entire dinner but I soon discover it's only the beginning. The boys' antics alternate between booger picking, booger eating, making fart sounds—some, I question the authenticity of—a stunning display of controlled chaos.

Jack Henry squeezes my hand as he leans over to whisper in my ear. "They're little boys trying to get the attention of my pretty girl. Ignore them or it'll get worse. Trust me."

He knows children. I don't so I take his advice. The night seems to take a turn for the better once I no longer appear preoccupied by the mischievous boys. And the fire-knife show holds their attention, preventing any further performance out of them.

I'm in the midst of clapping for the fire-breather when one of the performers comes into the audience and grabs my hand to take me on stage. I'm surprised because I didn't see it coming but I should've known. Shows like these always select people from the crowd to participate in the performance.

I turn to look back at Jack Henry and see him grinning and clapping as I walk away from the table. He probably volunteered me and paid them to put me in a string bikini so I could dance on stage for him. Horny bastard. I'll get him for this if I find out he's behind it.

I'm quickly given directions about my performance while shoved behind a divider to change into an orange bandeau top and green hula skirt. I come out and costume designers surround me—and the others pulled from the audience—to place flowers around our heads and ankles. I'm handed two feathered rattles. "The girls will demonstrate the motions. There will be a series of hand, hip, and foot motions. They'll introduce them slowly, one at a time—nothing complicated. All you have to do is mimic what they show you."

My man is so gonna love this.

CHAPTER FOUR
JACK MCLACHLAN

I watch the show with much enthusiasm but not because of a particularly spectacular performance. I've attended countless luaus. Although this one is quite good, it's L's performance I'm anxious to watch.

The audience members are led onto stage and L is the last one. That places her right in front of our table.

The people range in age from young children to, well, old as dirt. She's definitely the hottest one in the bunch. I'd say that about her even if she weren't my wife.

The hula dancers position themselves in front of the audience participants and demonstrate the first motion with their hands. Laurelyn mimics it slowly. Gracefully. Perfectly. They incorporate the hips next and I'm mesmerized by the way her body moves. I think she's better than her demonstrators. The foot motion is last but I'm already lost in her sensual motions when she peeks over her shoulder at me as she turns. Her body language is unmistakable. She's gonna let me fuck her ever how I choose.

My wife is hotter than hell. Every man—and woman—here knows it, including this guy with the wife and four-point-five kids sitting across from me. He's rarely taken his eyes off Laurelyn since the moment they were seated at the table. Surely, his wife has noticed, or maybe she hasn't since he completely turned the childrearing over to her so he could ogle my wife's tits.

This guy is blatantly staring and it is pissing me off, but I remind myself these aren't swingers in a club. This guy's here with his family but he should show respect toward his wife and mine.

I take a cleansing breath and exhale slowly. I'm letting this go because that's what mature men do. And it's what L would want from me.

When the show is over, Laurelyn returns to the table, changed back into her sundress. I rise and pull her chair out for her. "You didn't get to keep the costume?"

"Sorry, McLachlan. They made me turn it in." She leans over and lowers her voice. "But I'm sure we can come up with something for later."

Oh yeah. I'm definitely buying this girl a hula costume for the bedroom.

Everyone at the table resumes watching the show—except the ogler. Laurelyn has no idea she's being violated and I've had enough. No husband should have to watch some dick salivate at the sight of his wife's chest. "They're a great pair, aren't they?"

He turns at the sound of my voice and goes pale when his wife asks, "What was that?" His eyes become large as he reaches for his drink. "I said they're a great pair." I point at the kids sitting to the left. "Your older boys get along well while the younger son entertains the baby."

"Don't let those two fool you," she says as she gestures toward the rambunctious boys. "They're a handful. They don't always get along so well."

The show ends and I waste no time in leading L toward the car ahead of the crowd. "Wait. I need to go to the restroom."

I look at the horde around us and know they're all headed in the same direction. "We'll be at the house in ten minutes."

She shakes her head. "My bladder will explode if we get stuck in traffic."

"I really want to beat this crowd out of here so I can get you home and fulfill my promise." She crosses her legs and makes a face to convey agony. "But not at the cost of an exploding body part." I swat her bottom and she yelps. "Go—but hurry—because I have plans for you, Mrs. McLachlan."

I'm waiting for L and see our dinner companions as they're leaving. "Did you enjoy the show?" I call out as they walk by. I would never bring his indiscretion to his pregnant wife's attention, but I can't resist making the bastard squirm a little. He deserves that much.

He busies himself with one of the children, pretending to not hear me, so his wife answers. "We did. And you?"

"Loved it. It was Laurelyn's first luau so she especially enjoyed it."

"Laurelyn. What a pretty name. I'll have to remember that one when this baby comes—that is, if it's a girl. We didn't find out."

I hope it's a boy. I don't want this guy to have any lasting connection to my L. "I'll tell my wife you said so. Enjoy the rest of your evening."

"You too."

Laurelyn walks up from the opposite direction of the restrooms and is wearing that mischievous grin I love so much. "What have you been up to?"

She holds up a large shopping bag. "I wanted souvenirs."

We both know what's in that bag so I can't wait to get her back to the house to play dress-up. I grab her hand and lead her toward the area where our driver is to pick us up. "Where's the fire?"

"In my pants." That earns me a giggle from my bride but I'm not amused. I'm horny.

We're out a little earlier than expected, so I'm grateful when I see our driver waiting at the curb in a black Town Car. "That's us with the hazards on." I'm used to Daniel's reliability so it's nice to have someone do a good job of filling his shoes. Our temporary driver keeps up this kind of service and he'll earn a nice, fat bonus at the end of this assignment.

"What's with the hurry?"

I wave the driver off and open the door for L. "I'll tell you when we're in the car."

She's a woman so she doesn't get it. I know what's in that bag and what she's going to look like in it. She's going to dance for me—only me

—in a hula costume. Probably with nothing underneath. The anticipation has my cock hard as rock.

The car pulls away and I know I have at least ten minutes until we make it home, probably longer when you take traffic into account so I'm in pure misery. I bring her hand to my erection. "This is the hurry. I'm in agony because I want you under me so badly."

She leans up and removes her cardigan before spreading it over my lap. "If we don't do something about this, you won't last a minute once we're home. I don't think either of us wants that." She moves her hand up and slides it down the front of my pants. She grasps my cock in her hand and her thumb strokes the tip, spreading the moisture already there. "I think a little pregame show is in order so we savor the real thing later. Don't you agree?"

"I couldn't agree more." I lean my head back against the seat while L pumps her hand up and down. "God, you're the best wife ever."

She leans over to whisper in my ear. "I wish there were a divider. Remember all those naughty things we did in the back of that limo?"

How could I forget? Those were some of the best moments of my life. I grab her head and bring her ear to my mouth. "Hell, yeah. I remember it all. Every touch. Every kiss."

"You want to know what I remember?" She pumps faster as she talks, bringing me closer to the climax I need so badly. "You exploding inside my body, claiming me. You rubbed your cum into my skin, marking me like an animal, as if I was your possession for no other man to look at. And I loved it."

That's it. The first spasm begins, and then the others, followed by a full-on explosion. She doesn't stop until her hand and my boxer briefs are a wet mess and then she kisses the side of my face. "That's my boy."

She takes her hand out of my pants and opens her handbag to fetch a tissue. She wipes her hand and then passes a clean one my way. "Tissue?"

"Thanks." I take it from her and ease it down the front of my trousers. "Isn't my girl the prepared one?"

"Looks like I'd better be in case I need to do that again."

I can't lie and say it won't happen again, not with the way she makes me want her.

After we're back at the house, she has me wait in the bedroom while she gets into character. She's playful and it's only one of the many things I love about L.

I'm lighting the last candle in the room when she calls out through the cracked bathroom door, "Close your eyes."

She likes to do this—have me shut my eyes while she gets in place. It's all about staging for her. "Yes, ma'am."

I'm sitting on the edge of the bed and hear the sound of a ukulele begin. It takes several seconds before I recognize the familiar tune of "Somewhere Over the Rainbow" coming from her phone.

"Okay. You can look."

I open my eyes and L is completely decked out in hula gear, feathers and all. Her top is a yellow bikini and it's lovely against her freshly sun-kissed skin. Her skirt and headpiece are red, yellow, and black. Her long dark hair cascades over both shoulders and she's the most beautiful hula girl I've ever seen. I imagined something similar but the reality is so much better.

She's mimicking the dance she was taught at the luau, and the raging sexual urgency I expected isn't there. This type of dance leaves me feeling much different than when she pole dances for me. There's something surreal, and so very sweet, about the slow sway of her arms and hips to this particular rendition of the song. She looks so pure and deserving of much more than what I promised her I would do when I got her home tonight.

"This is the only Hawaiian song I had in my music library." She doesn't miss a beat in her rhythmic dance as she talks.

"Baby, it's perfect." And it truly is. It does something to me I can't explain.

"Each move has so much depth, every dance its own story." She makes coordinating flowing motions with her arms. "One of the girls backstage told me this is symbolic of a tree swaying in the breeze. It's beautiful, isn't it?"

She has no idea. "It certainly is." No woman has ever made it look so lovely.

She dances another minute and then shrugs. "That's it. I got nothing else. I wish I had more of a show for you."

I put my arms out for her. "Come here."

She walks to me and I wrap my arms around her waist to pull her close. I put the side of my face just below her chest and she cradles my head with her arms. I feel so much more for this woman than I ever thought possible. My love for her makes me ache deep in my chest. I never want to find out what it would feel like to lose her. "I love you so much, L. I don't ever want to know the pain of not having you in my life."

She leans back and tilts my face upward. "I love you and I'm not going anywhere. I'm here as long as you want me to stay."

I feel like I'll smother if I don't have her. "Swear you'll never leave me."

She smiles and it feels like a rush of breath expanding my lungs in a moment of suffocation. "I will never leave you."

"We've had a change of plans for christening our bed." I reach for her phone and pass it to her. "Put that song on repeat and forget what I said earlier. I just want to make love to you—as slowly as you'll let me."

She smiles as she thumbs the phone's screen. "I'm glad you like the song. I wasn't sure about it." She puts her phone aside and slides her hands over my shoulders.

"I love it." It makes me feel good about us. "Dance with me."

We sway in the middle of our bedroom. I'm in a completely different mindset than earlier. I know L likes my filthy mouth occasionally, but I use it far too frequently. I'm too much of a caveman with her at times. I should touch her gently and speak sweetly to her more often. She's a treasure—my precious one—and I'd be wise to always treat her as such.

The song comes to an end before beginning again but I'm done with dancing. I take L's hands in mine and lead her toward the bed. We stop when the backs of my legs hit the mattress and she unbuttons my white linen shirt before pushing it from my shoulders to the floor.

I take the floral wreath from her head and place it on the nightstand before I smooth her stray hairs. I twirl a lock of her long hair around my finger and marvel at how soft it is. "You are so beautiful."

She blushes and drops her face. It's still surprising to me how she can be so strong—even seek a career in the spotlight—yet she doesn't know how to take compliments. I'm certain it's because she never heard them while growing up. Or from that fool, Blake.

I place my hand under her chin and lift her face. "You better get used to hearing compliments because I plan on telling you often how gorgeous and loved you are."

CHAPTER FIVE
LAURELYN MCLACHLAN

My eyes are closed and I'm listening to the sound of the waves. I've only been awake for a few minutes but the resonance is hypnotic so I'm drifting back into slumber when the bed shifts. My eyes pop open when the bed sheet slides down my body and I feel Jack Henry's kisses against the bare skin of my lower back. "Are you awake?"

"I am now."

He runs his hand over the valley where my spine curves inward. "Have I ever told you how much I love this dip?"

Is he kidding? Only like a bazillion times. "I believe you may have a time or two."

His wet tongue glides upward and I bow reflexively, sending my bottom up from the bed, hitting him against his chest. My hair prickles as goosebumps spread from the top of my head to the tips of my toes. No matter how many times he does this, my body reacts the same. "Good grief. You'd think I'd become immune to that at some point."

His palm slides up my thigh to my cheek and he rubs it in a circular motion. "Please don't because I'll never tire of seeing your body arch like that."

I relax beneath his touch and his talented hands knead the muscles of my back as they make their way to my shoulders. I haven't said anything but my body is rebelling after our frolic against the pole yesterday. A massage is very welcomed. "Mmm... you can stop doing that sometime next week."

His fingers knead in circles and, again, my body erupts into chills. "So you like that, huh?"

"Mmm-hmm... just a little bit."

"A massage is the least I can do since it's my fault you're sore."

I lift my head from the pillow and peer over my shoulder at him. "I didn't say I was sore."

"You didn't but your body speaks to me in other ways."

Funny, I didn't hear it say a thing. "How so?"

"It wasn't your usual fuck-me-harder moan I heard when I pushed your legs back." He leans down to kiss the side of my neck. "Your legs were guarded so I knew you were probably feeling the aftermath of our pole excursion." He kisses the side of my face. "I'm sure it's worse today so we're taking a break from sex so you can recuperate."

I recall how gentle and loving Jack Henry was last night while we christened our honeymoon bed. His whole demeanor was different, but he was that way before, possibly discerning how sore I was. "Is that why you were so gentle with me?"

"Partly."

"What's the other reason?"

"I wanted to make love to you." He presses his nose against my hair and inhales deeply. "I'm boorish with you too often. I should be gentler."

I roll, forcing him to move from my back. "Listen up, McLachlan." He moves to his side and we're face to face. "I love your gentle side but I'm not a porcelain doll. I love it when you fuck me hard." I grab his chin and give it a squeeze. "Sometimes I need you to be a caveman. I crave it. Understand?"

He nods in agreement. "Yes, ma'am."

"This is our honeymoon so there will be no breaks from sex. Got it?"

"No argument here."

"Good." I push him to his back and straddle him. I place my palms against his chest and rub his pectorals. "Life is so much easier when you see things my way."

He licks his lips while reaching to palm my breasts. "You're always very convincing, Mrs. McLachlan. I'm afraid I'll never stand a chance with you."

I lean down so we're face to face again. "I'm afraid you're right." I suck his bottom lip into my mouth but let it go when his phone rings. It's Margaret.

"Shit. I haven't called Mum since we arrived. She's going to rip me a new one."

"No, she isn't. I've got this." I take his phone from the nightstand. "Good mornin', Margaret."

"Hello, darling. I'm sorry to call but my inconsiderate son hasn't seen fit to phone his mum to let her know all is well."

"I'm so sorry, Margaret. I'm afraid that's all my fault." I wink at Jack Henry. "I've been keeping him pretty busy." I'm still straddling him so I move my hips against him.

"It's okay. I totally understand but I needed to check in to make sure you were both all right."

He rises and puts his mouth on one of my breasts, sucking my nipple into his mouth. "We're having a great time. I love the house."

"I knew you would."

He moves to my other breast, rolling his tongue around the tip of its rosy pebble. "I can't believe he bought it for me."

"I can. He loves you so much, Laurelyn."

I look at the top of his dark head and run my fingers through his hair. "I know, and I love him."

"I know you do, honey. Any idea when you'll be returning?"

I remember him telling me we were here as long as we liked. I've been having so much fun, it hasn't crossed my mind to ask when we'll go home. I guess it's something we should discuss soon since Christmas is just around the corner.

"Just a minute, Margaret." I press mute. "She wants to know when we're coming home."

He takes a piece of my hair between his fingers and playfully twirls it. "Tell her we'll discuss it and let her know."

I unmute the phone. "We haven't decided yet but we'll let you know after we talk it over."

"Okay... as long as you're back in time for Christmas. I know Jack

Henry and how he thinks. I won't have my new daughter spend her first McLachlan holiday away from the family."

"I'll tell him you said so."

Jack Henry's interest is piqued. He mouths, "Tell me what?"

I wave him off. "I'm sorry, Margaret. Jack Henry was distracting me. What was that?"

"I said I'll let you go so you can go back to keeping your husband busy."

I feel heat in my face. I'm certain I'm blushing at my mother-in-law's reference. Nookie. She strongly encourages it. First, because she wanted me to snag Jack Henry as a husband and now because she probably wants me pregnant. She as good as said so at our wedding.

"All right. We'll talk soon."

"Have a wonderful time, darling. I love you and tell Jack Henry I love him."

I tear up after I hear my mother-in-law tell me she loves me. She accepted me so easily. Her arms have been opened in my direction from the moment we met—something my own father couldn't even do for me. "I will. We love you too."

I lean over to place the phone on the nightstand and then return to sitting astride Jack Henry. "She says to tell you she loves you."

"I owe you, sweet cheeks." He lifts my hand to his lips for a kiss. "I'm certain you just saved me from a Margaret-style arse kicking."

"We're husband and wife. That means we protect one another."

"I don't know what I did before you."

His words spark a reminder of what he did before me and a peculiar look comes over his face. We both know why, so I push it out of my mind and attempt a change of subject. "What day do you have in mind for going back?"

"I was thinking we might stay a couple of weeks."

I don't have to do the math in my head to realize that means staying here through the holidays. "And miss Christmas with your family?" Our family.

"I think it would be nice to spend our first Christmas as husband and wife here. I'll go out and get us a tree. We can decorate it together—anyway you want."

My heart plummets.

"What is it?"

I place my finger on his chest and before I know it, I'm tracing the infinity symbol. "This is my first chance at a normal Christmas with family. It's something I've never had before. I guess I was excited about it, but we can stay here. Spending the holidays with just you and me will be special."

He grabs my hand and kisses it. "I'm such an idiot. I wasn't thinking. Of course, you want to spend our first Christmas with family."

Being with Jack Henry is all I really need. "I want to make you happy. If being here together is what you have in mind, then that's what we should do."

"No. I'm making sure you have the Christmas you deserve. We'll leave Saturday so we can be back before Christmas Eve. What do you think of that?"

"I think it's perfect—just like you."

***

THE LAST SIX DAYS HAVE BEEN THE BEST OF MY LIFE. I'M SAD TO LEAVE MAUI but I know Jack Henry and I can return whenever we choose, so the sadness is lessened.

It's almost Christmas Eve by the time we land in Sydney, and I'm thankful Daniel is there waiting with the car. I'm so exhausted I practically fall inside. Jack Henry gathers me in his arms for the ride to our apartment and strokes his hand over my hair. "You see? This is what happens when you act like a sex-crazed maniac."

I gather all my strength to respond. "Sorry, McLachlan. It won't happen again."

That's the last thing I remember until we arrive at the apartment and Jack Henry attempts to gather me so he can carry me inside. "I'm awake. I can walk."

"I'm carrying you over the threshold."

"You did that already," I argue.

"I did it at our vacation house. Now I'm doing it at our apartment and you should expect me to do it again when we go home to Avalon."

I get out of the car and he scoops me up. "You're being silly, but I'm too tired to argue with you, freak, so take me to bed."

"Gladly."

I shake my head. "Not for that, McLachlan. To rest. I'm exhausted."

"You've been sleeping a lot the past few days. Do you feel okay?"

He's right. I spent more time in bed than usual but it was our honeymoon. Aren't we supposed to stay in bed far too much? "I'm fine... just exhausted by my husband's robust sexual appetite this week."

"Are you complaining?"

"Most certainly not."

"Welcome home, sort of, my beautiful bride." He chuckles as he brings me through the front door and sets me on the floor. He looks at me and then places his palm against my forehead. "You look pale. Sure you feel okay?"

"I'm really tired."

He takes my hand. "Let's get you to bed so you can catch up on your sleep. You'll need to be energized for tomorrow."

Shit! I have no idea how I'm going to get everything done. "But I don't have time to sleep. There's too much to do." I take a look around the living room but don't see any deliveries. I wonder where Daniel put them. "There should be a stash of Christmas packages here somewhere. They'll need wrapping before tomorrow. That'll take a lot of time because I make my own bows."

"No, ma'am. There's plenty of time for that. The first thing you're going to do is sleep and you can get to those other things later if you feel well enough."

I hate to admit it, but I'm too tired to argue with him. "Okay. Wake me in two hours."

It's dark when I open my eyes so that means Jack Henry didn't wake me as I'd asked. Shit! I've slept the whole day.

My head is pounding and I have chills. My body feels as though it's been run over by a semi... and then backed over again. I don't feel well at all and I can admit it.

I sit on the edge of the bed and flip on the lamp. The dim light is painful and I'd like to turn it off and lie back down but I have an urgent need to use the bathroom. I rise to stand at the side of the bed but my head spins so I lower myself to sit again.

As if on cue, Jack Henry comes into the room. "You're finally awake. You've been sleeping like the dead." He walks over and again places his hand on my head. "You're hot."

"Glad you think so."

"You're considerably chipper for someone with a fever."

I reach up and hold my head. "I'm dizzy but I really need to go to the bathroom."

"I'll help you."

He helps me to stand and my head feels like I've been whirling in circles, so I shut my eyes tight. "Oh God. I may throw up." And if I do, my bladder is going to explode. "Bathroom. Now."

He takes my hands and guides me in the direction I need to go but I don't open my eyes because I know I'll spew if I do. I feel his hands guiding me back toward the toilet before he peels my panties down my legs. "Sit."

We've done this before and he knows I don't want him around for bodily functions. "Hand me the trash can and then get out."

"I'm not leaving you alone on the verge of falling off the toilet into your own puke."

Seriously? He wants to argue about this now? I'm miserable because my bladder is about to burst. I squeeze my eyes, although I'm covering them with my hand. "I can't pee with you in here. You've got to go."

"I'm not leaving if you're unsteady."

"Grr," I groan. "I'm not going to fall but I may very well explode if you don't get out of here."

"You get one minute but you'd better call for me if you feel shaky. Got it?"

"Yes! Get out." I sound hateful—I don't mean to—but the wretchedness engulfing me is to blame.

The minute I hear the door shut, I'm finally able to relax enough to empty my bladder. And then it starts—the heaving, followed by the vomiting.

My eyes are still shut but I hear Jack Henry open the bathroom door. "You okay?" I heave loudly and I'm guessing he interprets that as a negative because he's by my side with a cool, wet cloth to the back of my neck. "What do you think is wrong?"

"I don't know. I guess some kind of virus since I have a fever." Even after vomiting, I don't dare open my eyes because I don't want to get started again. "Damn. This happened fast. I don't remember ever feeling so bad in all my life."

I'm sickened further when I realize I won't be able to attend Christmas with my new family. "No way I can go to your parents' tomorrow."

He rubs my back. "You don't have to make that call right now, but I'll bet you'll probably feel much better by tomorrow."

He isn't getting it. "I have a fever, so that means I'm probably contagious. Even if I feel better, I can't expose the family to whatever this is—especially the kids."

"You've been really tired and now you're throwing up and dizzy. Could you be... ?"

He doesn't finish but I know what he's thinking. I hate bursting his bubble. "Pregnancy doesn't make you feverish."

"Unless you're pregnant and you have a virus." Is he seriously wishing a pregnancy on top of this? I look up at him and my expression must convey my thoughts. "Don't look at me like that. You were right there with me on that bathroom counter the night before the wedding. It could've happened. Plus, it's not like we've been incredibly consistent in the birth control department lately."

I want to ask whose fault that is but I keep that comment to myself. "My period should start anytime."

He's rubbing my neck. "Want to try to go back to bed?"

I'm minimally better so it seems a good idea. "Yeah. I think I'm finished for now, but give me a minute. I'll let you know when I'm ready for you."

He sighs, a sign he doesn't appreciate my need for privacy, but I don't care. I have business to tend and it doesn't concern him. And I'm very glad I asked him to leave when I see the blood after I wipe. Talk about being on cue—my period has arrived so we won't have to wait to know I'm not pregnant.

Seeing the evidence of what I already knew leaves me unsettled. I didn't believe I was pregnant but I think I might have hoped, maybe somewhere deep in the back of my mind, that we had conceived. Is this disappointment I'm feeling?

I come out of the bathroom once I'm finished and he's instantly by my side, helping me to the bed. "I started my period just now."

"Oh." I hear his disappointment and I'm not sure how to respond. Saying I'm sorry doesn't feel right and neither does telling him we'll try. The truth is that I'm not sure what I want. I only know I love him and want nothing more than to please him, but do I agree to have a baby when I'm uncertain because I want to make him happy? How can that be best for our marriage?

I told him I'd think about a baby—and I will—but not now. I don't have it in me to do anything but climb into our bed and fall fast asleep.

CHAPTER SIX
JACK MCLACHLAN

It's becoming clearer as the hours tick by that L and I will not be spending Christmas at my parents' house as planned. I had hoped she would make a miraculous recovery so we'd be able to make it, but we've no such luck. If anything, she's sicker.

I hate waking her again but it can't be good for her to go so long without drinking. "L." I lightly shake her shoulder. "Love, you're going to get dehydrated if you don't drink something else."

She slowly wakes following a second shake. "I brought you some fresh water."

She closes her eyes. "I don't want anymore. I'll throw up if I put anything in my stomach."

I nudge her again. "Please try. Would you rather go to the hospital and get an IV?"

She puts her hand over her eyes. "I'm too sick to get up and go to the hospital."

Even sick, she tries to be funny. "I can manage getting you there if it's what you need."

She sighs, or maybe huffs is a better word. "Fine. I'll drink the damn water but bring me something to puke in. There's no way I can run to the bathroom when it decides to come back up."

I place a couple of pillows against the headboard and help her to a sitting position. She takes the glass from my hand but I don't release it because I'm afraid she's too weak to maintain her grip. "I've got it." I'm not convinced but I let her take it anyway. "What time is it?"

I look at the clock. "Almost two. How do you feel?"

"I'm still weak but I think I feel better than I did this morning." It's small, but she takes a drink and it doesn't immediately come back up. "We're missing Christmas. Is Margaret terribly upset?"

Very much so, but there's no way I'm telling L that. "She's disappointed but understands it isn't your fault you're sick."

She brings the glass to her mouth and takes another sip. "I think it's a twenty-four hour bug or something since I'm feeling better."

She has no idea how relieved I am to hear that. "I'm glad because I really considered gathering you up and taking you to the hospital."

She isn't too sick to give me her oh hell no look. "I think you know that wouldn't have gone over well with me."

She better figure out nothing will stop me from taking care of her. "It doesn't matter when it comes to your well-being."

"Good thing I'm better, then."

"Think you're good enough to open your Christmas present?"

She smiles and I'm reassured for the first time that she may actually be feeling better. "Absolutely."

I'm excited like a little kid. "Be right back."

"No. I want to come to the living room."

"Sure you feel well enough?"

"I won't be dancing a jig but I'm good enough to make it to the couch." She slides to the edge of the bed. "Give me a quick minute to freshen up and I'll meet you on the couch."

She's changed and freshened, looking quite different from the person I was so worried about twelve hours ago. She's sitting on the sofa waiting for her gifts, and I can't stop myself from wondering what her previous Christmases were like.

I remember last year. I found her alone when I drove from Sydney to Wagga Wagga and brought her home with me to Avalon—after Mum insisted. I was such a fool then. "Tell me what holidays were like for you growing up."

She looks puzzled. "Why?"

I shrug. "You're my wife. I want to know."

"Terrible until my mom got clean. I'd classify them as tolerable after that. My grandparents were the only joyful part of the holidays for me." That's not much detail about what it was like, but I'm guessing this is as far as she wants to go today.

"I wanted this to be the most special Christmas you've ever had."

She smiles and reaches out to touch my arm. "It is. I'm your wife and we're together. Nothing could spoil that, not even me being sick as a dog."

"You are so precious to me." I lean over and kiss the top of her head. I walk over to the Christmas tree Mum had delivered and decorated so we'd have our own for our first Christmas together.

I sit next to Laurelyn with her gifts. "I've been carrying your presents with me since the day we left on our honeymoon. I wanted to spend the holidays in Maui so I could have you all to myself on Christmas. Looks like I'm having my way, although this isn't exactly what I had in mind."

"I feel like shit. I bought your gifts before the wedding but they're under our tree at Avalon. I'm sorry. I thought we'd go home after we left your parents and have our own little Christmas there."

"I don't care about me, babe. This Christmas is only about you." I place her first gift on her lap and her face lights up like a child. "Open it."

She grins as she tears the paper of the small square box. She looks up at me when she sees the jewelry box. "You've given me a necklace, earrings, and a bracelet. What could this be?"

"Only one way to find out."

She flips the jewelry box lid and her eyes dance as she touches her new platinum and diamond drop navel ring. "Oh my God. You bought diamonds for my belly button." She takes it from the box and holds it up for a better look. "It's beautiful."

"I couldn't find one I liked so I had to have a jeweler make it." I point to the biggest stone. "This one is a third of a carat. The two smaller ones are quarter-carats each. The jeweler recommended keeping the total weight under a carat so it didn't become too much."

She lifts her shirt and holds it over her current ring. "What do you think?"

I can't wait to see it on her—but not now. "It's perfect, but wait until you feel better to put it in."

She reaches for my face and strokes it with her palm. "Always so thoughtful."

"You haven't seen anything yet, baby."

I give her the girly gifts my mum and sister helped me choose—nothing particularly special—and I'm down to the last one. "This is sort of a wedding-slash-Christmas present." I place the rolled set of papers across her legs. "I wanted to give this to you before we left on our honeymoon but it wasn't ready."

I see her intrigue by the way she scrunches her brow. "What is this?"

"Unroll it and take a look."

She slides to the edge of the couch and spreads the rolled papers out on the coffee table. "It's blueprints?"

"Yes."

"For... a house?"

"Not exactly." I move a picture frame to one side of the papers and a candle to the other to act as paperweights so I can show her the surprise. "This is the newest edition at Avalon—a music studio for you. It was designed by the leading acoustical engineer in the business. The guy is supposed to be some kind of genius when it comes to the science of sound and vibration in technology." I gesture toward the northeast corner of the drawing. "This room will have state-of-the-art recording equipment."

She's silent and I don't know what that means. "I know this won't be you traveling around the world with Southern Ophelia, but it's a way for you to hang on to your music. We live in a technical world and you can work with people in Nashville from here in Australia. I'm hoping you'll find it a happy medium."

"Happy medium means I'm settling for less than I truly want but that's not what this is—or what you are. You're everything to me—my number one. I love music but it'll always come after you and when we have a family, it'll come behind them." She waves her hand over the blueprints. "I love this. It's absolutely incredible and proves yet again how thoughtful you are and how much you love me." She puts her arms out for me to come to her—so I do. "I'd fuck you into this couch if I weren't sick."

That's my girl. "I accept rain checks."

"I'm sure you do."

"I have to call Addison to tell her about this." The doorbell rings and a puzzled look appears on Laurelyn's face. "Who in the world could that be?"

"There's only one person I can think of." Margaret McLachlan. I move to answer the door. "I guess it's a good thing I'm not getting fucked into the couch right now."

My guess is spot on. "Mum. This is a surprise." Not really. I knew she wouldn't stay away.

She's holding several plates of food and passes them to me. "I brought you something to eat." I take the food from her and she steps around me to go to Laurelyn. "How's our girl?"

"I'm much better, thank you."

She sits next to L and immediately begins her mothering by feeling L's forehead. I guess I learned that from her. "You're a little warm but you don't have fever. Any chills?"

"I did earlier but I haven't felt them in hours."

"Good. Whatever this is, it's passing quickly. I made soup. Do you feel like eating?"

Laurelyn nods and my mum motions for the cabana boy—me—to jump. "You're going to eat soup for her but you'd barely drink water for me." I sound like a pouty child.

"I feel better since I've gotten out of bed." She points to the blueprints on the coffee table. "And since I got this incredible Christmas gift."

My mum leans over to look at the plans. "What is this?"

"I'm building a music studio at Avalon."

Mum nods in approval. "What a great idea. You must be happy about this."

Laurelyn leans up and adjusts the pillow behind her back. "Beyond thrilled is more like it."

"My boy does good."

"He certainly does." I'm glad to have the approval of the two most important women in my life.

I take Laurelyn's empty soup bowl when she finishes and Mum follows me into the kitchen. "She's pale."

She's a hundred percent better than she was. "Pale is an improvement over the color she was early this morning. She scared me, Mum. She doesn't realize how very close I was to taking her to the hospital."

"She kept saying her wedding dress was tight so I thought she might have already been pregnant but just didn't realize it yet. I was hoping that was why she didn't feel well, but I see that isn't the case." So I'm not the only one hoping for a baby soon.

"I'd hoped the same thing but she isn't. We know for sure." I don't want to tell my mum about my wife's period, so I hope she understands what I mean.

She's grinning. "She may want to work on that as soon as she feels better."

I shrug. "I don't know. We discussed it in Maui. She told me she'd think about it."

"Don't look so discouraged. Thinking about it isn't a no."

"It isn't a yes, either," I argue.

"Son, she's open to the idea if she's thinking it over, but don't rush her. Pressure is the last thing she needs. You've been married a week. There's plenty of time for babies."

Laurelyn has plenty of time for babies. I'm not so sure about myself but I'm not going to upset my mum by going there with her. "I know."

"Enjoy being together while you can. Trust me, that special time is rare once little ones come along."

Isn't that the same thing Evan told me about Emma? That, along with a lot of other shit I didn't want to hear about him fucking her on their living room couch and kids nursing on her all the time. "I treasure every moment with Laurelyn."

"As you should." She takes the spoon and bowl from me and goes to the sink to wash them. "You couldn't have chosen a better gift than a music studio."

"Laurelyn quit the band but she didn't give up music. She wants to continue to work—maybe writing songs for other artists. I think the studio will be the perfect avenue for her to work from home instead of making trips to Nashville."

"Isn't Nashville where that man lives, the one who attacked her?" That whole situation weighs heavily on my mind.

"Yes and she'll have to go back to testify."

"How do you feel about that?" my mum asks.

She doesn't really want to hear me tell her how I feel about it, how I want to kill him. "I don't want them in the same room ever again, but I want that son of bitch locked up with the key thrown away. It'll take her testimony to do that."

"You've never told me about it."

And I don't plan to. "I can't. L doesn't want anyone to know what he did to her." She drops the soup bowl in the sink, shattering it, before she turns to me, looking sickened. "He didn't, Mum. I stopped him in time. But another minute and I don't think the outcome would've been the same."

She reaches for the dish towel and dries her hands before walking to me. "I had no idea."

"Don't say anything to Laurelyn."

"I wouldn't, son." She holds my face with her hands. "You've done a lot of things to make me proud but never more so than when you took Laurelyn as your wife. As her husband, it's your job to love her." She's unmoving as her eyes stare into mine. "She's one of us now and we protect our own... at any cost."

I nod in agreement with my mum. "With every heartbeat I have left, I will keep her safe."

I hear the echo of Laurelyn's phone and I recognize her mum's ringtone. "Jolie's calling, I'm sure to wish Laurelyn a merry Christmas."

"Good. Laurelyn needs her mother to be a presence in her life, even if from a distance."

CHAPTER SEVEN
LAURELYN MCLACHLAN

IT'S TAKEN SEVERAL DAYS FOR ME TO FEEL AS THOUGH I'VE RETURNED TO THE land of the living but I'm back. I hope I'm ready for the party scene because Daniel is driving us to Evan and Emma's house for their New Year's shindig. It's not a family party, meaning I'll be meeting Jack Henry's friends, so my stomach is fluttering a mile a minute.

"You're quiet, love."

I consider saying nothing but can't think of a good reason to keep it from him. "I'm your wife and I've yet to meet your friends, so I can't help but feel nervous about meeting your inner circle."

Jack Henry had no intention of introducing me to the people in his life when we began our companionship. Meeting his parents and siblings wasn't supposed to happen but even after we abandoned our original agreement, he didn't take me around his friends. He still hasn't, and I admit I'm troubled by this.

Our wedding was small with only family in attendance. I'd like to think that was because he didn't want me to feel bad about a huge crowd on his side when I had only four family members and a single friend, but the insecure person trapped inside me wonders if there's more to it than that.

"The people attending this party aren't my mates. They're Evan and Emma's, so we're acquaintances at best."

"Oh." So I still won't meet those he considers his buddies. "Why haven't I met your friends?"

He's grinning as he leans over to kiss my cheek. "I have none worthy of your company."

He's avoiding the question. "That's not an answer."

"I'm not hiding you from them, if that's what's on your mind." His arm is around me and I lean into him. He squeezes me closer and plants a kiss on the top of my head. "Or maybe I am. The whole bunch of them are self-proclaimed manwhores so I'd do well to keep you from them forever."

A manwhore, huh? Sort of sounds like someone I used to know.

"I assure you you're not missing anything, but I can have Mum invite a few to my birthday dinner next Saturday night if it's what you want."

That's right. My man has a birthday coming in thirteen days. Thirty-one. He sees age as a countdown but I don't. That's no way to think of life and I have to change his mindset. I also have to come up with a gift for him—a perfect one.

We arrive at my brother and sister-in-law's and the driveway is full of expensive cars. "Looks like they invited a lot of people." And it looks like some rich ones, which surprises me. I guess I didn't realize Evan and Emma rubbed elbows with a wealthy crowd.

"Perfect." The sarcasm is thick in his voice. "You should probably be prepared to be passed around. If you tire of it, let me know and we'll leave. I'm not opposed to ringing in the new year at home, just the two of us."

I wouldn't want to upset Evan and Emma by leaving before midnight. I look at the time. "We can survive anything together for four hours."

"We need a code word."

Is he kidding? "A code word? For what?"

"For when you've had enough and you need to get out."

Now I'm really afraid. "I don't know." I think for a moment, offering the first word that comes to me. "Infinity."

He grins. "May I say how fitting that is since it's what you trace with your finger when you're mulling something over."

We enter the house and it's more crowded than I expected. A lot of people must've come by taxi, or maybe they're like Jack Henry and have drivers. I hadn't considered that I might have to mingle with an elite crowd.

Shit. I may have married a man from the upper class but I've never rubbed elbows with these kind of people, not even in my music career. I'm a simple Southern girl with a twang I can't shake no matter how hard I try.

Please don't let me say or do anything to embarrass myself or my husband.

Emma's at my side almost instantly, placing a drink in my hand. "Evan's specialty—a painkiller."

I put it to my nose and sniff. "Mmm... smells delicious."

Jack Henry takes it from me and turns it up for a taste. "Be forewarned, L. Evan will fool you with these. He'll add more and more spiced rum in each one you drink. He wants you smashed—if for no other reason than to fuck with me."

Cock-block. I swear they're worse than two little boys hitting each other in the nuts. I bet they did that to each other all the time when they were growing up. Poor Margaret. I bet she wore their asses out every day whether they needed it or not.

Emma laughs. "Jack's not kidding. You should watch out for Evan. He loves nothing more than to fuck with his brother and he'll do it through you if he has to—just like Jack will use me." She hits my husband in the arm. "It never stops. I thought they'd grow out of it eventually—especially after we had kids—but they haven't. They're worse than my own children so I gave up hope a long time ago."

I don't intend on being curled over a toilet tonight or tomorrow morning. "Don't worry."

Emma grabs my hand and tugs. "Come with me. I want to introduce you around."

We make the rounds and my sister-in-law introduces me to one person after another. Jack Henry was right. I'm passed from one person to the next like some kind of novelty. Everyone at the party wants to meet the woman capable of lassoing Jack McLachlan's heart.

Meeting this many people at once, while trying to keep their names straight, is exhausting. I need a break from the crowd… and the alcohol. Jack Henry and Emma were right. Evan mixes much stronger drinks for me as the night progresses.

I catch Jack Henry's attention and motion toward the outside door. I fan myself and then point at the door so he knows I mean to step out for air. He gives me a nod, a signal that he understands, and I blow him a kiss.

I step out into the night air and sit in a patio chair with my feet resting on an ottoman. God, it's hot. I'm not used to bringing in the new year in the summer. I think I almost expected to see my breath in the cold air.

It's a reality I haven't considered—certainly not the end of the world —but I realize I'll never have a white Christmas in Australia. All of the things I associate with the holidays aren't the same here. I'm surprised by how bothered I am when I consider that my kids will never go out to play in the snow after they've opened their gifts from Santa.

"I see I'm not the only one needing some fresh air."

I turn toward the female voice interrupting my thoughts and see a beautiful, petite blond with silky hair flowing down her back. "Yeah. It's a lot to take in at one time."

She sits in the chair next to me. "I noticed Emma parading you around so I'm guessing you are her new sister-in-law, Laurelyn."

This woman knows my name but that's not surprising since everyone at this party is aware that I'm Jack Henry's wife. Still, it's unnerving. "That would be me."

"Your accent is adorable."

"Thanks. It sort of sticks out like a sore thumb. I've tried to tame it but I'm afraid it's no use."

"Don't. You sound like a sweet little country girl," she laughs. "You shouldn't change it to suit your husband."

It's true that I consider myself a country girl but I'm not sure I like this woman's tone as she tells me I sound like one. I believe she's trying to insult me—but in a catty way—as though I'm too stupid to see it. And

I didn't mention anything about changing my accent because Jack Henry didn't like it. "My husband loves my accent and would never want me to speak differently."

"You're the one who said you were trying to change it."

I know exactly what I said and it wasn't that my husband didn't like me the way I was.

I don't know this woman and I have no desire to argue with a complete stranger. I came outside to get a break from empty conversations and I don't intend on having another with her, especially if she's going to put words I didn't say into my mouth.

"If you'll excuse me." I get up to leave. "Jack Henry will be looking for me."

"Oh, look. You're right. Here comes Jack now." She emphasizes his name—as if she's correcting me about what I should call my own husband—and I'm taken aback by her nasty tone and sudden change of demeanor. Who is she? Did I get her name? I don't think so.

She walks toward Jack Henry and goes up on her tiptoes. I know what's she's going to do because I can see it coming a mile away. She intends to kiss him on the mouth. "Hello, Jack."

The bitch is quick, but he's faster as he turns his head and grabs her shoulders to push her away. "No, Lana." He sounds as though he's scolding a child. Or a dog—so the term bitch would be accurate.

Disappointment is etched all over her face. His reaction clearly isn't what she'd hoped for but then she breaks into a sneer directed at me. "I'm Lana and I can see from your expression that you've heard of me."

"Don't," Jack Henry warns her.

"Don't what, Jack? Tell her we were a thing and we used to fuck like champions?" She's smirking, trying to get under my skin—and as badly as I hate to admit it, it's working.

Fuck like champions. Perfect. My husband used the same terminology with me that he once used with this woman—the one who attempted to trap him into marriage by getting pregnant.

I'm caught off guard, my mind completely blank, so I don't have a response for my husband's former lover. I don't want her to know what an impact she has had on Jack Henry's life or how she has shaped who he became even years after they broke up. As much as I despise it, she has had a huge influence over my husband and the thought of her taking any kind of pleasure from knowing that sickens me.

What does she want? She didn't follow me outside for no reason. "Lana. I'm aware of your prior relationship with my husband and I'm also privy to knowing why he ended things with you. He, nor I, has any interest in reminiscing about the manner in which you once fucked. I'm his wife—by choice, not force. That means he fucks me—and only me—like a champion. And he enjoys the hell out of it when he does, which is often." I'm shaking on the inside. My upper lip may even be quivering. "Does that cover it, or do you need further discouragement?"

She looks at Jack Henry and reaches for his hand. "There's no possible way you could be happy with her. If you'll think about it, you'll remember how good we were together."

Un-fucking-believable!

Jack Henry moves from her reach and places his arm in front of me. It's to hold me back because he knows I could go for blood any second. "Lana, I don't remember us ever being good together. You're just somebody I used to know." He reaches for my hand. "I love my wife with all my heart and we couldn't be happier."

"I know you, Jack. You don't keep any woman around for long. You need variety—and I'm okay with that—but she won't be." She walks toward the house and calls out over her shoulder. "Emma will know how to reach me once the shine is knocked off your new bride."

That was absolutely humiliating—being told by a woman that she used to fuck my husband—and no less than like a champion. It's almost as if she said that knowing it would hit home with me. I want to strangle them both.

I stand motionless as reality sinks in. I married a man with many women in his past. This is the third time I've been humiliated by one of his previous lovers and I strongly suspect it won't be the last. "How many times do I have to go through this?"

He puts his hands on my shoulders, maybe because he's afraid I'll bolt. "I'm so sorry. I didn't know she was invited. We wouldn't have come had I known."

I'm guessing she's Emma's friend if she's at her party, so why wouldn't he have considered her being invited? "You never told me Lana was Emma's friend. Is that how you met her?"

"Yes."

I feel like I've been hit in the gut. Jack Henry's connection to Lana through Emma is a huge problem for me.

"Come on. We're going home," he says.

Oh hell no! Tucking my tail between my legs isn't my forte. Leaving would make me appear upset, which I am, but also weak, which I'm not, so I have no intention of giving her that pleasure. "No. It's too early to go home. We have a new year to ring in." I walk toward the house. "I think I'll have another painkiller since I'm due a stronger drink."

"L. Don't get smashed because you're angry at her."

"I'm not going to get drunk because I'm angry with her. I'm going to drink way more than I should because I'm pissed off at both of you."

"What did I do?" He tries to catch me but I make it into the house before he can grasp my arm.

I find Evan still acting as the resident bartender. "Hey, sis. Can I do you for another?"

"You certainly may, bro."

Jack Henry walks up and watches Evan mix my drink. "Get her hammered and I'm kicking your ass."

Evan gives him the bird and I sort of feel like doing the same thing.

He grabs my hand and leads me into Evan and Emma's bedroom. He shuts the door and presses me against it. "Why are you mad at me, L? I didn't do anything wrong."

L. Hearing him say that puts a thought into my head. Laurelyn. Lana. "Oh my God. Did you call her L too?"

"What?" He looks like I've injured him as he steps away from me. "No, of course I didn't. That's my special name for you."

He can wipe that hurt look off his face. "She used your words, McLachlan. Fuck like a champion. I can't believe you said that to me on our honeymoon when it's what you used to say to her."

He shrugs and puts his hands out. "It's a phrase that my mates and I used to say all the time. It wasn't something special I shared with her. In fact, I don't recall ever telling her I was going to do that to her."

I don't want to hear details about anything he might or might not have done with her. "Just stop."

He rakes his hands through his hair—a telltale sign of his frustration. "You are my wife. I love you. She and I were over a long time ago. You heard me tell her that, so why are you angry with me?"

I've probably turned an ugly shade of green because I'm so envious of the role she has played in his life. "I'm your wife yet this other woman has molded you into the man you are."

He cradles my face with his hands. "Dammit, Laurelyn. You make me the man I am today—the one who loves his wife and wants to be a father. When are you gonna see that you've undone all the damage she caused? You make me… unbroken."

She will always be a part of him. "She made you the way you are. I can't stand that you became a man that went from one meaningless relationship to the next because of her. It sickens me."

He backs away from me. "Because of you, I didn't feel broken anymore… but I can clearly see that you don't feel the same."

I didn't know that's how he felt, like he's fixed because of me. I'm so stupid. I just told him I'm sickened by the man he is. "I'm a foolish woman. I shouldn't have said those things. I didn't mean them." He places his hand on my arm to move me away from the door but I plant my feet firmly. "No."

He doesn't move an inch but looks me in my eyes. "Infinity." The moment he says the word, I know I've messed up. Bad. He's used our code word as a safe word. It means he's had enough of me and needs to get away.

I step aside so he can leave and I remain in Evan and Emma's bedroom. Alone.

CHAPTER EIGHT
JACK MCLACHLAN

I OPEN THE DOOR AND LANA'S STANDING THERE EAVESDROPPING BECAUSE that's what a nosy bitch does. I try to move around her but she steps with me, blocking my escape. I place my hands on her arms. She thinks I mean to kiss her because she closes her eyes and leans in but instead I force her aside.

She grasps my biceps tightly, pressing her long claws into my skin. "I heard what she said. Your wife doesn't want you the way you are—but I do."

The more Lana says, the more I realize how much I hate her. I can't believe I ever had a relationship with this bitch. "I'm not discussing my marriage with you."

She shrugs. "Doesn't sound like there's a marriage to discuss. Your wife is repulsed by the person you are—the man I made you, per her words." She advances toward me. "If she loved you, she'd be fine with who you are."

I continue to hold her at arm's length. "Stop. I don't want to hear this."

"I'd be okay with you having other women. You could bring them into our bed anytime you wanted." She grins and gestures toward the door of Evan and Emma's bedroom. "I've come to like it. Maybe you and me and Laurelyn could give it a try."

What the hell is wrong with her? "I punched the last person who suggested something similar."

"My tastes have matured since we were together. I like it rough." She unexpectedly shoves me. I'm caught off guard and my back slams against the wall, making a loud thud. "So would you if you'd let me show you."

She's not just a bitch—she's crazy. "You're nuts and I'm done here."

I push against her to escape but she locks her arms, pulling me with her against the wall. I stumble, landing chest to chest with her, causing another loud thump. "See? I knew you'd like it rough."

She holds on to me tightly and her intent is no mystery. She wants L to open the door and see me with her like this.

And she gets what she's after.

Laurelyn stands in the doorway staring at me tangled in Lana's arms. I'm fucked—and not the way I want to be. "L. It's not what it looks like." That's all I'm able to say before she storms past down the hallway.

"How fuckin' cliché! At least have enough respect for me to be original."

"Whoops," Lana laughs.

I've never been violent toward a woman in my life but I have to fight the urge to put my fist in this one's face. At the very moment I feel like I could explode, I punch my clenched hand through the wall next to her head. She appears somber and fear creeps into her eyes. She's frightened by my display and potential of what I might do to her. Good. I hope I've managed to put a stop to her game. "I never want to see your face again."

I push away from her to go find my wife and I see Evan still bartending as I pass through the kitchen. "Did Laurelyn come through here?"

"Umm... yeah. I think she went out the door to the garage." I'm guessing she has Daniel on his way and plans to sneak out. She won't if I have anything to do with it.

It'll take him at least twenty minutes to get here so I walk over to the kitchen sink to wash my bloody hand. Evan calls out, "Whoa, bro! Who'd you punch?"

It stings as the cold water hits the open skin. "Not who. Tell Emma she can pick a new color for the hallway if she wants since you'll be needing some sheetrock work."

"I'm assuming that was no accident."

"Definitely not. Laurelyn thinks she saw me fucking around with Lana." Even I admit it must have appeared that way. "You know I wasn't. She set it up to look that way."

"I knew she was up to something when she called Emma out of the blue. She was fishing for an invite to the party so she could get to you and Laurelyn."

Emma walks up. "Who wanted to get to you and Laurelyn?" She looks down at my hand. "Oh hell. What happened?"

"A shitstorm named Lana." I don't want to explain this again. "Catch Emma up. I gotta find L and explain."

I go into the garage and find no trace of Laurelyn so I call her phone. I hear the faint Hawaiian rendition of "Somewhere Over the Rainbow" and follow its melody toward the courtyard. She's sitting at the bistro table digging through her purse to find the noisemaker. I'm sure she wants to silence it so I don't discover her hiding place. Too late.

She's crying and it breaks my heart to guess what's she's imagining. "You'll go away if you know what's good for you."

"I've already told you I know what's good for me, and it's you. Always you. That's never going to change." I want to go to her but I'm afraid she'll push me away.

"Really? Because you sort of looked like you thought Lana might be good for you a few minutes ago."

"Does it make sense that I would walk away from you and fuck around with Lana two seconds later when you could come out of the bedroom at any second and see me? Come on, L. You know that was a total setup. Just like her cornering you outside." She doesn't reply but she doesn't dispute my allegation, either. "Babe, it's impossible for you to wrap your head around the malicious things Lana is capable of because your heart is so good and pure. Trust me when I say she's venomous. And determined. She'll do anything to get what she wants."

"She wants you."

"And you too."

She looks confused, as she should be. "What?"

"I'm not the only one she'd like to have. She proposed a threesome." She looks as though she's waiting to hear me say if I accepted or declined the offer. Shit, I can't believe she's at a point where I have to confirm that. "I said no."

Lana has successfully fucked me after all.

"I think there's been a lot of misunderstandings tonight and I want to clear them up." I drop to my knees in front of L and take her hands. "I don't want Lana, even though she tried to make it appear as though I did. I love you. You're the only one for me."

"That may very well be the case but I'm not ready to say all is well and get over what just happened." She looks down as tears fall from her eyes. "I'm just so... damn mad." Her words convey anger but her tears, along with the sob that follows, tells me she's something else—in pain.

How did it come to this? I didn't do anything wrong yet I feel like a bastard. My wife is upset and crying and I don't know how to fix it.

The car's headlights shine on us when Daniel pulls into the drive and I ask if she's going to let me come home with her. She has a habit of making me leave when she's angry. She doesn't answer immediately and my heart pounds. She sighs. I know she probably wants space but I don't want to be away from her tonight. I think being apart could cause more harm than good. "Please don't make me stay somewhere else tonight."

She reaches for her purse and gets up, leaving me on my knees. "Come on. Daniel's waiting."

She doesn't utter a single word on the drive home—and neither do I. I can only guess what she's rolling around in her head right now, but I'm predicting it isn't good.

We arrive at the apartment—our temporary home while visiting Sydney—and I can't believe this is how we've spent our first New Year's Eve as husband and wife. We walk toward our bedroom, me following her, and I totally expect her to slam the door in my face or tell me to find another place to sleep. She doesn't.

She's a little unsteady from Evan's painkillers so she leans over to hold the footboard as she kicks off her pumps. "I hope you know you're not putting your hands on me tonight."

I look at the time and see it isn't yet midnight, but it's close. This isn't how I want our first year to end so I decide to take a leap—one I hope doesn't land me on my face. "It's almost midnight. I don't want to go into next year like this."

Tonight's events aren't small, so I'm sure Laurelyn has things she needs to say. She's hurt and her wound can fester, causing damage to our marriage. As her husband, it's my responsibility to contain this infection known as Lana.

"We have five minutes before we begin two thousand fourteen. I want you to take these last moments to say anything you'd like. Rant and rave. Kick and scream. Tell me you hate the way I've lived and what I've done in the past. Tell me if I'm fucking up this marriage. Say or do whatever you feel you need to so we can move beyond this night. Let me have it good, babe."

I've stunned her speechless.

This is probably the stupidest idea I've ever had. She's incredibly hurt and angry so if she takes me up on this offer, I should expect her to say harsh things. But I want to give her this outlet. She needs it. "There's nothing you can say to make me unlove you, so go for it without looking back."

"I'm not doing it unless you do the same. Tell me the things you'd like to say yet choose to hold inside."

Is it possible to make these confessions, not discuss them, and move on as if nothing happened? It suddenly feels like a challenge—a game of truth or dare—and is no longer about Lana. This is something more and goes deeper than tonight's events.

Women are so different from men. We are pissed off for a little while but get over it quickly. Women have long memories and hold grudges so this might not go well for me. "I'm not sure that's a good idea."

"I can always handle anything you say, as long as it's the truth." I get this now. She wants my true confessions.

"I'll agree but only if you swear you'll have no regrets. You can't dwell on anything I say."

She's terrified but excited. At least that's what I think I see in her eyes. "Do your worst. Tell me your fears and the demons you hide."

I set the timer on my phone. "A three-minute confession. We squeeze in whatever we can in a hundred and eighty seconds. Say it, get it off your chest, and move on without discussion or explanations. When the timer ends, it's a new year, a new start. Do you agree?"

"Yes."

I press start on my phone. "Go."

She looks at me, bewildered. "I don't know if I can. I'm afraid."

She's overthinking this so I'll go first—starting with her sorry-ass mother and father. "If your parents ever treat you poorly again, I'm telling them to fuck off, especially your mum. She really pisses me off." Laurelyn's eyes grow large and she doesn't reply. I don't think that's where she expected me to start. "If you don't say anything, that means you forfeit your turn and I get to go again."

"I despise what you did with those first twelve women because of Lana. I understand it's irrational for me to be angry about things that happened before you knew me, but it doesn't stop me from being pissed off every time I think about it—which is often." This isn't surprising to hear. I often think about her being with Blake, as well, although their relationship came before us.

Speaking of Blake… this grievance is all on me but she should know the way I feel. "I'm furious with myself because I was tending to business instead of being with you the night Blake attacked you. I have to work very hard to not see the image of him on top of you with your dress shoved up to your waist." I look down because I can't look at her when I say the next part. It's bad. "And sometimes I wish I hadn't heard your voice telling me to stop because I wanted to kill him. I still do." I've probably scared the shit out of her, but damn, that feels good to get off my chest.

She doesn't give me time to dwell on what she thinks of hearing me say I want to kill Blake. "I worry you'll miss the thrill of being with other women."

I'd like to address that one—to tell her it isn't possible to ever be thrilled by the thought of being with a stranger after having something so real and true with her. But what we're doing now isn't about explanation; it's about confession. "I worry that one day you'll figure out I'm not worthy of your love."

"I'm terrified you'll decide I'm too complicated and not worth the trouble I cause you." Never. She's a complication I can't live without.

"I'm afraid you'll never get over my past and what I did with those other women." I'm worried more than ever now because she has admitted she thinks of them often.

"I'm still pissed off that you almost added a fourteenth to your list of companions." Can't blame her for being pissed off about that one—what a total fuck-up on my part.

"I'm scared you want to put off having a baby because you're not really sure you want to be with me forever." I check the time on my phone. "Thirty seconds left."

"I'm scared I'll be a shitty mother like my mom." Not possible. She's nothing like her mother.

"I wasn't unhappy when you told me it was your birth control patch I had pulled off."

She narrows her eyes at me. "I'd beat you senseless with a handbag right now if I had one handy."

How can she think she'd be a shitty mother? She already acts more like my mum than her own. "You're becoming more like Margaret McLachlan every day."

I hold up the phone and she announces, "Ten seconds."

It's her turn but I'm going again. We're almost out of time and I have something to say. "I want you to have my baby... please say you will."

She says nothing and the timer alarms, signaling the end of our timed confession. My heart and mind feel clear. Do hers? Or was that the worst thing we could have done?

That was stupid of me to ask her to have a baby during a three-minute confessional. I want to know what she's thinking, but dammit, I can't ask. We agreed this wasn't about discussion.

I bet she's pissed. She's already told me she'd think about it and I agreed I wouldn't pressure her. But now I have. And without giving her the option to respond if we stick to these stupid rules.

I have fucked up again. Why do I keep doing this? "I'll find somewhere else to sleep tonight. Just give me a minute to grab something to sleep in and brush my teeth."

I take my sleep pants from the chest and go into the bathroom. I'm changed and finished brushing when L comes up behind me. She slides her arms around my waist and places the side of her face against my back. She's shorter and smaller so her image is almost completely hidden in the mirror. "I didn't ask you to sleep somewhere else."

"You told me to forget touching you."

"It doesn't mean you have to leave our bed."

I'm not trying to convince her to kick me out of bed but I know when I've fucked up. "I wouldn't blame you if you did. Even I know I've done wrong, L."

"You've also done right." She kisses the bare skin on my back and then her touch is gone too soon. "Even I know that."

I watch her reflection in the mirror as she turns and lifts her hair. "Unzip me?"

I grasp the zipper of her black sheath dress and pull, letting my fingers graze her skin on the way down. I'm sure it's the most action I'll get tonight.

We're standing in the bathroom and I'm peeling her out of a dress following an incident with one of my former lovers. This is like déjà vu because we've done this before. I recall being sent away that night, but not this time. She's letting me stay.

I'd like to kiss her bare shoulder. It's right there, so close to my mouth, begging me to place my lips against it, but I resist because I'm still not sure where I stand.

She catches the straps of her dress and eases them down her body. She wiggles as it slides down and tosses it onto the bathroom counter, leaving her in a black lacy push-up bra and a G. She's hot as hell—like always—and I think this is my punishment for my earlier offenses.

I don't think I can take this. She needs to be covered if I can't touch her. And it doesn't need to be any of that sexy stuff she usually wears to bed. As much as I love her in it, I don't want to see her in it tonight if I can't touch her. "I'll grab you one of my T-shirts."

"Don't."

She reaches behind her back and unfastens her bra before tossing it on top of her dress. I'm surprised by what she's doing because even at her angriest moments, I've never known her to be cruel.

I close my eyes because it's agony to see her this way when she's already told me I can't touch her. "Please don't."

"Please don't what?"

"Torture me." I wave my hands back and forth in front of her near-naked body. "Using this."

"Torture isn't my intention." She pushes her panties from her hips and shimmies out of them. They drop to her feet and she kicks them to the corner, leaving her wearing only black pumps. "Something you said changed my mind. I want you to touch me."

L's forgiving me? Forgetting tonight's events?

"What did I say to change your mind?"

"Shh... it's against the rules to discuss anything we said during our confessional." She steps close so her body is pressed against mine. "It's two thousand fourteen. Let's start the year off right."

She brings my hand to her lips and sucks my index finger into her mouth. She makes a show of sliding it in and out of her mouth, her tongue swirling. Then she moves to my other hand to do the same.

Fuck, it's hot. I'm instantly hard.

She hops up on the counter, her bum landing on my hand towel, and motions with her finger for me to come closer. When I do, she yanks the front of my trousers open and drags my zipper down. She pushes my pants and boxer briefs to my knees and wraps her legs around me. I put my hand on her bum and easily slide her bottom to the edge of the counter.

She puts her hand around my rock-hard cock and slides it up and down her drenched entrance. I flex my hips, trying to get inside her but she pulls away. I expect her to tell me she needs to insert the spermicide but doesn't. "Tell me I'm the only one."

"You're the only one, forever. It'll always be you, L. Never doubt that."

She wraps her arms around me and tilts her pelvis so my tip is pressing against her. "You're the only one I ever want inside me." She reaches around to my bum and digs her nails in as she pulls me into her... without birth control.

I don't think she's ovulating but this is still me inside her without contraceptive so anything could happen. And she's not telling me no. Her body is telling me the complete opposite as her legs alternate between squeezing hard and relaxing as she rides me on the bathroom counter.

Her arms are wrapped around my shoulders and her mouth is pressed to my ear, enabling me to hear every sound her mouth makes as she grinds her body against mine. Every moan, every grunt. Even the soft, breathless sound of her saying my name when she comes, followed by her whispering how much she loves me.

Her climax comes before mine but moments later when I come, I squeeze her hard and close when I empty myself deep inside her womb. "I love you too, L. Only you."

CHAPTER NINE
LAURELYN MCLACHLAN

T HINGS HAVE BEEN SURPRISINGLY GOOD BETWEEN JACK HENRY AND ME SINCE our New Year's confessional. Good isn't the right word. Great is more like it. Who would've thought that telling one another our innermost thoughts would be so healthy? I like this newfound depth in our relationship so much that I may ask him if we can do it again.

Jack Henry asked me to have his baby. Becoming parents is something he began talking about before we were married, but it seems to be on his mind all the time now—which means it's on mine constantly as well.

A baby. That's what I'm thinking about as I stand in Margaret's kitchen preparing the lasagna I'm making for Jack Henry's birthday party tonight, per his request. My mother-in-law comes to me with a bowl of chocolate frosting. She's baking his favorite cake, something she does for every member of the McLachlan family on their birthday. "I have extra. Want to help me clean the bowl?"

"Absolutely." She passes me a spoon and I dig in. "Omigod. That is so good, Margaret." And it is. I've never tasted frosting this delicious. I can see why this is my husband's favorite but it makes me realize something. I've never seen him eat chocolate cake. Ever. I didn't know Jack Henry liked it. I'm his wife so how could I not know that? I bet it's this family history with the heart stuff. He exercises religiously and rarely indulges in things he considers unhealthy because he's fearful of ending up like his father and uncle. I'd like to ask Margaret about it but I don't want to introduce concerns if she hasn't already considered them.

"Did they start work on your music studio yet?"

"They poured the concrete early this week and said we could expect it to be finished sometime in May."

"I would think that's soon considering all the equipment that'll be installed."

One can anticipate fast progress when she's married to a man with money and high expectations. "You know Jack Henry. He sets the bar high and expects everyone else to as well."

Margaret grins. "He gets that from his father. Henry is a hard worker. I'm not sure he would have ever retired if I hadn't cut him off."

"You cut him off of what?"

"Nookie." I giggle because the word itself is funny but hearing her say it makes it even more so. "I'm going to give you some advice because you're still a new wife—and because my son can be a little shit at times. I know; I'm his mum." She looks around as though she's about to reveal top-secret information. "Nookie equals power and there's a reason he wants it from you all the time. It levels the playing field. Don't like something he's doing? Take the nookie away. Get the results you want. Need him to see things your way but he refuses? Withhold the nookie and he'll make the fastest attitude adjustment you've ever seen. Want your husband to retire because he's going to work himself into an early grave and miss his grandchildren growing up the way he missed his kids? Close the gates of nookie and get your husband home with you instead of burying him. That's how you work it, darling. You use the power of the nookie to get the results you want."

Oh, my. She's a sly one. I could learn a lot from her.

Henry comes into the kitchen and opens the refrigerator. He bends down, searching for something, and Margaret sashays over to him. She whispers something in his ear and gives me a wink before returning to the sink of dirty dishes.

Henry grabs a bottle of water from the refrigerator and takes a big swig. "You girls have been standing in here on your feet for too long. Go rest a minute and I'll wash these dirty dishes for you."

Wow. What a sweet father-in-law. "Thank you, Henry." I give him a kiss on the cheek as I pass by. "You're so thoughtful."

Margaret and I go into the living room and put our feet up. "Don't be mistaken, Laurelyn. That was not the offer of a thoughtful man."

"You used the power."

"Yes, I did, and you want to know what's so brilliant about it? I still love being with Henry after all these years so I'd have given it to him anyway. Hell, I'd probably have instigated it myself, so it's win-win."

"You are the master." Margaret is so cool. I think I just fell in love with her a little more. "What time is everyone coming?"

"Seven."

Perfect. That gives me plenty of time to go to the apartment and get ready. "Who should I expect?"

"It's normally only family but we're having extra guests tonight. Chloe is bringing the new guy in her life and three of Jack Henry's mates will be joining us."

"I didn't realize Chloe was dating anyone."

"It's still new so we've not met him, either."

Wow. A few weeks. I guess I've been too busy if I've missed something important like that. "That's great."

"I hope Jack Henry doesn't try to shake him down too much. I may need to speak to him before the dinner—maybe ask him to take it easy since he can be hard on her fellas sometimes."

I can see him being like that, but she's an adult, the same age as me. "Why is he hard on them?"

"It's how he is. He's always been incredibly protective of her since the day she was born." She laughs. "He wouldn't even let Evan near her for the longest time."

"I haven't seen him be overly protective with her."

"He's lightened up since you came along."

"I guess she's glad of that."

"I suspect she is," Margaret agrees.

We sit with our feet propped and Margaret tells me stories about Jack Henry as a child. I can't stop smiling because I'm picturing this beautiful boy with dark hair and bright blue eyes getting into the mischief she's describing.

I wonder if our babies will have his eyes. I hope so.

"What are you giving Jack Henry for his birthday?" Margaret asks.

I'm still smiling but for a different reason and I can't keep it from her. "I have a few things for him but one special gift. He asked for a baby and I've decided to give him one."

"Oh, Laurelyn." She cups her hands over her mouth to muffle a squeal. "A baby. That's wonderful news. Have you told him yet?"

"No. I'll tell him tonight." I have something very special planned but I'm keeping that part to myself.

"He's going to be thrilled."

"I know. I can't wait to see his reaction." I'm pretty sure it's going to be a huge smile and then involve him taking me straight to bed.

Margaret claps her hand like a child. "Will you start trying right away?"

"Is tonight considered right away?"

She grins. "I have a bit of advice for you since you're new at this." She lifts her brows and whispers, "Put a pillow under your bum... after he does his thing. You shouldn't get up right away; let gravity work for you."

Omigod. Margaret is giving me pointers on how to keep Jack Henry's sperm inside so his boys will swim upstream. This isn't awkward at all. "Okay." That's all I can say.

"Stay that way about ten or fifteen minutes before you get up." She giggles before giving me a wink. "I can't wait to get my hands on another grandbaby."

CHAPTER TEN
JACK MCLACHLAN

Mum meets us at the door. "Hello, birthday boy." She squeezes me hard before hugging my wife. "Laurelyn." She whispers something in her ear but I'm unable to make out what it is—just as she intends—and I'm reminded of another time when she did the same thing. These women get along too well. They're going to unite and plot against me.

The old girl is wearing an unusually large grin tonight. That can only mean one thing when it comes to Margaret McLachlan. She's up to something. "What's going on, Mum?"

"It's your birthday, son. I'm just thinking back on the day I gave birth to my firstborn."

I'm calling bullshit. "But you're smiling." She never smiles when she talks about having me.

"Of course I'm smiling," she says. "It was a happy day."

She makes a nice attempt at sounding sincere but I know better. This woman has told me about the day I was born countless times—mostly when I caused her some type of trouble or worry.

It's not really a story that will encourage Laurelyn to want to have our baby but she's bound to tell her about that day from hell at some point. "She was in labor, without any kind of painkiller, for twenty-one and a half hours. I weighed over ten pounds and she thought she would die pushing me out. I'm pretty sure she begged someone to kill her, although she's never admitted it."

Laurelyn's eyes grow large and her jaw drops. "Good lord. Over ten pounds?"

"I did not beg anyone to kill me." She playfully whacks my arm. "Not more than five times, I don't think. But I forgot all the pain when I saw him. He was so beautiful, Laurelyn. He had a headful of black hair... and I'm glad because he was face up when he came out and his head was shaped like a cone. But then he cried and it was music to my ears. He was worth everything I endured and yours will be too."

Laurelyn doesn't need my mum hounding her about a baby. I'm already afraid I've pressured her too much, so I lift my brows as a warning. "Mum."

"I'm zipping it." She makes a motion with her fingers across her mouth and we follow her into the living room. There's a crowd, probably twice as many guests as usual. I see several of my mates and I know Laurelyn will be happy to meet them. Then there's the usual suspects—my parents, Evan and Emma with their trio, and Chloe. And Ben-fucking-Donavon.

I'm blinded by red. "Why the hell are you here?"

"Jack Henry. Ben's a guest in our home." My mum's voice has an edge of warning to it but I don't care. She can whack me as hard as she'd like if she doesn't like what I have to say.

"No one's answered me yet. Who invited this dick?"

Chloe's giving me the evil eye. "I did, and he's not... a dick."

I'm feeling ambushed by my own sister—and maybe by my own wife. "Did you know about this?"

"No." Laurelyn's voice has a high-pitched edge to it, so I take that as a sign she doesn't like being accused. "I only knew that Chloe was bringing the new guy she was dating."

My sister is out of her damn mind if she thinks I'm gonna let that happen. "Oh hell no. You're not dating him."

"I'll go out with whomever I want and there's nothing you can do about it, so stop being a dickhead."

Fuck me. I can't let this happen. He's no good for her and I don't want him near my wife. "Chloe, there's things you don't know about him."

"Ben told me everything." I somehow doubt that.

"Hey, man," Ben says as he steps forward and gestures toward the patio door. "Could we step outside to talk this over instead of making a scene?"

Yeah. I'm sure he doesn't want to have this conversation in front of a crowd. It'll only prove how unsavory he is but I also fear what he'll say about me. He's aware that I didn't know L's last name after being with her for three months. I damn sure don't want him bringing that up in front of the family, so he has me over a barrel.

"We'll be back in a minute."

Laurelyn places her hand on my arm and whispers, "He's here for your sister—not me—so behave."

"Like that's supposed to make me feel better?"

L lifts her brow as a warning and it's the same look I've seen my mum give me a thousand times. "We're here to celebrate your birthday and I'd appreciate you not getting into a brawl."

"I won't, love. I swear."

We go out to the patio and I stand with my arms crossed as I wait for what he has to say. I can't think of a single thing I'd like to hear from this guy.

"I want to start by apologizing for my behavior with Laurelyn."

He's telling the wrong person. "Maybe you should apologize to her instead of me."

"I plan to, but I knew it wasn't possible if I didn't go through you first." He's right. I'm not sure I'd allow him to get that close to her. "I'm sorry I didn't give you the information you needed to find her, but it all seemed really weird to me. You were with Laurie for months and didn't know her last name. I assumed there was a reason for that and it was her own decision. I thought I was protecting her."

Protecting her, my ass! I know how much pleasure he took in denying me what I needed to know. "You did it while wearing a shit-eating grin. You loved seeing me grovel."

"I won't say I didn't enjoy it. I wanted Laurelyn, and you came between us. I couldn't see then that you were the one for her, but I realize that now. It was always you. I never had a chance."

I'm not interested in discussing how much he wanted to fuck my wife. That much I already know. I'm more interested in what his intentions are when it comes to Chloe. He stands to gain a lot professionally by being associated with this family. Or he could just be a bastard looking to give me a jab since he was unsuccessful at closing the deal with my wife. "What about my sister? You going out with her to piss me off or do you see her as an opportunity to further yourself?"

"I like Chloe a lot and our relationship has nothing to do with you or your family."

"Just how did this relationship come about?" I ask.

"I'm in Sydney with my internship, so Addie introduced us a few weeks ago and we hit it off. I asked her out and we've practically been inseparable since." A mental picture of an inseparable Ben and Chloe isn't something I need in my head. "I have my own business connections. I grew up in a family of winemakers just as you did, so I stand to gain nothing in that aspect by having a relationship with Chloe."

I still don't like this fucker. "I'm not gonna bullshit you. I do not care for you at all—and I really don't like you being with my sister—but she's old enough to make her own decisions. If she chooses you, then that's her mistake, but I've got my eyes on you. You fuck with my sister—or my wife—and you're mine."

"I have no intentions of doing either, but you need to get used to the idea of me being around. I don't plan on going anywhere as long as Chloe wants me here."

Fucking perfect. I'll need to thank Addison for this shit later.

THE PARTY WASN'T A TOTAL BUST. L MET THREE OF MY MATES—TREVOR, Ellis, and Wade—which made her extremely happy. I guess she feels like that's an area she knows nothing about since she hasn't met them before. But there are reasons. They've been thick as thieves this year. I'm not sure I want to know what they've been up to because it can't be good. And I'm sure I'd have been part of whatever they have going on if I hadn't been so wrapped up in finding Laurelyn, but I have my priorities in order. They have theirs too: T and A—tits and ass.

All three were checking out my wife right in front of me, but Ellis was shameless in his adoration of her breasts. They looked awesome in the dress she was wearing but I still ended up telling them all to fuck off. Doesn't matter who it is, no one looks at my wife like that. Assholes.

They cackled, thought it was fucking hilarious. I can't believe I was once just like those dicks, but that was all before Laurelyn. She can't imagine all the ways she's changed me.

I'm driving us back to the apartment we keep in Sydney. I'd prefer to be home with L at Avalon for my birthday, but I wouldn't dare go against Margaret McLachlan's plans when it comes to an annual birthday celebration. She loves tradition, even demands it.

L didn't seem to mind and I think it's because she enjoys her new place in this family. It's quite different than what she had growing up. She enjoys being surrounded by those who love her, and boy, is my family crazy about her, especially Mum. There was something different between them tonight and I don't know what. Whatever it is, I've never seen Mum like this with Emma, or even Chloe.

"You're not okay with Ben and Chloe."

"No, I'm definitely not but what can I do? She's not a child. I have to remind myself often that she's the same age as you." Laurelyn and Chloe are different kinds of twenty-three-year-olds. L was forced to grow up fast so she's always felt more mature to me. As much as I love Chloe, she's been spoiled by all of us, including me, so it's difficult to think of her as an adult.

"Ben isn't a bad guy. Take me out of the equation and you wouldn't have had a problem with him. The two of you have a lot in common. I could see you being friends."

Maybe, but L is in the equation. "I don't know if I could ever be friends with him. He knew you were mine and still went after you."

"But he didn't get me and he never will because I'm yours and that isn't going to change." She reaches for my hand. "He was very sincere in his apology to me and I truly believe he likes Chloe for the right reasons. Please try to tolerate him for her sake—she really likes him."

I better not regret this. "I'll give him a chance, but his ass is mine if he does anything to hurt my sister."

"I'll gladly turn you loose on him, McLachlan." L reaches for her phone. "Nothing from Addison. She and Chloe have been hanging out a lot since the wedding, but I'm puzzled about the reason she didn't tell me about them."

I'm not puzzled. "She didn't want you to tell me so I could ruin it before it got started."

"Maybe. She'd expect you to go apeshit crazy, so maybe that's it. But she's been weird lately—sort of like she's checked out on me the last couple of weeks."

Addison's never been great at being there for L so I'm not sure why she's surprised by this. "Ask her to breakfast when we get back to Wagga. Take her to Fusion and you can coerce the truth out of her with their Belgian waffles. They're magnificent."

"Speaking of breakfast, I'm going out to eat with your mum and the girls in the morning before we go back."

"That sounds good."

"What will you do while I'm gone?"

"Sleep in."

She looks at me skeptically. "You don't sleep in."

"I do once a year because I need my rest after my wife gives me birthday sex all night long." Her laugh tells me she must think that's pretty funny. "Don't tell me you find that humorous because I'm wrong."

"You're not entirely wrong but there's more to it than that."

"Partially wrong?"

"I refuse to answer that. You'll find out in two minutes when we're inside and you open your gift from me." Nice. I bet she's going to wear some sexy lingerie.

We go into the apartment. L tells me to sit on the couch while she gets my birthday gift from our bedroom. I'm not so sure it's what I was thinking. She isn't acting like herself—she seems nervous.

She returns to the living room and sits next to me before placing a small rectangular box in my hand. It's wrapped in chocolate-brown paper with a blue ribbon bow and definitely isn't big enough for lingerie —unless it's really tiny.

"Open it."

I remove the bow and tear into the paper as I ponder what could be inside. It's a simple white gift box. What is this? A bracelet? I hope not since I'm not a fan of men in bracelets, but I'd wear it if it's what she gave me.

I remove the top and I'm confused by what I see. "A pregnancy test?" She just had her period a couple of weeks ago, so she can't possibly need to take a test.

"No. It's an ovulation predictor. It tells me when I'm most fertile."

I can only think of two reasons she'd use this: to avoid having sex on the days she's fertile so she doesn't become pregnant, or the complete opposite—because she's ready to. "And you want to know when you're fertile because… ?"

"You asked me to have your baby, and this is me saying yes." A smile spreads across her face. "A baby… it's my gift to you."

I lean over to kiss her mouth and stroke my thumb over her cheek. "Best gift ever."

She lifts a brow. "I took a test earlier and I'm ovulating."

It's weird. Something about hearing her say those words makes me want to throw her over my shoulder and haul her down to our bedroom so I can bury myself deep inside her. "Does that mean you want to start trying now?"

"I do."

"I love when those two words come out of your mouth. It means something crazy good is about to happen."

I get up from the couch and tug so she'll stand with me. I put my hands on her lower back and pull her close. No hug. No kiss. I simply look into her eyes. "This is what you want, right? You're not agreeing because you feel pressured or because you know it's what I want?"

She strokes her hand down the side of my face and I reach up to cup my hand over hers. "It's all I've thought about since you asked on our honeymoon." She laughs. "It's totally insane to be married a month and try to have a baby on purpose, but it's what I want. I'm ready to start our family."

"Our family. I love the sound of that."

"Me too."

I clasp her hand in mine and lead her down the hall to our bedroom. "Can I have a minute? I want to change into something special for you."

Yes! I knew she'd be putting on some hot lingerie for my birthday. "Yeah. You can have two if you need it." She walks into the closet and comes out with a shopping bag. Whoa. I wonder what's in there? "Take as long as you need."

She gives me a naughty grin. "Be back in a jiffy."

This is it, McLachlan. You and L are going to make a baby. There's no going back after it's done. Hmm. I'm surprisingly calm about it, but I guess that's how it feels when you know it's right.

There's no reason to still be dressed when L returns. We both know what we're here for, so I take off my shirt and trousers and place them on the chair in the corner of the room. I'm only wearing my boxer briefs when she comes out of the bathroom and stops in the doorway, leaning against the frame. She shifts her weight to one leg and places a hand on her hip, pushing her breasts up in her ivory chemise. It's a bra at the top with sheer fabric flowing to the edge of the tiny triangle between her legs. It's the ultimate prelude to baby-making.

"What does the birthday boy think?"

I walk toward her and she moves to meet me in the middle of the room. I'm remembering the times when she's been her most beautiful: the night I met her; seeing her again after I thought she was gone forever; watching her walk down the aisle to be my wife. I thought she was beautiful all those times but the way she looks now as she comes to me so we can make a baby… it isn't something I know how to label. Beautiful doesn't begin to cover it. I'm in awe.

I'm overcome by the love I feel for this woman. My eyes fill and a single tear escapes. She's trembling as she comes up on tiptoes to catch it with her lips. "I know." This is a surreal moment for me. This beautiful woman has agreed to take a part of me into her body and join it with hers to make a new being—a little person who looks like us.

She puts her hands on my hips and walks backward toward the bed until the backs of her legs hit the mattress. She sits and glides to the middle. She lifts her foot and curls her toes around the waistband of my boxer briefs, pulling them, and me, in her direction. She uses her index finger to coax me. "Come here, birthday boy. I've got a little somethin' for ya."

I crawl up her body, taking my time as I leave a path of kisses beginning at her belly. When we're face to face, she grasps the back of my neck. "Kiss me," she says as she pulls me down so our mouths can meet.

Her mouth is making love to mine. Slow. Deep. Loving. "I love you, Laurelyn McLachlan."

She stares at my eyes as I hover above and runs her fingertips down my cheek where she kissed my tear away only moments earlier. "And I love you, Jack Henry McLachlan."

I kiss the side of her face and move my mouth down the length of her neck before reaching to unfasten her top. She arches her back, allowing me easier access to the clasp, and I can't resist placing a kiss between her breasts, over her heart.

When I'm finished removing it, she lifts her bum and we repeat the same process with her knickers. "I'm feeling a little underdressed here." She pushes at the waistband of my boxer briefs. "Maybe you should take these off so I don't feel out of place." She helps me push our last barrier away and I discard it over the edge of the bed.

Her legs are parted and I nestle my body between them until my hard cock is against her warm, inviting entrance. But I'm not quite ready. Making love is something we've done countless times, but it's never been for this reason. This time is different. "This is about so much more than us."

She's trembling beneath me. "I know," she whispers. "And it scares me to death, but in a good way."

I'm pressed against her, ready to enter, but I have to ask one last time. "You're sure?"

She lifts her hips and my tip glides just inside her entrance. "Yes." She squeezes her legs and brings me closer. "No doubts."

I press my hand into the mattress so I can wrap it around her lower back. I lift to pull her hips upward and sink into her as far as possible—I'm sure deep is best when trying to impregnate your wife.

Impregnate my wife. I like the sound of that.

I'm moving inside her slowly and my hands move to skim the underside of her arms. I push them over her head and lace my fingers through hers. Our hands are joined as one, just like our bodies.

This is it—two will become three. Maybe. If things go well, this could quite possibly be the last moment we'll share before our child finds its place in her womb.

I release her hands and move mine down her body. Her legs are bent on each side of my hips so I grasp them and push back. Laurelyn moans and I slide my hand between our bodies to the point where we become one. No beginning. No end. But I know L's body as well as my own. She needs more so I find that spot—the one that drives her crazy every time I touch it—and stroke my fingers against the nub. A moment later, her breath quickens as she grasps my back and pulls me against her tighter. She grinds her hips upward so I know I'm right where I need to be. "Right there. Don't stop."

This woman knows better. I never stop until she comes undone.

Her legs tighten and I know what to expect next. And then it happens. Her inner walls squeeze around me, contracting in rhythm. Once. Twice. And then again and again until I lose count because I'm lost in my own world coming apart. Exploding.

I push her legs back and apart as I thrust deeply one last time. I'm making this one count but it won't be a shame if she doesn't get pregnant and we have to do this again. And again. I enjoy it right nicely.

My upper body is braced on my elbows as I hover above her. I'm still inside, unmoving. I push the hair from her face and she smiles, giggling. "What's so funny?"

"I was thinking of all the extreme measures we took to prevent a baby and now we're trying to have one."

It's called irony. "That's what happens when your world is turned on its head. Things you once thought you'd never want transform into your greatest desire."

"You certainly did a one-eighty."

"I decided to go all in, baby. No folding." I kiss her before pulling out slowly and rolling onto my side. "I never imagined myself loving a woman the way I love you. You changed my everything."

She points toward the head of the bed. "Pass me a pillow."

"Sleepy so soon, love?" I hold the pillow out and she takes it. "I thought we might try that again in case the first time wasn't successful."

"It's not for my head." She lifts her hips. "Help me get this under my butt."

Okay. I get this now. She's taking advantage of gravity, which means she's been researching. It could be entertaining to go back and look at the history on our computer. "Where'd you find this tip?"

"Your mother told me to put a pillow under my hips and stay in bed for a while… after you've done 'your thing.' Her words."

Oh fuck. L told my mum? "She'll probably call to see how things went. She has no boundaries when it comes to her kids and that now includes you. You know that, right?"

"I love your mom. We're close so I caved when she asked what I was giving you for your birthday."

L straightens her legs and holds them in the air. Wonder if this is another tip from my mum? "Want me to stand you on your head and give you a good shake?"

"No, but I wouldn't turn you down if you came over here and let me prop these on you." I move over and hook an ankle over each of my shoulders. She puts her hands behind her head and her breasts have never looked fuller. Gravity always works for my girl, never against. "I'm not sure this helps the sperm get in there or not, but it won't hurt."

Shit, how's a guy supposed to have his wife's vagina staring him in the face and not pounce?

I smile down at her and she can guess what I'm thinking. "Don't even think about it for at least ten more minutes."

She's got to be kidding me. "Easier said than done, L." I reach down and run my thumb through her moist slit. "This is practically begging to be licked."

"Don't you dare, McLachlan." She warns me but I don't listen. I'm too captivated by what's in front of me screaming to be tasted. I lean forward but she locks her knees around my head. "It's not a Tootsie Pop. We're not gonna find out how many licks it takes to get to the center—at least not for nine more minutes."

CHAPTER ELEVEN
LAURELYN MCLACHLAN

Nine minutes seems much longer when your horny husband has his head between your knees staring at your stuff like he's starving and you're a buffet. He spent the entire time taunting me, using his filthy mouth to tell me what he was going to do as soon as I would let him.

And I am so turned on.

He's describing how he's going to lick me and I can't wait any longer. "Time's up."

"Hmm… I don't believe it is. I think there's at least two more minutes to go." Great, he wants to taunt me further.

I reach up and grab the back of his neck, pulling him down so we're eye to eye. "Your mouth. On me. Now."

He's amused, as evidenced by his grin. "Now I'm the one who has a little somethin' for you… and this drenched goodness below your waist."

Oh shit. I'm going to die if he doesn't put his mouth on me soon. Or touch me. Something. Anything.

I rock my hips on the pillow because I'm restless and needy. It's excruciating and he could put a stop to it—if only he would. "Please don't tease me because I don't think I can stand it."

He puts his finger on my pubis and presses against the bone. I lift my hips, hoping to coerce it downward, but he resists my coercion. "You mean don't tease you the way I was teased just now while I was forced to look at this?" He looks down and drags his finger through my center. I groan and bite my lower lip as I shift on the pillow. "You're so wet." He strokes one labia and then the other. "Did you know this whole area fills with blood when you're turned on? The action is very much like an erection." He strokes me a few more times before stopping. "It's magnificent to watch the physical changes that occur as you become more aroused. Your breathing increases and you get a flush across your chest. I've never sat back and watched your body change like this. It's beautiful."

Beautiful? I'm about to combust and he's telling me it's lovely? "Touch me. Lick me. Fuck me. I don't care which. It's your choice but do something. Please." Desperation. That's what I hear in my voice.

I'm this man's puppet and it isn't the first time. Nor will it be the last.

I'm still on my back with a pillow under my hips. Not for long. He yanks it out from beneath me and tosses it aside. "Touch you, lick you, or fuck you. My choice, huh?"

"Yes."

"I believe I'll do all three." He flips me over to my stomach and I make an unexpected high-pitched sound when I land on the mattress. Jack Henry finds it amusing; I can hear him chuckle behind me. Then he's at my ear and his voice is breathy. "You're gonna like this."

His promise sends a thrill straight through me and it concentrates in my core. "Whatever it is you're gonna do, I wish you'd hurry up and do it already."

"No instant gratification for you, Mrs. McLachlan. It comes fast and is gone too quickly. I want you to enjoy the anticipation." He slides his hand around to my stomach and then down to the cusp between my thighs. "This is me touching you." He cups his hand over me and moves it up and down. "And this is me licking you." His tongue starts at the base of my lower back and he drags it up my spine slowly. He gets about halfway up when my body bows uncontrollably, sending my bottom up from the bed, arching in response to the sensation. That's when I feel him enter me from behind. "And this is me fucking you. All three at the same time."

His weight presses my front into the mattress. I grasp the comforter and bring it to my mouth to bite so I can stifle my scream. All these sensations—touch, lick, fuck—are too much to bear at once. Each thrust forces a moan, sounding much like an animalistic grunt, from my mouth.

He does something new when he brings his palm down and smacks my bottom. It's not hard enough to hurt but I jump because I wasn't expecting it. And then he squeezes my cheek. Hard. It's not something he's done to me before.

How can he work the front and the back like this at the same time? There's only one answer. Talent.

His mouth leaves my back and is next to my ear. He takes it in his mouth and sucks it hard. I'm pretty sure it's gonna leave a hickey on my earlobe. "I'm so close, L, but I want you to come around me first."

And as if he holds the power to control my body, I do. Big time. I fist the edge of the mattress and scream, "Ohhh!" Each of his last few thrusts propel me across the bed and I'm glad to be holding onto something so I'm not sent face first into the floor.

Gah, he likes it rough sometimes. Good thing I do too.

He stills and lowers his body to lie against my back, kissing across my shoulders. He's so tender and gentle—a huge change from the man forcefully thrusting himself into my body just a moment ago. "I see that Mr. Hyde has returned to being Dr. Jekyll."

I feel him press his face to my back. "You don't like Mr. Hyde?" He rubs his hands up my arms.

"I most certainly do. A lot."

He gives my shoulder one last kiss before pulling out of me and rolling to the bed. He lies next to me, and I don't move when he gently dances his nails up and down my back. "It's fucking ridiculous how much you turn me on. It's like you have this crazy power over me and sometimes I feel like it takes over." He strokes my lower back in a circular motion. "You know I'd want you to tell me if I ever do anything you don't like, right?"

Is he talking about slapping and squeezing my ass? "I know, but don't worry—I love everything you do to me. Especially this new triad of sensation—touch, lick, fuck. I hope you do it again soon."

He lowers his fingertips to my cheeks and traces them back and forth, occasionally gliding one down my crack, but never close enough to touch the place that remains unexplored.

I wonder if he's doing it because he's toying with the idea of trying it. I think I assumed anal sex was something neither of us had experienced, but the truth is I have no idea what he's done with other women. Frankly, I'm not sure I want to know, but the question eats at me and I'm afraid it'll continue if I don't find out. His favorite position is from behind. Does that mean he really wants it the other way but isn't asking me for it?

"Do you think it would be a mistake to talk about sexual encounters we've had with others?"

His hand goes motionless. "I don't want to know anything about you and Blake. I'm content with pretending the whole thing never happened."

I've told him that Blake never made me come. Jack Henry's the only man who's ever done that for me, so he knows sex with Blake wasn't good. I'm sure that leads him to think we didn't do much exploring—and he'd be right. Sex with Blake was always missionary and it ended with him getting off as soon as possible. End of story.

"What if I wanted to know about the things you've done with the women before me?"

He sighs. "I'd say no good can come from talking about it." He begins stroking my back again. "You are my wife. Nothing before you matters. Nada."

But it does because it matters to me. I want to know if he's fucked another woman in the ass. More importantly, I need to know if he liked it, so I'm going for it. I'm pushing all my chips to the center of the table. No folding for me. "Did you have anal sex with the others?"

His hand goes motionless again. "What do you hope to gain by talking about things that happened before I knew you?"

Shit. That's a yes. Now I wish I hadn't asked.

I drop my face to the bed but turn away from Jack Henry. I don't want him to see how bothered I am. "I just wanted to know that I was the one to fulfill your deepest desires, not someone else who came before me."

"L. That's not my deepest desire."

"But you liked doing it?"

"I didn't say I'd done that with any of the others. I haven't." His hand returns to its previous motion. "I think all guys think about it. I know I do when I'm giving it to you from behind, but it's not something you've done before. I figure you'll tell me if you ever want to try it and we'd experiment, if it's what you want. If you never want to, it's fine."

The act seems so unnatural and unromantic to me. "It scares me."

"Then we won't do it. It's not a big deal."

"I'm sure it's something Addison has done. I can ask her to tell me about it." I lift my head and peer over my shoulder. "I would try it if it's what you wanted."

"My mates talk about it all the time, but this is what I know. Fucking you in the ass doesn't get us a baby." He kisses my shoulder. "I want all of my swimmers in the right place."

Good grief.

I lift my head and roll over so I can look at him. I'm almost shocked by his words. Almost. He just used the phrase *fucking you in the ass* and the word *baby* in the same sentence. I'm pretty sure that combination is just wrong, but that's my caveman. No filter. And I love him for it.

"If this whole conception thing works out tonight, then we'll have a baby before Christmas." And before our one-year anniversary. That's a little terrifying.

"If you got pregnant tonight, when would the baby come?"

"I'd be due on October first." He looks at me grinning and I shrug. "What? I Googled it."

Breakfast with Margaret, Emma, and Chloe turned into the two mothers giving me all kinds of tips on how to get pregnant. Between the two of them, they have six kids, so it appears they know what they're talking about.

I return to our apartment after spending the morning with the McLachlan ladies and find our bags sitting next to the door. "In a hurry much?"

"There's a rainstorm coming soon. I'd prefer to be home before it starts."

"You don't like driving in the rain?" Technically, I guess it's riding instead of driving since we'll be in the backseat.

"Not really. Dad and I were in a car accident in the rain when I was ten. I still remember the car hydroplaning." He stops to kiss my forehead as he walks by with the last piece of luggage. "I haven't been much of a fan since."

"Was it a bad accident?"

He puts the bag down and points to his upper arm. "Broke my arm so bad, the bone was sticking out through the skin."

I wince, thinking of the pain he must've endured at such a young age. "That sounds terrible."

He pushes his sleeve up and I'm able to see a faint scar—one I've never noticed before—and I stroke my fingertips over it. "It wasn't pleasant."

There's so much I still don't know about Jack Henry, but I plan to learn it all.

I place my purse on the table by the door. "Can I have a minute to do a walk-through? Just to make sure I'm not leaving anything I want to take home."

"Of course. You can do that while I take these bags to the car."

I walk into the bedroom and the linens on the bed are thrown about from our baby-making sessions. I guess he has someone who'll come in to clean after we're gone. Or maybe I've assumed too much and it's something I should've taken care of prior to leaving. Too late now.

I feel him come up behind me and his arms wrap me in a tight cocoon. "Remembering what we did in that bed last night? And this morning?"

"I am—vividly. There's a lot of biological material on those sheets. I should have washed them this morning since we're leaving." It seems gross, and maybe rude, to leave the bedding for someone else to clean.

"I have someone who will come in to take care of it."

Well, there's no time for worrying about it now. "Okay. Let me take a look in the bathroom and then we can go."

I go inside for a once-over and decide I'm all good. If I leave something, I can buy it in Wagga. Maybe. It's not exactly a large town with a lot of shopping options but it's where Jack Henry and I have made our home, and I love living there.

I'm walking out the door when something in the trash can catches my eye. I stop and look at the blue box I've become so very familiar with since our honeymoon—one of our many boxes of spermicide. I reach down to take it out and hold it up while standing in the doorway. I clear my throat to catch Jack Henry's attention. "I see you trashed this. Did you take pleasure in doing that?"

He gives me a crooked grin. "Hell yeah, I liked throwing that shit away. It makes our decision to have a baby feel much more real."

I'll agree with that. It's feeling very real right now.

CHAPTER TWELVE
JACK MCLACHLAN

We arrive at Avalon with about thirty minutes to spare before the bottom drops out of the sky and a raging thunderstorm descends. Laurelyn's standing at the wall of windows overlooking the vineyard, watching the sheets come down. "I love rain. It relaxes me."

I approach from behind and wrap my arms around her waist. "I don't dislike rain, only driving in it."

"It's perfect for napping."

"Then you should go lie down for a while and I'll get you up in a couple hours."

"I am pretty tired." She looks at me over her shoulder. "Both of us were up late, so I think you should join me." I'm not sure but I think this is an invitation for something besides napping? "It's Sunday—Mrs. Porcelli isn't here." Yes. This is an invitation for daytime sex and perhaps a nap afterward. Both work great for me.

I tug on her hands. "I'm in."

I lower the roman shades, darkening the bedroom. "You're right. Today is perfect for napping."

She crawls onto the bed and then moves to her knees. She pulls her dress over her head and drops it before reaching around to unfasten her bra. "It is, but I think today is even more perfect for making a baby."

She's going full force at Project Conception and it's a total turn-on. "You're really in to this." I kick off my shoes and unfasten my jeans. I pull my T-shirt over my head and let it fall to the floor.

She wiggles her bum as she pushes her knickers down her hips. "I don't do anything halfway."

I'm moving to the bed when she tosses the white lace at me, successfully landing it on my shoulder. I grasp the nearly nonexistent piece of fabric and bring it to my nose. Her scent is intoxicating and I'm positive it's impossible to ever get enough of it. I'm completely possessed by her. "Do you realize you hold complete authority over me?"

"Funny, I've thought the same thing about you on many occasions."

"I once chose to do things only if they pleased me. Now everything I do is for you because I want you to be happy."

She crawls to the edge of the bed to meet me and puts her arms around my shoulders. She drags her mouth across my jawline toward my ear. "And I am. You can't imagine how happy you make me."

"Bet I can."

She backs away and moves to sit on her bum before sliding to the middle of the bed. She spreads her hair as she lies down, a precaution she takes so it doesn't get caught beneath her back. It's crazy how great she looks—sexier than any woman I've ever seen photographed in a nudie mag—and she's for my eyes only. I covet that.

She's lying on her back with her feet apart and knees closed. She looks so timid and innocent, but I know better, so I kneel and place a hand on each leg and push them apart. She lifts her arms over her head and arches her back as she grasps the edge of the mattress. She knows something good is about to happen and I wouldn't dare disappoint.

Touch. It's so simplistic in certain aspects, and so very complex in others.

I place my thumb against Laurelyn's clit, applying the slightest pressure, but I don't move it. The brain is the largest sex organ for a woman, so I want her to anticipate what's coming… to crave it. I want to hear her ask me to give it to her. I won't deny that I enjoy holding this kind of power over her, the same as she enjoys the control she has over me.

She begins rotating her hips but my hand remains stationary, frustrating her to no end. I give her a few rotations of my thumb and she moans once before I stop. "Come on, McLachlan. Don't do this to me."

"Don't do what?"

She lifts her foot to my shoulder and pokes me with her toes. "You know what. You're teasing me."

"I need specifics."

She rolls her eyes. "You want me to talk dirty."

"Yeah. I want to hear you say filthy things like a bad girl." She rocks against my hand and I move it away. "Uh-uh… you don't get what you want until you ask for it."

I wait in anticipation of the nasty things she might say. What will it be? Finger-fuck her? Suck her clit? Put my tongue inside her? I'm hard with anticipation but she shocks me with her words, as she often does. "I want you to put a baby inside me." Her voice is soft and so sweet. It crumbles any of the bad-boy exterior I pretend to have.

I was set to have fun, to play dirty. I wanted to make her beg for an orgasm but hearing her ask me for a child changes everything. It brings out my tender side, a part of me I didn't know existed until she came into my life, and it's something she sees far too little.

I place my hands on her hips and rub my thumbs over her hipbones. "I can't wait to watch you grow with our child." I lower my mouth to her stomach and place a kiss below her navel. "I'm going to kiss your swelling belly every day."

Her hand is at the back of my head, her fingers stroking my hair. "You'll make a wonderful father."

I move up so I'm hovering above her, careful to not press too much of my weight against her. "You told me you were afraid you'd be a shitty mother, like Jolie."

"We aren't supposed to address anything said during confessional. We agreed, McLachlan. That's the reason we can feel safe to say the things we wouldn't normally confess to one another."

"I know, and I'll only make an exception this one time because I want you to go into this knowing you are nothing like Jolie. You are the most self-sacrificing person I know and your love stretches beyond measure. It isn't possible for you to be anything but a wonderful mother."

"I love you."

"I love you too." She bends her knees and I pull back so I can move into position. She pulls me down so she can kiss my mouth and I whisper against her lips, "And this baby will be loved." Her hands find mine so she can intertwine our fingers. She squeezes them into a tight fist and watches my eyes as I enter her. "He or she already is."

She doesn't take her eyes from mine as I move in and out of her. It feels so intimate, like she's seeing straight into the depths of my soul, and it leaves me feeling spread wide, exposed. I've never felt a moment like this with anyone, and I love it. I want her to see all of me.

I'm sliding in and out of L slowly when I feel her legs come up and around my body. She's coaxing me deeper so I thrust harder, bringing me closer to climax. I push her legs back and apart as I thrust the last time, filling her body with a part of myself.

When I'm finished, I pull out slowly and reach for a pillow at the head of the bed. I motion for her to lift her bum. "Upsy, love." She lifts and I slide the pillow under her hips, repeating the same routine as the night before with her legs in the air resting on my shoulders.

"I don't think my legs have to be up. I'm sure there's been plenty of babies conceived without being in this position."

She tries to take her ankles from my shoulders but I hold them firmly in place. "But the view is so very lovely, Mrs. McLachlan. It would be a favor to me personally if you stayed this way for a while."

She grins while shaking her head. "You're going to do it again, aren't you?"

"Do what?"

"Taunt me until you can have your way with me... again."

"The first time, we make love because it's about the baby. The second time, we fuck because it's about us." She pretends to gasp in outrage, but I know she's used to the things I say so I rarely shock her anymore. "You didn't come just now so tell me, Mrs. McLachlan, what it is you want."

"I want you to rub me with those talented fingers of yours." She takes my hand and places my finger over her clit. "Right here."

I begin moving in a circular motion. "Like this?"

She closes her eyes and her words come out as a breathy whisper. "Yes."

"You're one orgasm behind me. I don't think it would hurt a thing to play catch-up while we're waiting. Do you agree?"

She's rocking her pelvis against my fingers and can't sit still. "I couldn't agree more."

"Then I have a task before me. A very beautiful one." I use my thumb to stroke her center up and down several times before concentrating on the tight nub at the top. It's her most sensitive spot and I alternate between fast and slow, hard and soft. She's building. I can tell by her body's reactions but I want to finish her off with a bang, so I lower my mouth and suck her clit. I'm inconsistent with the pressure and speed so she's unable to predict what will come next.

A moment later, she fists my hair and moans, "Ohh... ohh... ohh." She unclenches her hand and her entire body goes limp. That's when I know she's in that place, the one where she's blissful and euphoric. There's no other feeling in the world like it.

CHAPTER THIRTEEN
LAURELYN MCLACHLAN

I can't believe it. Jack Henry and I are trying to get pregnant. Addison is going to shit when I tell her.

Daniel drops Addison and me at the Castlebury Hotel where we'll be dining at the restaurant Jack Henry recommended. She was running late, as usual, so we're doing brunch instead of breakfast.

An attractive hostess escorts us to our table and calls me by name—Mrs. McLachlan—when we're seated. How does she know?

I lift the menu but I'm not reading it. "That was weird, right?"

I can see that she doesn't know what I'm referring to. "What was?"

"The hostess called me Mrs. McLachlan but I don't know how she knew. I didn't make reservations, so there's no reason for her to know my name." My mind immediately goes to that place: is this woman one of the twelve and she knows who we are?

"You're married to Jack McLachlan. People know him and they make it their business to know who his wife is." Addison lifts her menu. "She's probably green with envy that she'll never get to fuck him."

I hope that's the case, but if she's one of the companions who came before me, then she already has. Many times.

The hostess is older than me but still young—not at all the type Jack Henry would've chosen.

I need to stop this. He's my husband so nothing before me matters. He told me so last night.

Another woman walks up to our table. "Mrs. McLachlan. Welcome to Fusion Restaurant. Julie is your server and she'll be with you shortly. May I get you something to drink while you look at the menu?"

I think I need alcohol. "I'll have a mimosa."

I expect the same from Addison but she surprises me. "Orange juice, please."

I feel a little weird drinking alone. "Why aren't you getting a mimosa? I know how much you love them."

Addison touches her hand to her forehead. "I have a headache. I don't figure it's a good idea to put champagne on top of that."

I pick up my purse and begin digging because I know she hasn't taken anything for it. That's how she is. "I'm sure I have something in my purse that you can take."

"I'm good, Laurie. You don't always have to take care of me like I'm a child."

She's never minded it before. "You're being pissy this morning."

"I'm sorry. I was restless last night. You know I'm a bitch when I haven't had my sleep."

She's worse than a child without a nap when she's tired. "It's supposed to storm again later. It'll be a perfect day for napping."

We place our order and the food arrives. I still haven't brought up Ben and Chloe but I can procrastinate no longer. "Last night was Jack Henry's birthday party with the family and I gotta tell ya, Addie... we were pretty shocked to see Ben there with Chloe."

"Oh hell." Her eyes grow large.

"Why didn't you tell me they were dating?"

"I'm sorry. I know I should have—and I meant to—but I've had some pretty serious shit going on lately."

Addie always has serious shit going on. "So bad you forget to tell me my sister-in-law is dating your brother, whom my husband despises? Doesn't make sense that you would forget something like that."

Addison's eyes fill with tears. She squeezes them tightly and big messy drops roll down each cheek. "Laurie. I've messed up big time. I mean, I've really fucked up." She carefully wipes the tears from her eyes using the corner of her napkin in an attempt to prevent smearing her perfect makeup.

I'm not oblivious to Addison's tendency to be dramatic, but dread grows deep within my gut. "I'm sure it isn't as bad as you think."

Her eyes appear larger than usual as she looks up to. More tears roll down her cheeks as she nods. "Yes, it is, and I don't think I can do the only thing that would fix all of it." She's sobbing and it scares the shit out of me because this isn't my Addie.

I love my best friend but she's selfish as hell, so there's only one thing that would make her react this way. Something must have occurred between her and the man she adores with all her heart. "Has something happened between you and Zac?"

She makes the ugly cry face and then uses her hands to conceal it. "Oh, something has definitely happened between us. I've joined that statistic they warn you about—the less than one percent of people whose birth control fails even when they take it correctly." Her body shakes because she's crying so hard. "I'm pregnant."

"Oh, shit."

"Yeah," she laughs, but not the humorous kind. "Me having a baby is definitely an 'oh, shit' moment."

I know they aren't married, so the timing isn't ideal, but I don't understand why her reaction is so extreme. She loves Zac. He loves her and they're great together. I have no doubt they'd marry and be together forever anyway. "It's a shock. I'll give you that, but I don't understand why you're so upset."

"Are you kidding me, Laurie? I'm not mother material. I'm too into me and what I want." She's shaking her head and looking at me like she thinks I may have lost my mind. "My mouth is too damn filthy. The kid's first word would be fuck. No doubt."

"I think you'll make a wonderful mother and I'm sure Zac agrees. What did he say when you told him?"

Addison looks away. "I haven't told him."

"Why not?"

She looks so sad. "Do you really think he wants to hear that I'm knocked up?"

I can only stare at her as I think of how happy Jack Henry would be if it were me telling him we were having a baby. I can almost see the broad smile on his face, his bright blue eyes dancing with happiness. I imagine him scooping me from the floor and spinning me round and round as he tells me how much he loves me and how happy he is.

But this isn't happening to me, so I shove the daydream from my mind and return to reality. Addison's reality. "I'm sure a baby will come as a shock for Zac but he loves you. I don't think it'll be an unwelcome surprise."

She sighs while shaking her head. "You're wrong."

How can she know? "Has he told you he doesn't want kids?"

"He wants children." She covers her face with her hands. "But I don't think he wants them with me."

Addison is clearly shaken and lacks her usual confidence. "Why would you say that?"

"We've been together a year and he hasn't proposed. Shit, he never even talks about marrying me. The only future we ever discuss is one with him owning his own vineyard. I'm never part of the equation."

Wow. I had no idea. But that doesn't mean he has no plans to marry Addison. I've seen the way he looks at her and I know he's head over heels in love with her. "He's ambitious. I'm sure he's waiting because he'd like to have a way of supporting you and your habits before he makes you his wife. Zac's no fool. He's figured out that you're high maintenance."

She grins but it's halfhearted. "Then we could be years away from him being able to afford me. Or maybe he's years away from being ready to be a husband and father."

"Zac might have a choice on the husband part, but he doesn't on the parent thing. Kids don't wait around for their parents to be ready. They come when they decide they want to." Look at me. It took over twenty years for my parents to finally act like a mother and father. Sort of.

"Maybe he thinks I'm good enough to fuck but not good enough to be his wife or the mother of his kids."

"There's no way he thinks that. I'd bet money he asks you to marry him as soon as he knows there's a little Zac inside you."

"But don't you see? That's exactly what I don't want. He needs to marry me because he loves me more than anything in this world. Even more than his dream of owning a successful vineyard. I want him to love me the way Jack loves you. I won't settle for less."

That's probably one of the most mature things I've ever heard come out of Addie's mouth. "And you shouldn't have to."

"Oh my God, Laurie. I'm going to have a sweet little adorable chubby-cheeked... shit machine." She leans over and rests her forehead against her palms. "I'm going to get fat and have stretch marks. And hemorrhoids. You know that has to be a total turn-off. Oh God. My sex life is over."

And here we go with the exaggerating. "I'm sure there are measures you can take to prevent those things, or at least reduce them. You should do some research so you'll know what to expect."

Her head spins so she can see me. "Let me guess. You're suggesting I read that book about pregnancy expectations."

Addison makes no bones about it. She is no intellect and doesn't claim to be. The world is lucky if she reads stop signs. "It might be a good place to start... after you tell Zac."

She shakes her head, her face stern. "No way. I'm not ready to do that."

She's being unreasonable. How long does she plan to hide this? This secret has an expiration and it will reveal itself with or without her permission. "You can't keep this from him for long. He's going to figure it out and I can't imagine that going over well."

"I know. It won't take long before he figures out I'm missing my period. God, he's such a control freak. He keeps up with my cycles better than I do, but I need a little time to sort out how he might take the news."

A control freak is exactly what Addie needs—someone to steer her in the right direction. I know her and I understand what she's saying without hearing the words directly. I'm afraid it won't go over well if she baits Zac to get his reaction. She's not considering the whole picture. It's easy to say what one would do when they're not actually in the situation. No one truly knows how they'll feel about a circumstance until it happens to them. "Please don't try to make Zac speculate about a proposed pregnancy. Your baby isn't hypothetical. It's real and he deserves to know as soon as possible."

"And I'll tell him but I need to know how he feels about me—minus a baby—first. If he asks me to marry him, I want to know it's because he loves me, Laurie. Not on account of an obligation or because he wants to hang on to me because he's afraid his child will slip away."

Okay. I understand her desire to want to know his true feelings for her before he finds out about the baby. I would feel the same if standing in her shoes. "Be smart about the way you do this. The last thing you need is for him to feel deceived."

A shocked expression comes over her. "What if I've been looking at this the wrong way? I've imagined him asking me to marry him because he wants to do the right thing but what if I'm wrong and he tells me he never wants to see me again? Or wants me to get an abortion? He has so many dreams for the future and I'm afraid he'll think a baby will ruin it all."

I hadn't considered that possibility and I'm not sure why. Isn't that sort of what my dad did to my mom? "If he does, then screw him. He can piss off because you have me. I'll always be on your side and will help you raise this baby."

Addison reaches across the table to cup her hand around mine. "You're always the stable one and I'm the loose cannon. It should be you having a baby. Not me."

This is probably the one time Jack Henry would completely agree with Addison. "It will be one day." Hopefully one day very soon.

※

JACK HENRY'S SITTING AT HIS DESK LOOKING AT A VINEYARD MAP. "HEY, babe." He puts his arms out for me so I go to him. He pulls me onto his lap and nuzzles his nose against my neck. "How did brunch go with Addison?"

He's really asking if I got an explanation out of her regarding why she didn't tell me about Chloe and Ben. "She said it slipped her mind."

He pulls back and looks at me. "And you believe her?"

I put my hand up, indicating that I need to explain. "Not at first, but then she told me about everything going on in her life and I knew it was the truth. She's been preoccupied."

He leans back in his chair, taking me with him. "What has little Miss Self-Absorbed gotten herself into this time?"

"She's pregnant."

He lifts his brows. "Is it Zac's?"

I slap my hand against his chest because I can't believe he's asked. "Of course it is. She's not a whore."

"Did she do it on purpose so he'd marry her?"

Wow. His opinion of Addison is even worse than I thought. "No. She hasn't even told him yet because she's terrified he'll tell her to get lost."

"Zac's not in the best place to take on a baby right now, but he'd be a motherfucker to turn her away. You think he'd do that?"

I'll kill him if he does. "I don't believe so because I know he loves Addison."

"Haven't they discussed marriage?" he asks.

"She says they never talk about it and it's eating at her. That's another reason she hasn't told him. She wants to figure out his thoughts about marrying her without a baby in the equation."

Jack Henry shakes his head. "Shit. Those two are in a damn mess. So glad that's not us."

"I know."

"Did you tell her we've decided to have a baby?"

I wanted to so badly but it was the wrong time. "No. I couldn't after she told me she was knocked up."

"Don't worry about it, love. It'll all work out for them." I know. My best friend and I will be pregnant together if all works out the way I hope. Our babies will be born close together. It may not seem like it now but it's actually pretty perfect.

"You're right. Zac's crazy in love with her and he'll drop on his knee as soon as he hears her say the word baby."

※

IT'S ONLY BEEN A FEW WEEKS SINCE WE WERE IN SYDNEY TO CELEBRATE JACK Henry's birthday, but now it's time to return to my in-laws for mine, although my actual birthday isn't for a few more days. The best part is that I get out of doing the cooking this time and Chloe, a professional chef, is preparing dinner. Another plus? Margaret is baking my cake of choice. Chocolate—yes, sweet baby Jesus—definitely chocolate. I could easily become hooked.

I finish packing early and go out to Jack Henry's office to see how much longer he'll be. I'd like to get to Henry and Margaret's early so I can talk one on one with Chloe since I'm certain she'll be inviting Ben tonight. I'd like for that to go a little smoother this time around.

Jack Henry isn't over the whole Ben thing and I don't suspect he will be any time soon. He still hates him for pursuing what he considered his. Too bad he failed to inform me that I belonged to him. It would've saved us a lot of grief and time apart, but I know in my heart that everything happens for a reason.

I tap on Jack Henry's half-opened door. "Hey, handsome. I wanted to see how much longer you'd be." I stop dead in my tracks when I see the leggy brunette in a short skirt reaching across his desk—across him. Her blouse is so low cut, I expect a nipple to jump out if she stretches any harder.

He appears oblivious to what she's doing—of course he would with me standing right here—but how can he be? It's so blatantly apparent that she's trying to make him notice her great rack. Hell, they're so nice, they catch my attention.

"This is Bianca, the intern I hired for the semester." I remember him saying he took on an intern but he never mentioned it was a female and he damn sure didn't tell me she was hot. "This is my wife, Laurelyn."

I smile and offer my hand. "It's a pleasure."

"I've heard a lot about you." Hmm… funny. I haven't heard a single word about her.

"I hope all good."

"Absolutely."

"I'm finishing up, babe." Jack Henry uses a red pen to circle an area on the map they're looking at. "This entire section needs to be scouted for downy mildew. I've seen a few suspicious areas and it's imperative to head it off early. You'll be looking for yellow oil spots on the leaves. The infected ones are usually on the outside of the canopy but not always. You can find it on the top too."

I understand very little of what he's just said but she does. He's speaking vineyard, and she understands it perfectly.

"Got it, Jack." She's calling him Jack? I don't like that. With the exception of Mrs. Porcelli, all of his employees call him Mr. McLachlan. This woman's not even a paid employee; she's an intern.

"I'm finished here if you're ready to go."

Oh boy, am I ever.

We're not fifteen minutes into the drive when I can stand it no longer. I have to ask. "You've not mentioned Bianca. When did she come to work for you?"

"December."

Oh hell. He's been working with this woman for two months and hasn't mentioned her once? What gives? "Why haven't I seen her before today?"

"She's rotating through the vineyards. This is her first week at Avalon." A beautiful woman has been roaming around my home vineyard for a week and I didn't know? What kind of dumb-ass wife isn't aware of that?

"I find it a little strange she was dressed in a short skirt and low-cut blouse for intern work. Wouldn't that be a little inappropriate for scouting?"

"She was dressed like that because she had an appointment in town this morning. She won't go out scouting in that." He glances at me and then back at the road. "Where are you going with this, L?"

I recall the way her breasts were thrust in his face. "She looked like she was trying to breastfeed you when I walked into your office."

"You're being ridiculous. I've known that girl since she was a child. She's Mr. Brees's granddaughter. You remember him, right? One of my very good clients who gave us the tickets to Madama Butterfly. Accepting her as an intern is a favor to him."

He's wrong. That child is all grown up and, outfit aside, I saw something in the way she maneuvered her body around him. She wanted him to want her. I know because a woman has the gift of intuition and mine is screaming at me, Beware of this woman, Laurelyn. She wants your husband.

He doesn't see it, or maybe he just refuses to admit it to me, but my radar is on high alert. I won't be taking my eyes off her any time soon. "Of course I remember who Mr. Brees is. He's responsible for my first opera house orgasm."

"Really, L? You're giving Randall Brees, a man who very much resembles a Keebler elf, credit for that orgasm?"

"You know what I mean. He's the reason I met your family. If he hadn't sent you those tickets, I wouldn't have been with you in Sydney on the night Henry was taken to the hospital. Meeting the McLachlans set our whole arrangement into a different motion—it changed everything. Mr. Brees has no idea but he may very well be behind me becoming your wife."

"Wow. Here I was thinking all this time that I was the reason you became my wife."

I roll my eyes. "Ha ha."

"All joking aside. You have no reason to worry about Bianca. She knows you're my wife and I'm not interested in her."

I hate looking like the jealous wife. It's not an attractive look for anyone, but I'd choose it over the naïve, played wife any day. "I'll cool my jets because I trust you but let's be clear about one thing. She makes one false move—one—and she's gone."

He grasps my hand and brings it to his mouth for a kiss. "Anything you say, babe."

We arrive at Henry and Margaret's a couple hours before my party. Jack Henry plants himself in the living room with his dad so he can check out the score of some game on TV. Suits me. I want to talk to Chloe about Ben, so I go into the kitchen. I see my chocolate cake on the counter and have an incredible urge to grab a fork. "Someone is eyeing that dessert very intently."

"I've been craving this cake since the last time we were here. I almost called to beg you for one last week. I was willing to drive four hours to pick it up."

"You should've called me. I would've made one and brought it to you." Margaret's grinning. I'm sure she's assuming I have this special craving for a particular reason, but I don't. I think it's just a delicious cake and I didn't get enough of it before.

I can tell Chloe is processing this conversation. "I've seen that same reaction from some of the people at the restaurant and they're always pregnant. Think you could be?"

Margaret knows we're trying but I'm not ready to go there with the rest of the family. And yet I don't want to lie to Chloe. She's my sister-in-law, and also a good friend, but I don't want to say anything to spur more questions. I shrug, attempting to appear nonchalant. "Not that I'm aware of." I walk over to take a look at what she's preparing—and change the subject. "What did you decide to go with?"

The birthday girl, or boy, always get to choose the meal. I couldn't come up with anything that sounded great so I told Chloe to choose for me. "My version of chicken and biscuits. I thought you might like it since it's sort of similar to your southern cuisine."

"That sounds so good. I need a huge glass of sweet tea to go with it."

"Done. Jack told me you'd want that rather than wine so I gave it a try." Smooth one, McLachlan. You got me out of having to refuse alcohol.

She takes out a pitcher from the fridge and pours some over ice. "Try this and tell me if it's sweet enough for you."

It's really good. "You nailed it. Tastes just like Nanna's."

"It tastes like syrup to me but Jack said it had to be really sweet."

"He knows me well."

Margaret leaves the kitchen saying she wants to check on the game's score. She gave me a wink when she said it so I'm certain she has an agenda—to quiz Jack Henry on how the baby-making efforts are going since she can't ask me in front of Chloe.

"How are things with Ben?"

"Really good. I know Jack hates him but I like Ben a lot. He treats me well—better than any of the other losers I've dated lately." She gets a giddy look on her face. "It's crazy, Laurelyn. It's only been a little over a month since we started dating but I think… I think he could be the one."

I never thought Ben was a bad guy. He just got a little zealous when Jack Henry started swinging his weight around. Honestly, I think he liked the challenge Jack Henry presented more than he liked me. "It's not crazy at all. I knew very soon after I started dating your brother that Jack Henry was the only man I'd ever love."

"Ben's perfect for me, although I never thought I'd want to be with someone in the business. They don't make the best family men." She looks up at me and scrunches her face. "I'm sorry. I didn't mean that the way it sounded. Jack has changed because of you and he'd never be absent like Dad."

"It's fine. I know what you mean... but you should probably be prepared for your brother to cause problems. He's not happy about your relationship."

"I don't care. His approval isn't a requirement for me to be happy."

"I'll work on him."

Chloe comes over to give me a hug. "I'd appreciate that. I say I don't care if he approves, but that's not the truth. I want him to accept Ben."

"I think he will in time. All of this is still fresh. Be patient with him."

She puts a baking dish in the oven, sets the timer, and then comes back to sit with me at the bar. A huge grin spreads across her face. "This isn't something I could say to Addison but I've been dying to tell someone." She giggles before leaning over to whisper, "Ben is supremely fucklicious." She groans. "Mmm... the man is damn good at what he does."

Okay. So, I don't have to ask if they're having sex—not that I would anyway. "It certainly helps when it's good, doesn't it?"

"Oh yeah. No man has ever done to me the things he does. I just thought I was having good sex before. But umm... no. Is that how American men are?"

"I only had one sexual relationship before Jack Henry, and it was terrible, so I think you lucked out with Ben being... supremely fucklicious. It has nothing to do with him being American."

She's wearing a shocked expression. "Laurelyn. You only had one sexual partner before my brother?" Her eyes are huge. "You were almost a virgin when you met him. I bet he fucking loved that."

"Actually, he hates it. He wishes I hadn't had the one."

"I can totally see that; he's a greedy bastard. But you're his wife so I guess he's supposed to feel that way."

Jack Henry comes into the kitchen to grab a beer. "Smells good in here, sis." We both go silent and he knows he's interrupted something. "What are you up to in here?"

"Nothing," we say simultaneously and then look at one another and burst into laughter.

"Girl talk?"

"Yeah. You could call it that."

He twists the cap off his beer and tosses it into the trash. "I like girl talk."

"You wouldn't like hearing this. It's not your flavor."

"Try me."

For a moment—like, a nanosecond—I consider telling him how supremely fuckable his sister finds Ben but then decide I can't do it; I don't want to sour his mood. "I love you too much to do that to you, cave man."

CHAPTER FOURTEEN
JACK MCLACHLAN

I'M THE ONLY ONE WHO DIDN'T HAVE A GIFT FOR LAURELYN AT MY PARENTS' house on Friday night but she understood since it wasn't her actual birthday. However, today is. She's going into town for lunch with Addison and that couldn't work better for me since I'll be picking up her gift and driving it home. I want her new Cayenne here, but hidden, when she comes back from her day out in Wagga Wagga.

She comes into the office to say goodbye. "Ooh, I haven't seen Mr. good-looking suit in a while."

She's right. I haven't worn a business suit in quite some time. "You like?"

"Oh yes. It reminds me of the way you looked when we first met. You're still hotter than the devil's ass."

"I have a business meeting in town with a new client. He has two hundred storefronts. Not huge but this guy has established these businesses in a ridiculously small amount of time, so I'd expect him to double it within the year. I think it's going to be big." I'm not obsessed with work like my dad was but I'll be pretty damn happy to score this account.

"That's great news."

I sort of need to know what her plan is for the day. "How long will you and Addison be out?"

"I'm not sure. We're doing lunch at Alfredo's and I'm hoping I can talk her into doing some shopping. She really needs a pick-me-up. Hiding the pregnancy from Zac is wearing her down." That's just like Laurelyn to take her special day and turn it into a way to cheer up her friend. Sometimes I get mad at her for always putting others ahead of herself, but it's who she is.

Addison deserves to be worn down. It's no small thing, what's she's doing. That baby is Zac's too and he deserves to know it exists. "Maybe that should be a sign to her that she shouldn't be doing this."

"No argument there. You know I'm supporting her, not her decision, right?"

"I know. I guess I thought she'd come around in a day or two."

"I'd hoped for that as well but Addison's stubborn once she makes up her mind about something."

That's the pot calling the kettle black. "Sounds like someone else I know. Maybe you should take her vibrator shopping to get all this off her mind."

"I was thinking the same thing."

Is she serious? "I was kidding, L."

"I'm not. I think it would lift her spirits."

This could work out well for me if Laurelyn buys something fun for us. "Well, if you do, I don't want you coming home with one of those vagina pleasers that performs like a circus monkey."

"A circus monkey vibrator?" she laughs. "Really, McLachlan?"

"They have them in performing rabbits and dolphins. Why wouldn't they make a monkey?"

"Okay. Nothing in the form of an animal or anything that penetrates."

Good. She remembers. "Because?"

"Nothing goes inside me but you. Got it." She says it like a child reciting a rule to her teacher.

I roll my office chair toward her and reach out to grope her bum under her light denim dress. I pull her between my legs, my face level with her stomach. I kiss it atop her clothes. She's wearing her boots. I haven't seen her in those in a while. I wonder if I can talk her into wearing them tonight. "Mmm... now I'm a little excited about what you might bring home for us to try."

"Any requests?"

"Mmm... choose something adventurous."

She giggles—very much like a child instead of the mature woman she is—and it makes me smile. She looks so innocent when she laughs that way, especially while wearing this little country sweetheart outfit. But I know better. There's very little this sweet girl enjoys more than a good ol' hard fuck. "Adventurous. I can do that."

She leans down and kisses my mouth. It's brief, just a sweet goodbye not intended to make my dick stand up. "Don't forget we have dinner reservations at seven thirty."

"You never told me where you're taking me."

"And I'm still not." I want to see the surprise on her face when we return to Ash and sit at the same table where I propositioned her fourteen months ago. I wish I could've taken her there for the one-year anniversary but it wasn't possible, considering we were at Avalon becoming husband and wife. Our lives have been a little crazy since so this has been my first chance to get her back there.

"I'll be sure to return in time. Should I dress casually?"

"I have something in mind for you to wear so I'll have it laid out for you."

"You choosing my clothes is a little weird."

"It's not weird." Okay. It is strange but there's a reason. I want her in the dress she wore that night—the floral one with only one shoulder. I hope I'm able to find it. "It's something I haven't seen you wear in a while and I like the way you look in it."

"Now you have me wondering if you're a closet cross-dresser. Am I going to come in and find you wearing my lace panties one day?"

"I'm choosing something for you to wear, L, not me."

"Okay. I gotta go. Thanks for letting me drive the bullet."

She calls my Sunset that since it's so fast. She says it gets away from her because it's such a smooth drive. "Please be careful. And don't speed."

I stand at the window and watch her disappear down the drive before I phone Daniel. "She's gone. I'll be ready to leave in fifteen minutes."

I'm finishing some last-minute details on a new order when Bianca comes into my office, without knocking. She's traded her short skirt for short khaki shorts and her low-cut dress shirt for a thin, tight white T-shirt with a deep V neckline. I'm glad L isn't here to see this because she wouldn't like it at all. In fact, it makes me a little uncomfortable after the things she brought to my attention on the day she met Bianca. In light of that, I think it's best if I finish the paperwork later. "I'm going into town for a little while but I'm expecting a delivery and I'd really like it if you could take care of it for me."

She places her hand on my shoulder. "Anything for you." I lean away from her touch to reach into my drawer for nothing in particular. I really hope she isn't going to be a problem, but my gut is telling me otherwise. One wrong move and she's out of here. That's what L said. I definitely foresee that being a problem, but my business relationship with Brees means nothing if this girl causes a problem for L and me.

Please, Bianca. No wrong moves. It'll screw us both.

I get out of my chair and move around my desk in the opposite direction of her as I head toward the door. "I have a business meeting and I have to make a pickup, so I'll be out until this afternoon." L's new Porsche SUV had to be purchased at a dealership in Sydney and driven to Wagga Wagga, so it's waiting in the parking garage at the hotel where my business meeting will take place. It couldn't have worked out better.

I run into Harold on my way out to meet Daniel. "Glad I ran into you. I have a single bag of a new potassium-deficiency product coming in today. Bianca is going to be watching for it and will bring it out to you. I thought we could try it on that area in the southwest corner and see if it does a better job than the old product."

"Sure thing, boss."

When I finish landing my new client, I go into the parking garage to fetch L's sleek black SUV. It's sharp, even if it's a family vehicle. I could've gone with something flashier but she's chosen to become a mum, so this fits her. It's classy without looking like a muscle man should be driving it. I hope she isn't disappointed I didn't buy her a sports car. I'm certain she'll understand that wasn't a sensible choice.

She isn't ovulating so tonight isn't about us trying. It's about us having fun and boy, do I have a little bit of naughty in store for her. I told her to buy something adventurous but the truth is I already have. I can't wait to see her in the sexy lingerie I bought or try out some of our new toys. I have to adjust myself inside my pants. I'm getting hard thinking about it.

My meeting ran longer than expected so I'm a little later than I'd like when I get back to Avalon. Harold flags me down in the driveway from the edge of the vineyard, and I know something's up. "You told me Bianca was bringing the potassium today?"

"Yeah."

He shakes his head. "She never brought anything to me."

"Did you ask her about it?"

He shrugs. "I haven't seen her to ask."

Hmm... that's not right. I told her to accept the package and take care of it and she agreed. "I don't know what happened with her, but don't worry about it. We'll get it out tomorrow."

Harold steps back to admire L's new vehicle and whistles. "That's one good-looking ride, Mr. McLachlan."

"It's Laurelyn's birthday present. You think she'll be happy?"

"I don't doubt it for a second."

I pull the Cayenne around back to a spot where L won't see it when she comes home. I'm going to blindfold her when I bring her out to see it, the same way I did with the house in Maui. And I'm going to do it again later tonight as part of the fun I have planned.

I go into the house and check the spot where Mrs. Porcelli leaves my mail. Fuck! It didn't come. The expected delivery date is supposed to be today, so I take out my phone to track it. Hmm... says it was delivered. I relax, assuming Mrs. Porcelli placed it in a different spot, but I have to find it before L gets home.

I leave the kitchen and go out to my office to see if her gift arrived in my business mail by accident. I find a package on the desk but it's the potassium, returning my thoughts to Bianca and why she wouldn't have taken this to Harold like I asked.

"Crash Into Me" begins playing on my phone. It's still Laurelyn's ringtone more than a year later. The song still makes me think of her on that stage every time I hear it. "Hello, love."

"Hey. I was calling—just in case—to let you know I'm on my way back a little early."

"Just in case of what?" I ask.

"I don't know. It's my birthday and you're being all secretive about tonight so I don't want to walk in and ruin anything you might be up to."

"You're safe. I've already taken care of everything." Except finding that package of naughty goodies.

"All right, Mr. Organized. I'll see you in fifteen."

Fifteen minutes does not give me long to find that package, so I decide to call Mrs. Porcelli. She has no idea what I'm talking about so I check the front door. And the back. Nothing. Fuck, I really want L to dance for me in that outfit tonight since her pole days are limited. Once she's pregnant, there'll be no more of that for a while.

I still haven't found L's naughty surprise and she'll be here any minute, so I give up and decide to search for her floral one-shouldered dress instead. I hope I have better luck finding that.

I enter our bedroom and go motionless, the blood draining from my face. What the fuck is going on in here?

Bianca's lying across the bed dressed in L's new red metallic pole outfit and has all of our new kinky toys spread around her. "You are a very bad boy, Jack McLachlan."

Fuck! She got L's package and thought it was the one I intended for her to receive. "I'm afraid there's been a terrible misunderstanding."

She moves to her knees and motions for me to come to her. The top barely covers her breasts so I quickly look at the floor. "I get it, Jack. You were afraid to approach me so you had these things sent to me. Well, I get the message and I accept your invitation."

I'm walking around the room looking for her clothes. "You were supposed to open the package with the potassium in it, not this one. These things aren't for you."

"What?" She sounds terribly confused.

Fuck! L is going to kill us both if she walks in and sees this. "My wife is on her way home. You've got to get your clothes on and get the hell out of here."

I hear a sound so I stop to listen. Too late. I hear L coming into the house. "Oh hell. She's home. Get your motherfucking clothes on while I try to explain this shit."

Of course she heads straight for our bedroom because she needs to get ready for our dinner reservation, so I try to head her off before she can see Bianca in her outfit. "Hey, you. How was…"

I interrupt her. "Stop, babe. Don't go in there."

She laughs. "What are you up to? Some kind of birthday surprise?"

Of course she doesn't suspect there's a near-naked woman in our bedroom. She trusts me but I swallow hard as I prepare to tell her what's happened. There isn't a way to present this that isn't going to look heinous so basically, I'm fucked. Thanks a lot, Bianca. "L, hear me out before you totally lose it."

"You're scaring me. What's happened?" I look toward our bedroom door, dreading—yet hoping—a fully dressed Bianca will appear at any moment. I really don't want L walking in and seeing her without her clothes on. "Why are you acting so weird? And why are you watching the door?"

"There's been a misunderstanding."

She knows something has gone awry—I see it all over her face—as she pushes past me into the bedroom. "Well, let's not make it two."

I enter behind her and it looks really fucking bad for me because Bianca is topless and pulling on her shorts.

Laurelyn gapes as she stands in the doorway, I'm sure unable to believe her eyes. "What the fuck?" she yells before she charges Bianca and punches her. I go after her but she hits her a second and third time in the face with her fist before I'm able to restrain her.

I pin her arms behind her back and she uses my hold on her as an opportunity to lift her legs up and kick Bianca in the arse with her boots.

I've never seen Laurelyn like this—she's a total scrapper—and I'm surprised at how stout she is for her petite size. "You need to get out of here."

Bianca's nose is bleeding and the blood smears down the front of her white shirt as she pulls it over her head. "I know you're pissed off but please don't think Jack had any part of this. It was all a misunderstanding on my part and I'm so terribly sorry. And embarrassed. This will never happen again."

Laurelyn is unmoved by Bianca's promise. "You say that as though you think there'd be an opportunity. This isn't baseball, honey. You don't get three strikes before you're out."

"What? But I need this internship if I'm going to graduate on time," she says.

"Well, that sucks for you since you won't be back," L tells her.

"Jack, I have to have this," she pleads.

I don't give her time to make an argument. "You'll have to find another internship because you can't come back here ever again."

My birthday plans for L were shot to hell and back last night. Imagine that. Neither of us was in the mood for celebrating after Bianca's little stunt, so we're having dinner at Ash tonight. It's not a surprise like I had planned but they're going to give us our corner table when it becomes available.

I had a last-minute business meeting come up so L is driving into town to meet me. She says she doesn't mind because she wants to drive her new SUV. At least that part wasn't ruined.

I text L to let her know I'm finished with my meeting and waiting for her at the bar. I take a seat on a stool to wait and order two Pinot Noirs—not from my own vineyard—because I'm curious about the competition. It's decent at best, certainly nothing to brag about, so I gloat because I know mine is much better.

I check the time and see that Laurelyn is considerably late, which isn't like her at all. "Get stood up?" The voice belongs to a woman sitting a couple seats away. I briefly glance in her direction and see a leggy blond wearing a plum business suit, a fitted jacket and short skirt with very high heels. I can't see her face because she's looking straight ahead but I can tell she's beautiful.

I choose to reply since I don't wish to be rude but probably more so because I want to let her know I'm not on the market. I don't want her flirting with me when Laurelyn arrives. "Nothing like that. I'm waiting for my wife."

"Her mistake. If she was wise, your wife wouldn't leave you sitting alone in a hotel bar for me to invite upstairs."

I'll be damned if I'm not stunned. I haven't even made eye contact with this woman and she invites me up for sex. Sure, it sounds a lot like what I once did, but now it just sounds insane. "Sorry. You'll need to find someone else."

She leaves her chair and moves to the one next to me. "I don't think your wife will mind." She unexpectedly places her hand on my head and pulls me close so she can whisper in my ear. "I know for a fact that your wife won't mind if you take me upstairs and fuck me like a champion." Her faux Aussie accent is gone, replaced by a more natural southern twang.

I turn to look at the woman next to me and recognize the golden-brown eyes staring back. "Laurelyn?"

"Shh... no names. I only want a companion for the night. No complications. No communication afterward."

My brain registers the fact that my wife is sitting next to me in a public place wearing a blond wig and a sexy business suit and I get what this is. It's all for me. L admitted during our confessional that she was afraid I would miss having different women, so she's become someone else for me tonight. I push L's glass of wine in her direction and hold mine up. "A toast to the best wife ever since she has no objections to this."

She clinks her glass to mine and takes a tiny sip before putting it on the bar. I forgot. She's avoiding alcohol since we're trying to conceive. "Would you like something without alcohol instead?"

She puts her hand on my leg and slides it up. She brushes my still-soft cock, causing it to stir. "No. What I'd really like is this."

"Well, who am I to stand between a girl and what she wants?" I toss some bills on the counter in front of the bartender. "No change."

"Thank you, sir."

We leave the bar and enter the lobby area. "Do I need to get a room?"

She holds up the keycard. "Already taken care of."

"Perfect." I wasn't looking forward to standing at the check-in desk with a raging hard-on.

We enter the elevator and I wait for the doors to close so I can descend upon… hmm. What do I call her? She isn't Laurelyn tonight. "I need something to call you."

She tilts her head and grins. "You can call me yours for tonight."

"Then you may call me incredibly pleased."

She extends her hand for a shake. "It's very nice to meet you."

She releases my hand as an older couple enters the elevator. Dammit. I'd hoped to get her heated on the ride up.

The woman in the elevator is judging us. It's clear as day by the expression on her face. She saw us introduce ourselves to one another and has now taken notice of only one elevator button pressed. I'm guessing she thinks Laurelyn is a hooker and I'd bet all the money in my wallet that she's checked my hand for a wedding band.

"You didn't say how much this was gonna cost me."

Laurelyn turns a deep shade of red and lowers her head, giggling.

"I have until morning. That was the agreement, right?"

Laurelyn straightens and wipes the smile from her face. "Yes, sir. Your wife arranged for you to have me all night."

"Like I said before… best wife ever."

The elevator pings and the doors open for our floor. I gesture for Laurelyn to exit first. "After you, milady." We exit and I can't resist looking back at the couple in the elevator—she gives me a look of disapproval while he appears envious.

We say nothing as we walk the hall to our room. "This is us." L slides the card into the door. I step behind her and push her blond hair away from her neck so I can kiss it. She moans and I slide my hand under her short skirt and explore, finding her panties so my fingers can dive into her wet center. "Damn. You're already slick." She's struggling to get the keycard to unlock the door while I finger-fuck her. "I'm going to bend you over and give it to you so hard."

The green light flashes on the door and she pushes it open. "I'm going to come before we even get inside if you don't stop."

I take my fingers out of her, but only because I want her to come with my mouth on her. I want to taste her.

I lead her to the bed and she sits. I drop to my knees and kneel between her legs before I pull her bum to the edge. I reach under her skirt and drag her panties down her legs. I bring her sexy red G to my nose and inhale deeply. "You smell so fucking good, I could almost get off just sniffing these."

I drop her knickers on the floor and grab the back of her thighs, pushing them back and apart. She props on her elbows, readying herself to look at what my mouth is going to do to her. It's fucking hot as hell when my girl watches me lick her.

She's looking down at me, blond hair spilling over her shoulders. Our eyes—light blue and golden-brown—are locked when I place my tongue against her center and drag it in an upward sweep. "Oh, filet-o-fuck. That feels good." I lick her from the bottom toward the top and then circle my tongue around her clit. I push two of my fingers inside her and she calls out, "Omigod, yes!" It's a plea for me to make her come. And then she does. I feel the contractions around my fingers and I taste the saltiness of her orgasm in my mouth. It's absolutely delectable.

She falls back on the bed, her legs propped on the mattress. They're trembling so I place my hands on her knees to steady them. "That good, huh?"

"Yeah. It was just that good."

She comes up and pushes me onto the bed. She unbuttons my trousers and yanks, anxious to get them down. "I'm not sure you've been given a proper blow job recently. I think you need one."

"I couldn't agree with you more."

Once my trousers are off, she moves to her knees on the floor. She pulls me to the edge of the bed and begins by licking my cock from base to tip. She grasps it in her hand and her eyes watch mine as she drags her tongue across the tip from side to side. "I love the taste of your pre-cum." She licks her lips and swallows before sucking me fully into her mouth, taking my entire cock in to the back of her throat.

"That feels amazing." But as great as it is, I have to close my eyes because I can't watch the blond head bobbing up and down over my dick, even though I know it's Laurelyn.

"Babe, I'm about to come." I still tell her before I do. I always will but just as L always does, she sucks even harder. She always wants me to come in her mouth.

Laurelyn isn't ovulating but it still feels like that shouldn't have been wasted in her mouth. Then again, this isn't us trying to have a baby. This is us role-playing because L wants to keep me happy and satisfied. She has no idea how unnecessary this is because all I want is her. No other women.

I pull her into my arms and brush my mouth against hers. I want a sweet, soft kiss fresh on her lips when I bend her over the bed and fuck her senseless. "Remember this delicate kiss."

"Okay." She has no idea what I mean. But she will.

I take a pillow from the bed and put it on the floor. "Turn over and kneel." She does as I instruct and I stretch her arms over the bed. I take my shirt off and pitch it across the room. I lean down and place my lips at her ear. "Pretend to be someone else and I'm gonna fuck you like you're someone else."

I drive my cock into her hard and fast, causing her to gasp. I still until I feel her relax and then start moving in and out of her slower, testing the water until I build up to a faster pace, one she can tolerate. I grasp her hips and squeeze, pulling her body against mine to meet my thrusts. This sex is faster and rougher than what she's accustomed to.

I look at the blond hair falling over her shoulders and down her back and realize this isn't what I want. I don't want to fuck other women. I don't even want to fuck Laurelyn while she's pretending to be someone else.

I pull out of her. "L, take that fucking wig off. I can't stand looking at that blond shit. It makes me feel like I'm fucking somebody else."

She's on her knees with her upper body stretched across the bed, squeezing the comforter tightly in her fists when I hear sobs. "L, why are you crying?" She releases the bed linens and uses her hand to wipe her face. "What's wrong? Did I hurt you?"

She doesn't reply so I physically turn her over and see her tear-stained face and red eyes. "Talk to me, L. Tell me what's wrong."

She refuses to meet my eyes. "You were different with me just now."

"Only because you came to me as someone else."

"You've never fucked me like that before. Is this who you are with other women?"

I use my hand to turn her face toward mine. "I'm not with other women."

She finally looks me in the eyes. "Is that who you became when you were with the other twelve? And with Lana?"

"No."

She gets up from the floor and straightens her skirt. "This was a bad idea."

"I'm sorry." I roll to sit on the floor with my back against the bed and press my palms to my forehead. "I don't know what happened." But that's a lie. I know exactly what happened. I gave her a punishment fuck because everything she did and pretended to be tonight was a reminder of the repulsive things I've done. And my own wife was the one forcing me to walk that path again.

"I shouldn't have done this." She cups her hands over her mouth and then pushes her hands to her forehead. "I'm sorry. I need to get out of here."

"I'm coming with you."

"Please, don't." She can't look at me and I don't know what it means. Is she angry? Hurt? "I need some time to think."

Laurelyn leaves without another word and I'm left sitting in a hotel room wondering what the hell she needs to think about.

CHAPTER FIFTEEN
LAURELYN MCLACHLAN

I CRY ALL THE WAY HOME. I'M CONFUSED ABOUT WHAT HAPPENED, BUT MORE embarrassed than anything. I don't know what I was thinking when I decided I'd pretend to be another woman for Jack Henry. That's clearly not what he wants.

What should have been a night of hot sex turned into a total disaster. Jack Henry seemed to be into the role-play thing. I thought we were having fun and then it felt like he suddenly turned… angry. "Pretend to be someone else and I'm gonna fuck you like you're someone else." I don't even know what that means.

I left Jack Henry at the hotel and now I don't want to be alone. That's why I've called Addie and begged her to come stay the night with me at Avalon. "Jack is staying in a hotel? Shit, I feel sorry for him and I don't know what happened."

Addie knows about his past. She thinks it's fucked up, and it is, but she's the only person I have that I can talk to about this. "We were meeting at a hotel for dinner and I showed up dressed in a business suit like his former companions… wearing a blond wig. I propositioned him to be my companion for the night. No names. No commitments."

"Holy shit. Did he take you up on the offer thinking you were someone else? I'm gonna kill that fucker!"

"No. That's not what happened at all. I pulled off a phony Aussie accent and he didn't know it was me at first. He turned me down cold—even said he was waiting for his wife."

"I'm really confused here, Laurie."

"I had this crazy idea to role-play—be someone else for him—so he could feel the excitement he used to get when he took a new companion." Shit, that sounded so much better in my head than hearing it come out of my mouth.

"That's the stupidest idea you've ever had!" Addison yells. "He loves you to death. Why would you even put the idea of him being with another woman in his head like that?"

Yeah, hindsight is twenty-twenty. "I wish I hadn't. It turned to shit so fast, Addie. Everything was good at first. We went up to the room and we were having fun but then something happened to him." I remember what he said and chills come over me. "It's like he became someone else and all I could think was that I came up to this room pretending to be someone else, so this must be what he was like with those other women."

"How was he different?" she asks.

"He got rougher—more vigorous—than usual but I really liked it. It gave new meaning to sex on fire but then I freaked out because I started thinking about how he must've fucked those other women better than he does me. Then I started crying."

"Oh hell, Laurie. That's just so silly. You know he didn't fuck them better than you. He was probably really turned on that you would do something so nuts just to get him off so he got a little carried away."

"It was weird. He wasn't himself."

"Well, you damn sure weren't his sweet L, so why would you expect him to be your precious Jack Henry?" She's right.

"He told me to take the wig off, that he couldn't stand it because it made him feel like he was fucking someone else."

She gives me her duh look. "Sounds to me like he went along with that shit to make you happy but he doesn't want to be with other women. I don't think he even wants to be with you when you're trying to look like other women. He hates his past and you forced him to relive it. It's like a slap in the face to him."

I only wanted to have fun. I never considered this outcome and it's my fault. None of this would've happened if it weren't for me. "Omigod. You're right. I'm a terrible wife. And to top it off, he's sleeping in a hotel because of my stupid insecurities."

"I wouldn't say you're a terrible wife. Maybe you could just say you suck tonight."

"He's told me time and time again that nothing before me matters." Why am I so insecure when it comes to Jack Henry? He made me his wife. What more can I ask of him? "I have to go to him."

I knock on the door once. Twice. And a third time. "Jack Henry." I remember the second keycard in my purse and take it out. I unlock the door and push it open. "Jack Henry? Are you here?"

I walk through the suite's living room but I can't see if he's in bed. It's hidden from view behind a wall but I see a red thong lying at the foot of the bed. It's the one I left during my hasty departure—which reminds me I'm still not wearing panties.

I walk through the bedroom door and Jack Henry is sound asleep, a half-empty bottle of whiskey at the bedside. I pick it up for a look at the black label—Jack Daniels. "This one is all on me, caveman."

He holds his liquor pretty well. I'm guessing his stamina for alcohol can be accredited to what he does for a living. A winemaker can't be an easy drunk so maybe he isn't plastered. We've had lots of pivotal discussions after he's had a little too much to drink. I tend to like the answers I get from him because they're honest.

I shake his arm. "McLachlan, wake up."

He opens his eyes slowly. "L?"

"I came back."

He reaches out for my hand. "I'm so sorry for what I did."

"No, I'm the one who's sorry. I shouldn't have done that but I understand now and I'll never do it again."

He runs his hands through his hair, tugging at it. "I'm such a motherfucker. I lied to you. I know exactly what happened and I gave you a punishment fuck because of it. I was too rough with you and I'm so sorry. Oh God, I might have hurt the baby if you're pregnant. Do you feel okay?"

"I'm fine."

He looks toward the curtains. "Is it morning? Did you take the test yet?"

"No. It's still night but I brought it with me so I can take it in the morning." Thank God I had the good sense to go back for it.

He puts his arms out for me. "Come here." I climb into bed with my somewhat drunk husband. "I love you so much, L, and I can't stand when there's disharmony between us."

"I will never, ever do this again."

He pulls me close and kisses my forehead. "It's late and I've had a lot to drink, so let's go to sleep before I say something foolish."

It's only a matter of a minute or so before Jack Henry is drunk-snoring. Perfect. I get to hear that all night. But I admit I'd rather hear it than miss it.

I get up from the bed and take off my jacket and skirt. I'm already panty-free so I toss the matching bra to the floor. I should've brought something to sleep in but I didn't, so I'm completely naked when I crawl into bed next to my sleeping husband. He rolls toward me and drapes his arm and leg across my body. He's naked except for his boxers, his choice of underwear since we started trying for a baby. I think he read somewhere that boxers increase sperm count.

I lie beneath him wide awake as he continues to snore—in my ear. I'm not drunk but I wish I were—or at least sleepy—because the alternative is that I'm horny. I want makeup sex, but I'm guessing that's probably impossible since my husband drank a shitload of whiskey.

I sigh, staring into the darkness, and then close my eyes. Maybe sleep will claim me if I lie motionless.

Jack Henry stirs and his hand moves to cup my breast. It doesn't help matters at all.

I should probably feel ashamed for what I'm about to do but I don't. What man would be angry about being awakened for sex? I can't name a one. "McLachlan." He doesn't stir so I shake his arm. "McLachlan."

"Hmm." It's a groan, but not the sexy kind. "What is it, love?" His words are slurred.

I decide words aren't the only persuasive tools I possess, so I slip my hand down his boxers. Damn. He's totally limp, a state I've not known him to be in too often. The man verges on having a perpetual hard-on so this may not work at all. He's still half lying on me so I wrap my free leg around him. "I really want you to fuck me."

"I'm up." He shoots up to a sitting position and I feel his cock stirring. "Did you just tell me to fuck you or did I dream it?"

"You didn't dream it. I want to have makeup sex. I need it so I can feel okay about us."

"We're fine, but I'm more than happy to make up with you if I can. I had a lot to drink so it might not be my best work. You'll probably have to get on top."

I don't think I care how good it is or if I get off. I really just need to feel the intimacy that only that kind of nearness will bring.

He's hard for me so I move over to straddle him. He puts his hands on my hips and groans when I sink down on him. "You feel so good, babe." And it does, but I already know I'm not going to come. Jack Henry's too incapacitated to do the necessary things to get me there but I still want this. I need it.

Jack Henry barely comes before he passes out again but I'm still satisfied.

We fought.

We forgave.

We fucked.

It's our thing, so I know we're all good.

A HUNGOVER JACK HENRY STILL WAKES BEFORE ME. AMAZING. I DON'T know how he does it.

I'm lying on my stomach and the bed sheet is pulled lower. The cool air hits my skin and then the slight scrape of Jack Henry's facial scruff moves along my lower back, followed by the kiss of his mouth. "It's morning, sleepyhead."

I lift my pillow and bury my head beneath it. "Go away."

"No, my love. I ordered breakfast and it's waiting for us in the other room. Cold omelets aren't good, so get up."

I remove the pillow and glance over my shoulder at him. "How are you so cheery this morning?"

"I can't lie; I feel like shit, but I don't care because I'm excited about you peeing on that stick."

Oh, that's right. It's time.

It was hard as hell but we declined doing an early detection pregnancy test for fear of a false result. That would've been devastating so we chose to wait until today to see if we're going to be parents.

"Want me to do the test now or do I need to eat my omelet before it gets cold?"

He crawls up my back and lies on top of me with his mouth at my ear. "Get your sweet bum into that bathroom and do that test." He swats me across my ass as he's getting up.

I yelp and sit up on the side of the bed. "Here's the plan. I'll do the test, come out and wait how ever long it says it takes, and then we'll go in and read it together."

"Sounds good to me."

I get up to go to the bathroom and he catches my hand. "You know it's fine if it's not positive, right? That just means we'll get to keep trying, which isn't a bad alternative at all."

I nod. "I know."

I go into the bathroom and my bladder feels like it'll explode as I open the box and prepare myself for the deed. A pregnancy test is pretty self-explanatory but I read the instructions anyway because I've never taken one and I don't want to screw it up. I follow the instructions to a T and place the test on the counter. I slip into the hotel-provided robe and open the bathroom door, but I stop dead in my tracks when I hear the conversation in the living room between a woman and Jack Henry.

"I've been trying to find you for a while," she says.

"There's a reason you didn't and it's because we agreed to no contact afterward."

"I didn't know who you were until I saw your wedding announcement in the paper. Then I couldn't believe my luck when I saw you in the lobby last night."

"Isn't it against some kind of policy for you to look up guests when you work here?" He's angry.

"It is, but I don't care. It was worth the risk because I had to see you," she defends.

"I'm married now."

It's clear this is another one of the twelve and I'm so fucking sick of this. It's ridiculous. This one is ruining our potential baby moment—what could be one of the most epic moments of our lives.

I walk into the living room and Miss Number X is all dolled up for my husband. I'm immediately pissed off. She's beautiful—I'll give her that—but she's not young. She totally fits his type before me.

I could play coy. I could play nice. But what I feel like playing is neither. "I'd like you to leave now."

"I can do that, but there's one thing first." She places a photograph on the table next to our breakfast. "This is my two-year-old son. He belongs to you and you're going to start supporting him. You can either voluntarily take a paternity test or you can be ordered. The choice is yours."

I can tell she enjoyed saying that, and I'm sick. I swallow back the puke rising in my throat. I won't do it in front of her.

She walks toward the door and calls out over her shoulder, "My number is on the back of the photograph. I look forward to hearing from you, Jack."

I go through a series of emotions all at once but none are more prevalent than the hurt I feel in my heart.

Jack Henry sits in the chair and puts his head in his hands. "I'm assuming there's a possibility this child could be yours since you aren't trying to convince me otherwise."

"I was with her for a few weeks but I don't remember when. I'd have to do some thinking on it."

"You'll have to do some thinking on it?" I feel the tears coming. "Well, I don't have thinking to do about this shit. I can't take it anymore."

"Don't say that, L."

I walk to the bed where my clothes are and strip off the robe so I can dress and get the fuck out of here. "You don't understand what this is like, how humiliating it is for me every time a new one pops into our life.

They chip away a part of me each time I'm confronted by another one. I thought I was strong enough to handle it, but I'm not."

I'm sitting on the bed dressed and putting my shoes on when Jack Henry drops to his knees in front of me. "Don't leave me, L."

"I can't stay."

"We need to talk about this."

Tears stream down my face. "Another woman may have had your baby. Not me, your wife." I place my hand over my chest. "And it breaks my heart because I wanted to be the one—the only one—to give you babies." I look into his eyes. "Infinity."

He immediately recognizes our code word. He steps out of my way because he knows the best thing he can do at this point is let me go.

CHAPTER SIXTEEN
JACK MCLACHLAN

Un-fucking-believable! I get my ass out of one shitstorm only to be sucked into another.

I look at the child in the photograph. He's blond with blue, maybe green eyes. Nothing about him resembles me. I took biology and briefly studied basic genetics so I know he doesn't have to look like me to be mine, but it seems there would be some kind of semblance.

Although Evan and I are different, we both look like Dad and all the other McLachlans. Evan's three kids look like him in one way or another, especially his son, but is it fair to make a comparison?

I look at the picture and feel no connection to this boy. Shouldn't my heart be softened or filled with some kind of excitement about finding out I may have a son? It's not. I'm mad as hell—not at this child, but at myself. How could I fuck things up like this with my carelessness? L and I were about to have it all and something I did three years ago has shot all of that to hell.

My gut tells me this isn't my kid, but there's only one way to find out. I flip the picture over and immediately recognize the name. Jenna Rosenthal. She didn't even give me an alias when we had our short relationship a few years back.

I call the number and she immediately answers. "That didn't take long. I knew it wouldn't, so I already have the kit."

"No. I want to speak with my lawyer and have him recommend a reputable doctor to do the test." We're doing this by the book. No way she's hoodooing me with false results. I'm sure that kind of shit happens all the time to dumb fuckers, but I'm no sucker. "I'll take the first available appointment because I want this done as soon as possible."

"I'm sure you do want it done and over but it doesn't end with the test. Ashton is yours and I'm going to make sure you take care of him."

I can't see myself with a son named Ashton. It doesn't feel right. "We'll begin with the paternity test. Prove he's mine and I'll take care of him, but let's get one thing straight. Never be under the impression that anything will happen between us. I'm married."

"Judging by the look on your wife's face, you may not be for long." I can tell she took great pleasure in saying that.

"Not your business."

"That's where you're wrong. Ashton is about to become a huge part of your world—and I'm his mother—so that means I'll be in your face whenever I feel like it. Every part of your life will be my business, beginning with your home life."

I'm not fighting with this woman about a child who may or may not be mine. "My assistant will set everything up and will phone you with the appointment date and time." I end the call, not giving her time to argue further.

I need to go to Laurelyn. I don't know what I'll say but I have to see her. And I can't go smelling like sour mash whiskey.

I go into the bathroom to shower and see L's pregnancy test lying on the counter. We agreed we were going to look at the results together but Jenna Rosenthal ruined that.

So what do I do? We wanted to find out together. It doesn't feel right to do it without her. Nothing about this situation is right. L should be here with me and we should be doing one of two things: celebrating the new life we've created or making a game plan on how we're going to make our baby happen. But we're doing neither because of me and my fucked-up past. If he turns out to be my kid, he was conceived long before I met Laurelyn. Can she hold that against me? She's not here, so I'm beginning to think she can, and will.

I debate looking at the test, but not for long. I want to know if my wife is pregnant. Everyone knows two lines means pregnant. One line means not pregnant but I want to be sure, so I get the box out of the trash and verify what I'm seeing.

Two lines. Laurelyn is pregnant. "We did it, baby."

I once told Laurelyn she is the only angel in my life. Now I'll have two.

CHAPTER SEVENTEEN
LAURELYN MCLACHLAN

I GO INTO THE HOUSE AND STRAIGHT TO THE SHOWER. I TURN THE WATER TO full hot but I can't feel the heat beating down against my skin. I'm cold—inside and out.

How did my life turn to this overnight? Jack Henry and I had everything. We were on top of the world one minute and cast into hell the next. I know I need time to absorb this shock, but I'm not sure I'll get over this one, especially if he's had a baby with another woman.

It all happened so fast but that's generally how a kick to the gut feels. I was so giddy to read that fucking pee stick with him but instead I find out he had a baby with one of the twelve. Maybe.

"Laurie?" I'm startled when I hear Addison's voice. I forgot she stayed last night.

"Yeah, it's me. I'm alone. I left Jack Henry at the hotel. Addie, something bad happened this morning. I mean, really bad." I want to throw up just thinking about saying the words. Another woman had my husband's baby. I'm not sure I can force that to roll from my tongue.

"Laurie, I'm bleeding." I wipe the water from my eyes and open the shower door. "How much?" She doesn't have to tell me. I can see the stream running down her legs.

"It's a lot."

I attempt to appear calm. "It's okay. Go lie down on my bed and I'll get dressed."

I'm trembling as I dry off and pull on clothes. I tie my wet hair into a bun. "Hey, girl, how you doing in there?"

"Not good. I can feel blood gushing when I move."

"Then stay really still. I'm almost ready." I put my shoes on and go into the bedroom, following the trail of blood on the floor. Holy shit. My bedroom looks like a crime scene.

"I'm sorry, Laurie," Addison cries when she sees the look on my face. "I think I've ruined your bedding."

"No worries about the linens." She needs a pad—a huge one—but I only have small pantyliners. "You can't go to the hospital in this so hold up. I'm going to grab you something to put on." I fetch a pair of Jack Henry's sleep pants and a towel from the bathroom. "Take your panties off and put this between your legs." I spread his pants on the floor for her to step into. "Foot in. Foot in." I pull them up and pull the tie so they fit her snuggly in the waist. "Can you walk?"

"Yeah, but I think blood is gonna gush out with every step I take."

"It's okay." But is it? I'm scared shitless. I've never seen so much blood.

We begin the walk from my bedroom to the car. It isn't a long distance but I swear it's never felt so far.

She's crying. "I'm losing this baby, Laurie."

"You don't know that for sure." I want to be reassuring but she's probably right. I don't know how she could bleed that much and not be having a miscarriage.

"I still haven't told Zac. I guess that won't be a problem now."

"Don't talk like that."

"I'm being realistic," she argues.

"Mothers are optimists, not realists."

We get into my SUV and I'm driving much faster than I should. "I need them to tell me everything is okay because I really want this baby, Laurie. Even if Zac doesn't. I've already decided I'm keeping it and raising it alone if I have to."

I reach for her hand and give it a squeeze. "Pray, Addie. Ask God to protect your baby."

"You know I don't do that." Like right now is the time to be stubborn and think you don't need the help of a higher power.

"Well, maybe you should."

Addison is taken into the emergency room and they begin her assessment quickly since anyone could see that she's bleeding way too much. "Any idea when your last period was, Miss Donavon?"

"The last normal one was on October seventeenth. I spotted in November but I don't know if it qualifies as a period."

The woman types the date into the ultrasound machine. "Okay. We'll use the one in October since November doesn't sound like a period. That gives you a due date of July twenty-fourth, which makes you... fifteen weeks. Looks like you probably conceived on or around October thirty-first." The woman grins. "I guess you had a fun Halloween."

"Yeah, it was a good one."

"Addison! You didn't tell me you were so far along. You should've already seen a doctor." How could she be so irresponsible?

"I didn't know I was that pregnant. I thought I was two, maybe going on three months at the most since I spotted in November."

"You're almost four months. Shit, it's almost half over."

"Let's do a scan and see what's going on here." The woman squeezes a bottle and clear jelly squirts onto Addison's stomach. She places a probe in the wetness and makes swirling motions, spreading it across her belly. All of us are silent, staring intently at the screen. The difference is she knows what she's looking at. Addison and I have no idea.

She points at a white flashing on the screen. "This is your baby's heartbeat. Can you see it?"

"I do." She stares at the screen, tears streaming down her face. "I haven't lost my baby?"

"He or she is hanging in there. I think I see what's causing all this bleeding but I need some better scans for the radiologist to read. Take a breath and relax while I get the pictures I need."

We stare at the screen because it's so amazing. "Omigod, Addie. Look. It already has arms and legs and I can see them moving."

"I prayed to God, Laurie. I begged Him to not take my baby and He didn't." Addison squeezes my hand. "Will you call Zac and ask him to come to the hospital? He should be here with me."

I hate that it took something so catastrophic to bring her to her senses, but thank goodness she's finally going to tell him. "Of course—but what do you want me to say? He's going to panic when I tell him you're in the hospital."

"Tell him I'm fine but that I'm asking for him. I want to be the one to tell him about the baby."

"I'm on it." I'll have to use a public phone since I left mine at home in the mad dash to get here.

Addison is admitted to a room and is all settled when Zac does just as I predict—he barrels into the room panicked, although I've assured him she is fine. His eyes grow huge when he sees a very pale Addie in the bed. "What happened to her?"

"Addison wants to be the one to tell you." I put my hand on her arm. "Addie. Zac's here."

She stirs and opens her eyes before a wide smile spreads. "Hey, baby."

He's instantly at her side, crouching so he's face to face with her. "What's wrong?"

It's time for me to go. "I'm going to leave so you can talk."

Neither acknowledge me or my exit; they're both too terrified, but for completely different reasons.

CHAPTER EIGHTEEN
JACK MCLACHLAN

I'M DRIVING TO AVALON, KNOWING THE WHOLE WAY THAT LAURELYN WILL kick me out when I get there. It's her thing—what she does when she's angry with me. And she's super pissed right now. There's no way she'll let me stay after the way this morning went, but I can't sit back and do nothing. I have to try.

I enter the house through the kitchen and toss my keys onto the counter. L isn't in the kitchen or the living room. "Laurelyn?" I'm not sure she'll answer if she isn't speaking to me but I call out her name again anyway. "Laurelyn." No reply—that's no surprise.

I enter our bedroom and nothing can prepare me for what I find. "What the fuck happened in here?" There's a huge pool of blood on Laurelyn's side of the bed with a trail leading into the bathroom. And a path going out the door down the hallway. I had to have walked through it on my way to the bedroom. How did I not see it?

This is no small amount of blood. Something significant happened here.

I take my cell out and call her. The sound of my personal ringtone echoes from the bathroom. She doesn't have her phone and I'm further alarmed. I pick it up and look at her recent calls. The last one was made to Addison last night, long before she returned to the hotel, so I dial Addison and get no answer. Shit!

I look at the pool of blood on the floor and begin mapping it out in my head. I smell her body wash so she took a shower. She left a wet towel on the floor, something she never does, so she was either in a hurry or something happened, like a sudden case of profuse bleeding. There's a trail leading from the puddle to the bed. She must have gone to lie down after it started, hoping it would stop, but from the looks of things, it only worsened.

Oh fuck! I'm panicking because this is very bad.

There's a pair of blood-soaked panties on the floor so she has to be miscarrying—it's the only possible scenario that fits. And it's all my fault. I did this to her and our baby.

I follow the trail from the bedroom, up the hall, and through the kitchen to the garage. Her car is gone. I wasn't here to help her so she must've gotten into her car to drive herself to the hospital. Why didn't she call an ambulance? Or me?

There's more than one hospital so I have no idea which she would have gone to. I take my phone out and start calling. "I'm trying to find my wife. Laurelyn McLachlan."

I'm put on hold at least a dozen times before I finally speak to someone who can give me answers. "Sir, we don't have a patient by that name."

I hang up to call the next hospital and I'm told for a second time that Laurelyn isn't a patient at their facility. My mind races. Maybe she didn't make it to the hospital because she passed out from the bleeding. It's possible. There is a fuckload of blood on our bed, not to mention what's on the floor.

Her car. It can be traced. I'm in the process of finding the number to call when I hear the garage door open and then close. I dash to the kitchen and see Laurelyn, safe and sound. I drop my phone and rush to her, taking her in my arms and squeezing. "Fuck, you scared me. What the hell happened in our bedroom?"

I lessen my hold because I'm afraid I'm squeezing too hard but I don't let go. "Addison started bleeding. Bad."

"Are she and the baby okay?"

"Yeah, but can we go inside? It's been a crazy morning and I'd really like to sit down."

I let go of her and we go into the house. She sits on the couch and kicks off her shoes before putting her feet up on the coffee table. "The doctor says she has a previa. Her placenta attached itself at the bottom of the uterus next to her cervix instead of the top where it should be."

That doesn't sound good. "How serious is it?"

"They say it'll probably resolve itself because it'll grow up away from the cervix as the baby develops, but they put her on bed rest until that happens since her bleeding was so heavy."

"And if it doesn't resolve on its own?" I ask but am afraid to hear the answer.

"They won't let her go into labor if the placenta is still attached to the cervix. She'll stay on bed rest the remainder of the pregnancy and get a C-section when her due date comes."

"Which is when?"

"July twenty-fourth." I'm trying to do the math in my head but they figure that pregnancy stuff differently. "She's almost four months."

"Whoa. She's that far along and still hasn't told Zac?"

"She told him and he was happy about it—like, really happy. He proposed—already had the ring and everything. He'd been walking around with it for weeks and was just waiting for the perfect time to present itself."

I understand that. "And it never did so he seized the moment. Sound familiar?"

"Yeah. It sort of does."

I don't want to address the latest shitstorm, but I have to. "We're scheduled to go in for a paternity test at the end of the week. It's the soonest we could get in with the doctor my lawyer recommended. He says it'll take a little longer to get the results since we're doing a legal paternity test and not a personal."

"How long?"

"Probably a week." She sighs and looks up at the ceiling as tears form in her eyes. "Look at me, L." She lowers her face and tears spill onto her cheeks. "If that boy is mine, I have to take care of him. You know I do."

"I know and it's one of the things I love about you. You'd never turn a child away like my father did."

She's going to think I'm talking nonsense but I have to tell her how I feel. "But he's not mine. Don't ask me to explain how I can be so certain without proof, but I'm not wrong about this, L."

"You can't possibly know that," she argues.

"I don't feel a connection to him at all."

"You've never seen him. You wouldn't feel something for a child you've never laid eyes on."

I place one of my hands on her stomach. "I've never seen this one and I'm already connected to it. I love this baby with all my heart."

"So I'm pregnant?" She sounds… I don't know. Angry? Disappointed? Definitely not thrilled. She's probably pissed off because I looked, but I don't regret it. This baby is a goodness I need so badly in my life right now.

"Yes. The test was lying on the bathroom counter staring me in the face. I debated but couldn't bring myself to trash it without checking the results first." She looks at my hand on her stomach and a sob escapes, leaving me wondering if it's one of joy or sadness. "Please don't cry, L. It breaks my heart in two."

"This isn't the beautiful image I had in mind for us finding out we were having a baby. I imagined us having this really special moment filled with ecstatic joy and tears of happiness. I pictured us making love afterward, maybe you'd kiss my belly and tell me how much you were going to love seeing it grow with your baby."

This isn't what I wanted, either, but it is what it is. "Listen to me. There's a part of me growing inside you and he or she isn't any less special because of what may or may not have happened three years ago. No, this isn't the way I envisioned it, but we've created life, L. We deserve our moment of happiness so please don't lessen how special our child is because of what happened this morning."

"Omigod. You're right. That's what I'm doing." She looks at her stomach and puts both of her hands on top of mine. "I'm so sorry. I don't know what got into me."

I do. Jenna Rosenthal. She's done a hell of a doozy on us both.

I kneel on the floor at Laurelyn's feet. I pull her bum to the edge of the couch and push her shirt up so I can kiss her stomach. It's flat as a washboard but not for much longer. "I love you and this baby so much. I can't wait to see him or her growing in your belly every day."

She strokes her fingers through my hair. "I love you and this baby more than anything in this world."

I feel like I can breathe again. "You don't know how happy that makes me hearing you say that."

"But at the same time, I don't feel like I'm being honest if I don't tell you how pissed off I am about your past reemerging to disrupt our lives again."

I really wish I could snap my fingers and make it all go away. "I'd give anything if I could change it. You deserve so much more than the shit I put you through. This is what I was talking about when I said I was terrified you were going to wake up one day and see that I'm not worthy of your love."

"I've told you before… I despise what you did. It's a hard pill to swallow every time it's shoved down my throat."

"I know. I hate it as much as you—and it seems the ghosts of my past are going to keep showing up in our lives—so I need to know if you can handle it." She said she couldn't this morning, but she'd just found out about this possible son of mine and she didn't know she was pregnant. I hope she's changed her mind.

"I knew what I was getting myself into when I married you, and the decision to have a baby was half mine. I can't back out now."

That's not the answer I was hoping for. "Would you back out on me if you weren't pregnant?"

"I can't say what I would or wouldn't do if that were the case. It isn't possible for me to know."

She's so hurt and angry. I'm inclined to believe she would leave me if it weren't for the pregnancy so I have to wonder if she's rethinking her decision. "Our baby is not a mistake."

"In light of this morning's events, the timing isn't perfect, but I would never think of our child as a mistake."

No child should be viewed that way but it's all I can think when I consider Jenna's son being mine. And I'm a son of a bitch for feeling that way. "Will you go with me for the paternity test?"

"Will we be called back with them into the same exam room?" she asks.

"No. I made our appointments an hour apart so I wouldn't have to see them. There's no point in having contact with the child if he isn't mine."

"Then I'll go with you."

"Thank you." I place my head in her lap and stay that way for a while as I consider how things will go if Jenna's son is mine. "I'm scared, L. I'm terrified nothing will be the same for us if this turns out badly." She says she wants to hear my fears and know my demons, but I don't think she would want to know how I really feel. It could bring up memories concerning the way her father felt about her so I keep it to myself.

CHAPTER NINETEEN
LAURELYN MCLACHLAN

PATERNITY TEST DAY IS HERE. I TOLD JACK HENRY I WOULD GO WITH HIM BUT I want to back out. The whole thing scares the shit out of me. To top it off, I'm nauseated as hell. I lie motionless, waiting for the wave to pass but it lingers. I guess this is what I have to look forward to in the mornings—and it sucks.

We've been sleeping in the same bed all week, but we haven't made love. He hasn't even tried. I guess I should be glad since it would complicate this whole situation further, but I don't like living as roommates. I desperately miss the intimacy I share with my husband and the more we grow apart, the more I see how unhappy I would be without him.

He comes into the room and sits on the bed next to me. He cups his hand around mine and produces a crooked smile, but there's no joy in it or his eyes. "The appointment is in an hour and a half."

"I know. I was just waiting for this nausea to pass so I could get up and get ready."

He brings my hand to his mouth and kisses it. "I'm sorry you don't feel well, but it's a sign of a healthy pregnancy. It means your hormones are climbing."

"How in the world would you know something like that?"

He shrugs. "Seems I remember my mum saying something like that when Emma was pregnant. Want to try a few crackers to see if it'll help?"

"I guess you remember Margaret saying that was a remedy too?"

"No. Everyone knows it is."

I scoot up in bed. "Yeah. I'll try one or two."

He returns a few minutes later with crackers and a fizzy drink. "Mrs. Porcelli sent ginger ale. She said it might help."

"You told her I was pregnant?" I ask. He better say he didn't or I'm going to be pissed off.

"No—only that you weren't feeling well."

"What are we going to do about telling people?"

"I would tell the world if it were up to me, so I guess it comes down to what you want." I don't think he's kidding. I wouldn't put it past him to run an ad in the paper.

But I'm not ready for anyone to know. "I don't want to tell anyone yet."

"Because you want to wait until the miscarriage risk has passed?"

"Yes." No. That's not the reason at all. "No. I don't want to announce my pregnancy and then have it overshadowed by the announcement of you having a two-year-old son with another woman." I know this hurts him but it's how I feel. "Can we just agree to get through today, see what the results are next week, and then go from there?"

"I'll do anything you want. You have all the say-so."

I bite into the cracker and roll it around in my mouth. I don't have a clue how eating can make my nausea better because the simple thought of swallowing my own saliva right now makes me want to yack. "I gotta spit this out." I come up from the bed and run toward the bathroom when I realize there'll be stomach contents following the cracker.

Jack Henry is instantly by my side helping to pull my hair away from my face and placing a cool washcloth on the back of my neck. "I'm so sorry you're sick, love."

"A normal part of it all, I'm afraid."

"I'd take it from you if I could."

"Yeah, I know you would." I have no doubt about his sincerity because that's how much he loves me.

WE ARRIVE TEN MINUTES LATE FOR HIS APPOINTMENT BECAUSE OF ME. I HAD at least three more dry heaving episodes before we made it out the door. I told him to go ahead without me but he wouldn't.

He's scared shitless. I see it in his eyes. And I think I detect nervous trembling in his hands as he flips through a parenting magazine. "Do you feel better?"

"No. I'm still really nauseated. I think I could lie down on this floor and happily die right now."

"Would you think less of me as a man if I did the same?" I'm actually amused for the first time in days. We're a sight—two adults sitting in this pediatrician's office more terrified than any of the kids surrounding us.

"Jack McLachlan." He's called back and we're led into an exam room by a short, round nurse. "You're here to submit a DNA sample for a paternity test regarding Ashton Rosenthal."

"That's correct."

Holy shit. I've not heard his name until now. I think I've been pretending he didn't have one, that he didn't really exist, but hearing it makes it all too real. "I'm going to throw up."

The nurse scrambles to grab an emesis basin from the cabinet and hands it off to me just in time. More dry heaving—of course it is. I have nothing in my stomach.

"Looks like you may need to see the doctor while you're here." She wets a paper towel and passes it to me.

"A pediatrician isn't going to help what's wrong with me."

"My wife's pregnant. It's morning sickness." He sounds so proud.

"Oh, well, congratulations." An awkward silence ensues and I'm sure it's because she's remembering why we're here in the first place. I feel the pounding heat of humiliation rising in my cheeks. I shield my face. "The doctor will be with you shortly."

I look at Jack Henry. "See. That's why I don't want to tell people yet."

He sighs. "I get it, babe, but please try to understand my side. I'm excited about our baby. It felt good to tell someone my wife is pregnant. It makes me proud."

"You can't always do something because it feels good! That's why we're sitting here in a doctor's office for a fucking paternity test." I'm irritable, on edge, and I could burst into tears at any moment. I have no right to say these hurtful things to him. "I'm sorry. I don't know why I'm being such a bitch. I don't wanna be."

"It's the pregnancy, love, and this situation isn't helping." He puts his arms around me. "Just a few more days and hopefully this will be over for good so we can get back to being us."

Being us. There's nothing I want more, but it seems these bitches from his past won't allow it.

The physician comes into the exam room with his nurse. He's polite—not the best bedside manner in the world—but I assume he's used to dealing with children. He collects a swab of the inside of Jack Henry's cheek and places his patient label around it. He holds it up for Jack Henry to verify. "All of that looks correct to you?"

"Yes, sir. That's me."

"Good. The lab will send the results to us and we'll notify you by letter."

"I prefer to be called," he requests. "Mail will take at least two days longer and I'm anxious to know the results."

"Okay, but I'm sure you'll want something in writing as well. I'll have the office call so you can come by for the lab report."

So, that's it. Now, we wait.

We leave the exam room and wait at reception to check out. "Did you like the doctor?"

That's sort of a weird question. "Not really. Why do you ask?"

"We'll be needing a pediatrician."

"Well, it won't be him." Not only was his bedside manner lacking, I wouldn't want to be remembered as the wife who accompanied her husband for a paternity test. "I want a female doctor."

"What if our baby is a boy?" he asks. "Don't you think that would be awkward for him to let a female pediatrician look at his doodle?"

I slam on my mental brakes. "His doodle?"

"Yeah." Really? That's what Jack Henry's going to call our son's penis?

"I don't think it would be any more awkward than a male pediatrician looking at our daughter's tutu."

"Her tutu? That's what you'll call it?"

We look at one another and laugh. "Is this an example of what our vocabulary will be reduced to? Doodle and tutu?"

"I'm pretty sure it is. Three kids in and Evan only speaks fluent buffoon now."

"I didn't expect to see you here." I turn at the venomous sound of a woman's voice but I already know it's her—Jenna Rosenthal. She has her son on her hip and looks none too pleased about my presence. "You're pretty cheery for a woman whose husband just submitted proof that he's this little boy's father." She points at Jack Henry. "Look at him, Ashton. That's your daddy and you look just like him."

This woman is delusional. That child looks nothing like Jack Henry.

"Don't," Jack Henry grits through his teeth and then looks at the boy and softens his voice. "Don't tell him that."

"The test will prove it. You'll see."

"And if it does, you'll introduce me into his life appropriately, not standing in the hallway of a doctor's office."

"Next," the receptionist calls out and we step to the counter to pay for the visit.

Jack Henry folds the receipt and shoves it into his jacket pocket. "Don't look back, even if she says something. Just walk out of here."

"Okay." He puts his arm through mine and leads me out.

"Ashton, tell your daddy and the wicked step-monster bye-bye."

He feels me twist in his arms so I can turn to respond, to let that bitch have it good. "Don't do it, L. It'll reflect poorly on you if you physically or verbally attack her while she has a child in her arms. It's what she wants."

He's right but it's hard as hell to let that one go. "I'm fine." I straighten and hold my head high. "I'm good. Really."

He releases my arm and I wait until we're in the car to have my come-apart. "Why you always gotta fuck the crazy ones?" He looks at me but doesn't answer. "Damn, McLachlan. First Audrey and now her. Two of the twelve are nutjobs—three of thirteen, if you include Lana. That isn't a great statistic. What do you do to these women to drive them to the point of insanity?"

"Can we not talk about the others or what I did to them?"

"Sure. I don't really want to know, anyway." The topic of his former lovers is beyond old for me and I'm quickly developing the same feelings about this paternity test issue.

"I only want to concentrate on you and our marriage." He puts his hand on my stomach. "And our little one."

I place my hand on top of his. "We haven't celebrated this baby yet."

He leans over to me in the passenger seat and grasps the back of my neck with his free hand. He pulls me closer until our foreheads are pressed against one another. "Oh God, L. Things have felt so delicate between us this week. I was afraid to try for fear I would make you angrier."

"I didn't mean to make you feel that way." I embrace his face with my palms. "I've been selfish, wallowing in self-pity. I haven't allowed you to express happiness about the baby because I was punishing you. I've been unfair and I see that now. I'm sorry." I lean in and kiss his mouth. "Let's go home."

"Anything you say."

I'm thinking of all the ways I want to show Jack Henry how much I love him, but they seem awkward knowing our housekeeper will be roaming the house. "Would you want to call Mrs. Porcelli and give her the rest of the day off?"

"I don't think that'll be necessary for what I have in mind." He reaches for his phone and makes a call. "Hi, it's Jack. I have a favor to ask. Would you prepare a picnic for me and Laurelyn?" He gives me a crooked grin, showcasing only one of his beautiful dimples. "Thank you very much. We'll be home in about fifteen minutes."

He ends the call and makes another. "Harold, I'm taking the rest of the day off." He gives me the same crooked grin. "No, everything's fine. I just want to spend time with my wife so I think it's fine for you to knock off as well. We'll pick up tomorrow morning."

He pulls into the garage and leans over to kiss my mouth. "Stay here while I grab the basket."

"Okay."

I wait in the car and he finally returns. He's carrying two armloads of stuff, including the comforter from the guest bedroom. "Need help there?"

"Nah." He walks over to the ATV and unloads everything onto the backseat. He gestures toward the passenger seat. "Your chariot awaits, milady."

"What are you up to, Mr. McLachlan?"

"All in good time, Mrs. McLachlan."

I join my husband on my chariot and he drives us out to the vineyard. I open my mouth to ask where we're going but shut it because he isn't going to tell me. He means for this to be a surprise but I put the pieces together before we get to where we're going. He's taking me to the wine cave.

The realization flips a switch to my groin, setting me on ready, and I recall the first time Jack Henry brought me here. I had not yet agreed to his crazy, indecent proposal but he was so determined I would. He used some rather unorthodox moves in order for it to happen. It's also the day he told me he'd never marry or have children. My, what a difference a year has made. Give us another and we'll be parents of a... four-month-old.

He parks by the entrance to the wine cave. "You figured it out half a mile back, didn't you?"

"No." He looks at me skeptically. "Yeah. But it only gave me time to think about what we're going to do when we get in there."

"I recognized your squirm."

What does that mean? "My squirm?"

"You're fidgety and restless when you're turned on but have to wait on me to give it to you."

This isn't news to me but I didn't realize it was so blatantly recognizable to him. "Do you know all my secrets?"

"I doubt it."

He unlocks the entrance and we enter the dark cave. He flips the switch for the lanterns and our path is illuminated. "I love this place so much."

"I do too. I'm sorry I haven't made time to bring you back sooner, but Harold stalks this place, constantly checking to make sure everything is as it should be. He does a top-notch job when it comes to my vineyard but he throws a wrench in me being a caveman."

That needs to change because it's been far too long since we were here last. "Then you should give him more time off so we can sneak down here more often."

"I might just have to do that."

We walk the corridor and I wrap my arms around myself. The cave is drafty. "Cold?" he asks. I nod and he pulls me into his warm side.

We stop at the entrance to the room where our reception was held. "I still haven't forgiven you for smearing wedding cake across my face."

"It was cute."

I didn't find a thing cute about it. "It was not. Addison worked on my makeup forever to get it perfect. Do you know what it was like to have her in my face for that long?"

"L, you still looked perfect after I kissed it off."

We move into the room where he brought me on our first day at Avalon. Fond memories rush back. "I was spread across that table the first time you made me come. Then our wedding guests sat there and ate cake on it."

"I'm pretty sure your dad sat at the table in the exact spot where I hoisted you up and went down on you." He enjoys taking a stab at my parents any chance he can. He does it because he hates the way they've wronged me, so I'm okay with that.

He spreads a thick quilt on the flagstone-covered cave floor and then the comforter from the guest bedroom so it's nice and soft. He kicks off his shoes and sits on the linens before he holds his hand out. "Sit with me."

I step out of my sandals and kneel before lowering myself to sit next to him. He takes a bottle of wine from the basket and removes the top. He pours and passes a glass to me.

"I can't drink this."

"It's just sparkling grape juice." I take it from him and he pours a second glass for himself. "I knew you wouldn't be able to drink wine so I wanted to have something else on hand when we found out you were pregnant." He pats the floor between his legs. "Come sit here." I scoot over and back until he's able to cocoon me in his arms. My back is against his chest and he brings his glass to mine. "This toast is to you, my wife and the mother of my son or daughter. You've filled my life with so much love and joy this year. It's something I never thought I'd have. I love you, L, far more than I think you know, and I swear I'm going to do better so I can be the kind of husband you deserve. I'm becoming a better man because of you and this baby."

Omigod, he is so amazing.

I put my glass down and turn in his arms. "That was so beautiful, I don't even know how to respond." There's only one way I can think of, and it's not with words.

He puts his glass down when I move to my knees so I can pull my dress over my head. He reaches out and pulls me to him, gently kneading one of my breasts. "Are you sore here?"

"A little." He unfastens my bra and takes my already hard nipple into his mouth. He rolls his tongue around the tip and the sensitivity echoes in my groin, causing me to tremble. "But that feels good." He moves to my other breast and mimics the same movement before flipping us so I'm lying on my back.

He plants a kiss over my heart and then moves down the center of my body. He stops when he gets to my belly and places his fingertips against it, rubbing in a circular motion. "You're already so much more than just a child in my head. You're a miracle growing right here inside your mum." He places his hands on my hipbones and presses his lips below my navel for a kiss. "You're already loved more than you know."

He moves lower and I lift my hips so he can get my panties off. When they're discarded, I begin working on the top button of his shirt. "You're overdressed. Help me."

He yanks at the waist of his pants and I recognize the sound of his zipper sliding down. I hook my toes in the waistband of both and help him push them to his feet and then off. We're bare and pressed against one another. His erection is right there, ready to dive in, yet he waits. "This won't hurt you or the baby?"

"No. He's in a safe little cocoon." I bend my knees and part them further before shifting my hips upward to push his tip inside.

I know he's dying to. I am too. We've never gone so long without making love except when we were separated, but I see the hesitation on his face. "We're fine."

He presses his forehead to mine. "You'll tell me if something hurts or doesn't feel right?"

"Yes."

He enters me slow and easy, then stops. It's frustrating as hell. "I didn't suddenly become breakable because I'm pregnant."

"I know. I'm just being gentle."

I can't take this. "I'm taking control so get on your back. I'm topping." He pulls out of me slowly and does as I tell him. I climb over and sink down until he fills me completely. "Mmm… see? Doesn't that feel much more satisfying?"

He puts his hands on my hips and guides me up and down. "You can ride me anytime." And I do until we both come.

CHAPTER TWENTY
JACK MCLACHLAN

It's been five days since the paternity test and the pediatrician's office just phoned to let me know I can come by to pick up the results—but it'll have to wait. I have more important business to tend. Laurelyn has her first prenatal visit in two hours and I won't allow a special moment like this to be ruined.

Her morning sickness has reared its ugly head every day this week, so it's taking longer for her to get up and get going. Her face is so pale and thin—I'm pretty sure she's already lost weight. That can't be good for her or the baby. "Mrs. Porcelli mixed a home remedy for you." She glances at the glass and looks as though she might vomit any minute. "She seemed sure it would help."

"So she knows?"

"She must since she made this for you, but I didn't tell her." She slides up in the bed slowly with her eyes closed. "It wouldn't be hard for her to figure out since you've been sick every morning this week."

She takes the glass and looks at it. "What's in it?"

"I have no idea. It just looks like water to me."

She brings it to her nose for a sniff. "I smell something familiar but I can't put my finger on it." She brings the glass to her mouth and takes a tiny sip. "It's not terrible. There's a little tanginess with something sweet

—maybe a touch of honey." She takes another sip. "I don't care if it's bad if it helps this feeling go away. I hate being nauseated."

"What about some toast?" I want her to eat because she doesn't need to lose another ounce. I worry she and the baby aren't getting what they need.

"Maybe a little later." Not what I want to hear.

"Promise me you'll try."

"I will." She puts her hand on my arm. "Don't worry, McLachlan. I'll feel better in a few hours and I'll eat something then. I'm not going to let the baby starve."

I hate not being able to help her. "I can't control this situation and it makes me feel helpless. I take care of you—it's what I do—but I'm not able to with this."

"This will pass in a few weeks and I'll eat you out of house and home. I'll probably gain way too much weight and get lots of stretch marks. You'll wish I had morning, noon, and night sickness."

"Never. I want you and this baby to have the nourishment you need."

Laurelyn sips on her drink until she has about half of it down—and it stays. It's mainly water, I think, but it makes me feel better to see her at least get a little hydration.

It's a slow process but she gets out of bed to shower and dress for her appointment. We somehow manage to get out the door at a decent time. Despite her present condition, she looks beautiful and I can't stop looking over at her as I drive.

"What is it?"

"You're beautiful and I love looking at you."

"Well, find a time to look when you're not driving."

"Yes, ma'am."

We do the necessary paperwork as we sit in the waiting room, but we don't get called to an exam room for an hour and a half. "Waiting this long is fucking ridiculous."

She turns and gives me the shut the hell up face. I know it well. "I'm seeing an obstetrician. She has to leave the office to go deliver babies at the hospital. That's nonnegotiable so expect delays. We'll get our turn at making people wait when she comes to deliver this one."

L pees in a cup, gets weighed, and has her blood taken. All of that happens before she's even put in the exam room. "What else are they gonna do to you?"

She starts taking off her clothes to change into a patient gown. "I'm sure I'm getting a Pap smear since it's my first visit. She'll probably feel around to make sure everything is in good working order and I'm hoping for an ultrasound. I really want to see the baby."

She sits on the exam table and we wait some more—long enough for the doc to deliver at least a dozen babies. I'm becoming very irritable and L knows it. "Be patient, McLachlan."

"You shouldn't have to sit and wait like this. You haven't had anything to eat and it's well past lunch now."

She opens her mouth to reply—or argue—but doesn't when the doctor finally comes into the exam room. "Hello, Mrs. McLachlan. I'm Dr. Sommersby. I'm really sorry you've had to wait so long. I don't usually run so behind but I had two deliveries this morning and one was twins so it took longer."

"It's not a problem." Yes, it is. I won't have L sitting for hours like this every time she has an appointment.

They talk a few minutes about things I know nothing about as she feels L's breasts. That's awkward, having another woman touch my wife like that, but I guess it would be worse if it were a man. Dr. Sommersby asks L to slide down on the table and her feet are placed in metal footrests. I hear a lot of clanking and keep my place in the chair by her head. I don't even want to know what's going on under that drape. "Everything looks good. Now let's take a look with the ultrasound so we can document how far along you are."

This makes L very happy. And me. I want to see the baby and know everything is all right as well.

The doctor squeezes gel on L's belly and spreads it around. She takes notice of her navel piercing. "That's very pretty but I recommend you change it out to something flexible when you get a little further along. Sometimes these stiff rings leave ugly scars."

"I expected you to tell me I had to take it out."

"I'm pretty lax on most things, but I do want it out on delivery day in case of emergency. It's terrible trying to get those things out when everyone is scrambling around in a mad rush." An emergency—I hadn't considered anything like that happening. I guess no one goes in to have a baby and thinks something bad will happen to them.

I take Laurelyn's hand in mine as Dr. Sommersby adjusts her glasses and straightens the monitor screen of the ultrasound for a better view. She moves the probe one way and then another. I can't guess what she's seeing but for me, I see nothing but white noise on a black screen. "I was hoping we could see something with an abdominal scan but you're too early. We'll need to do a transvaginal." She returns the probe in her hand to the machine and exchanges it for one that looks like a huge dildo. What the fuck is she gonna do with that?

My thought isn't quite completed when she rolls a condom over it and I find out. "Relax your legs and let them fall apart, Laurelyn." Her hand and the dildo disappear under L's gown. "This doesn't hurt but it does feel full, especially if your bladder isn't empty."

L looks at me with large eyes and takes a deep breath before releasing it. She makes a face that tells me she's uncomfortable and squeezes my hand. "Whew! That's a lot of pressure."

"Hang in there, Laurelyn. It'll get better once I stop moving the transducer... which should be right about... now."

Laurelyn sighs a breath of relief. Her grip on my hand relaxes but it trembles as she searches the screen, waiting for the doctor to say something. Anything.

"This is just a two-dimensional ultrasound so the picture isn't the best. I basically only want to document the gestation. We'll do a three-dimensional when you're further along and have something to see that you'd recognize." She finally points to the screen. "Looks like you're six weeks, give or take a couple of days. This big dark area is your uterus and that white circle is the sac. And if you'll look right here..." She adjusts for a better look and points to a white area. "There's your baby."

Laurelyn squeezes my hand. "It's amazing. We're looking at our baby for the first time. Do you see it, Jack Henry?"

It's truly an incredible sight to behold, this tiny little person inside my wife. Part me, part her, but whether boy or girl, I hope to see more Laurelyn than me in him or her. "I do. It's incredible." I'll be forever changed by it.

We leave the office and Laurelyn can't stop looking at the ultrasound picture the doctor printed for us. "I haven't been able to get the bleeding episode with Addison off my mind since I found out I was pregnant, so it's a relief to know everything looks okay at this point."

"Everything is going to be perfect. No worries, okay?"

"I'm excited. I decided I don't want to wait about telling everyone since we got a good report."

I debate bringing up the test results. I don't want to taint our good news but I'm certain Laurelyn wants this over as much as I do. "Dr. Gates's office called this morning to tell me the paternity test results are in. Do you want to go by and pick them up while we're in town or wait?"

She sighs. "I don't want to put it off. It's better to get it done so we can either stop worrying and move forward or begin the process of accepting that boy as yours."

Laurelyn waits in the car while I go in to retrieve the report. The woman at reception smiles and wishes me a good evening as she places a sealed envelope in my hand. My name is typed across the front in all caps but all I can think is how it should read, JACK McLACHLAN'S FATE.

Laurelyn and I didn't discuss how we'd do this, but I don't open the results. I think it's something she and I should do together in the privacy of our home—mainly because I don't know what either of our reactions will be—but I'm giving her all the power. It's her choice to decide when and how.

I get into the car and hold the envelope out for her. "Tell me how you want to do this."

She takes a breath and her cheeks puff out as she exhales. "I think we should do it at home."

"Agreed." I toss the envelope on the dashboard and steer her Cayenne toward Avalon. The drive has never seemed longer.

I pull into the garage and grab the envelope. "I think we should be alone when we look at this. Do you mind if I give Mrs. Porcelli the rest of the day off?"

"I think that's best."

I go in ahead of Laurelyn and relieve Mrs. Porcelli of her duties for the rest of the day. L waits until she's gone to come into the house and I see why when she comes inside. She's already crying. "I'm sorry." She cups her mouth with her hand. "I told myself I wasn't going to be like this but I can't help it."

"It's okay, L. Your hormones are all over the place so you can't help this crazy emotional roller coaster you're riding." I hold my hand out to her and after she takes it, I lead her to the couch. "Is here okay?" She nods and tears roll down her cheeks as I break the envelope's seal.

She stops me, placing her hand on mine. "No matter the results, I love you. If he's yours, I'm not going anywhere. I'll stand by you and be the wife you need me to be."

I'm instantly relieved, and for the first time since my life spun out of control, I feel like my world won't end by what could potentially be on this piece of paper. "I can't tell you how much it means to me knowing you'll be here with me either way."

"I wanted you to know before so you could be assured that negative results aren't why I stayed."

I take the paper out and it isn't what I expected. I thought it would be a letter stating I was or was not the father of Ashton Rosenthal, but I'm wrong. I panic, trying to decipher its meaning. "It's the actual lab result." I search through lots of words and numbers I don't understand about alleles. One set is for: child. The other for: alleged father. And then I see what I believe to be the results.

Based on the DNA analysis, the alleged father, Jack McLachlan, is excluded as the biological father of the child, Ashton Rosenthal, because they do not share sufficient genetic markers. Combined Direct Index: 0. Probability 0%.

I'm not his father.

"Gah!" I put my hands into my hair and fall back against the couch. "Fuck." Is it wrong for me to be this relieved when the result leaves a little boy fatherless? I don't have time to sort that out in my head because I'm pulling L into my arms. "Zero percent probability. Jenna Rosenthal's son is not mine."

Thank fuck. I've managed to put another shitstorm behind me.

CHAPTER TWENTY-ONE
LAURELYN MCLACHLAN

I'm awakened when I hear Jack Henry on the phone, yelling, and I get up to see what's going on. "Your son isn't mine. There's nothing else for us to discuss." I don't have to hear another word to know who's on the other end.

He's quiet for a moment but then I'm startled when he throws his phone across the room hitting the wall only a few feet from me. "Motherfucking-bitch!" He's so angry, he's shaking. It's frightening to see him like this.

He sees me standing close to where he just busted his phone into pieces and his eyes grow large. "I'm so sorry. I didn't see you standing there."

"What was that about?"

He sinks into the couch. "That, my dear wife, was the sound of me being threatened and blackmailed by Jenna Rosenthal."

"With what?"

"She began by accusing me of having someone change the paternity test results. I told her we could take a hundred paternity tests and they would all exclude me as her son's father. Once she realized she wasn't going to hoodoo me into claiming her kid, she threatened to expose my past. She said you'd leave me for sure, out of embarrassment, if everyone knew what I used to do."

"What does she want?"

"What she wanted from the beginning—money."

Of course she does. Money-hungry bitch. "What kind of numbers are we talking?"

"She asked how much money I was willing to part with to keep you."

She's going to play hardball. "She probably thinks I don't know about your past."

"Or if she suspects you were a part of it, she thinks I'll pay to keep you from being humiliated as one of my companions."

I don't really give a rat's ass what people think. "I'm not going anywhere, so I don't want you to pay her one damn cent unless you think you can't live with people knowing."

"I really don't give a damn but I don't want that for you. It would kill me to see your picture in the gossip column with some stupid heading about me once being some kind of bizarre sexual deviant." He's still shaking.

"It might not stick. You're no longer one of Australia's most eligible bachelors. Your days of making the papers may have ended when you put a wedding ring on your finger."

"That's not really how it works. What I did was illicit. People love a scandalous story—especially when it's real. It's way more interesting than the happily ever after." He fists his hair and groans. "Fuck, Margaret McLachlan will kill me if she finds out."

"Then we should tell her about the baby as soon as possible. She won't want her grandchild to be fatherless."

"I don't know about that. She's going to be mad as hell."

Margaret isn't dumb. She's going to put the pieces together. Everyone will. "I spent three months with you and left. She's going to figure out I was one of them. I'm not really crazy about that idea. I don't want to disappoint her."

"My mum loves you, L. She won't think less of you." He gets up from the couch and walks over to gather the pieces of his phone. He takes his SIM card out and inspects it. "I need your phone. I have an important call to make."

I retrieve my phone from the bedroom and give it to Jack Henry and he makes the card exchange. He's standing with his back to me when he dials a number and waits for an answer. "Jim, I have another job for you. I need you to look into someone—a woman named Jenna Rosenthal."

Jenna Rosenthal. Another bitch I'd like to kick in the ass while wearing my boots. And I will if the opportunity arises, with a big-ass smile on my face.

※

WE DECIDED WE WANTED TO TELL MARGARET AND HENRY ABOUT THE BABY in person, but because of work Jack Henry needed to do at Avalon this week, we had to wait until the weekend to make the trip to Sydney. I'm sure my mother-in-law suspects why we're coming again so soon. I could hear the exhilaration in her voice over the phone. We'd only hung up for a few moments when she called back to tell me she's baking a chocolate cake for me—one I can take home when we leave—and even gave me permission to not share with Jack Henry.

We've taken my in-laws out to dinner instead of cooking at their place. The restaurant is formal, and overpriced, but it's what the McLachlans are accustomed to. There's even a woman walking around serenading diners. She stops to sing for a couple and belts out "At Last." I'm watching the scene happen from a distance but it's quite clear at the end of the song that the man is proposing to his dinner companion when he drops to one knee. The diners around them begin clapping and it spreads throughout the entire restaurant, most patrons likely believing they're applauding the songstress.

Everyone at our table has ordered wine, except me. Henry pays that little tidbit absolutely no attention but Margaret takes notice. I know because she's suddenly giddy and it's not from the wine.

"Jack, Randall tells me you brought his granddaughter on for an internship."

Uh-oh. "I did, but she found another one. She wanted to be closer to her college friends. She was more concerned with partying than learning to manage a vineyard." Nice one, McLachlan. The only good thing I can say about Bianca is that she had the good sense to go away quietly so

Jack Henry and Mr. Brees didn't experience a hiccup in their business relationship.

Jack Henry and his dad speak the vineyard language and I'm mostly lost. I think Margaret understands a lot but chooses to not join in. I think she still holds a little resentment for that life, although it made her and Henry a nice living. "Do you understand anything they're saying?"

She lifts her glass and takes a drink. "More than I care to know."

"I'm interested in learning. I want to understand so he can talk to me about things happening on the vineyards."

"I'm going to give you some advice." I smile, remembering the last bit she gave me. She grins too and leans in, lowering her voice. "Some more advice. A vineyard is work to him. It's his profession and he has employees he discusses that with. He pays them quite well for that service and you aren't his employee. Don't allow the vineyards to enter your home life and make damn sure you don't let them into your bedroom. Be his outlet—a safe place where he can escape—when all the shit that goes along with that life becomes too much for him."

Margaret has a different way of looking at things. Here I thought I would be bringing myself closer to my husband by becoming part of his work life, but she's telling me the opposite. And I think she's right.

"Trust me, Laurelyn. He will hold you in a different regard if he views you as his refuge and not his confidant." She returns to her entree and I can only think of how I hope to be the kind of mother she is. I want to be strong and confident, yet gentle and loving. I wish I'd had her as my role model instead of my own mom.

Jack Henry takes my hand and gives it a squeeze under the table after we order dessert. I'm guessing that's my cue he's ready to spill the beans. "Laurelyn and I have an announcement." Henry is yet to be in tune with what we're about to say but Margaret can predict it easily. She literally looks ready to burst. "Laurelyn's pregnant."

Henry does the manly, fatherly slap on Jack Henry's back as he congratulates us. I almost think I see his chest inflate, like some sort of pride thing about his boys being able to swim hard enough to impregnate me on the first try.

Margaret comes out of her chair and I do too. She pulls me into her arms in a tight embrace. "I knew it. Ohh… I'm so happy for you." She releases me and holds my arms out for a look. "When can I expect my new grandbaby?"

"October first."

"You have a date. Does that mean you've already had a visit with a doctor?"

"Yes. I have an ultrasound picture. Would you like to see it?"

"Absolutely." She pulls glasses from her purse, slips them on, and looks up at me. "It sucks getting old eyes. I can't see anything without these ridiculous things."

"I think you look really good in them." Margaret never looks anything less than classy.

"Bullshit. I look old as hell," she laughs. She holds the printout at a distance for a better view. "I do believe that is one of the sweetest little dots I've ever seen."

I laugh because she's right. The baby is tiny. "It's quite early—only six weeks. The doctor says it's the size of a rice grain. Most people don't announce their pregnancies until twelve weeks but we're too excited to wait that long."

"Will you tell everyone or are we privy to the information because we're the grandparents?"

I don't know. We haven't discussed anything beyond telling Margaret and Henry in case this story gets out about his past. "What are we doing?"

"I told you from the beginning, love. I want the world to know my wife is pregnant."

Okay, then. I guess we're telling the world.

I call my mom from the car as Jack Henry drives us home from Henry and Margaret's. I'm excited to hear her reaction. I hope she's as happy as Margaret is.

We begin our conversation like normal, her catching me up on everything going on in her life, before I move on to the news I called to share. "Mom, Jack Henry and I have wonderful news. I'm pregnant."

Silence.

"Mom, are you still there?"

"Laurie, why would you allow that to happen? A baby is going to ruin your career."

Just because I ruined her life doesn't mean my baby will ruin mine. Why can't she understand that? "We chose to have this baby because we want to start our family."

"You're being stupid. You don't know what you're getting yourself into."

I can't take hearing these things from my mother. "I have to go."

I end the call and let her reaction soak in for a minute before I tell Jack Henry the terrible things she said. I wait for his temper to engage, but it doesn't. He pulls the car to the side of the road and takes me into his arms where I cry until I have no more tears to shed.

❧

It's almost been a week—that's how long that blackmailing bitch said she'd give Jack Henry before she called again—so we expect to hear from her tomorrow. My decision still stands. I'm supporting my husband, even if this goes public. I say that with incredible allegiance but then I become afraid when I think of the remaining ten women I've not had the displeasure of meeting. Will they come out of the woodwork? There could be more false paternity claims. Or true ones. Are we making the wrong decision by not paying her off? I don't know.

Jack Henry is expecting a call from Jim today. I hope he is the best—as my husband believes—and tells us he's found something we can use to rid ourselves of that woman.

Jim phones while Jack Henry is sitting at my bedside during my morning routine—lying in bed nauseated, sipping Mrs. Porcelli's remedy while nibbling on crackers. He sits with me every morning and helps me to the bathroom when my nausea progresses to something more.

He's listening intently when the nearly overwhelming wave hits me. I close my eyes, wishing it all away, but it refuses to obey so I'm scrambling to get out of bed. "Just a minute, Jim." Jack Henry drops his phone to the bed to help me up.

I rush to the bathroom but wave him away. "Take the call," I tell him between heaves. "I'm fine."

He's hesitant as displayed by how long he stands in the bathroom. "Call out if you need anything."

I nod, my head hanging over the toilet.

I wash up following my vomiting episode and I think it's possible that I feel better. Yes, I believe I do.

As I come out of the bathroom, Jack Henry is finishing his call. "My man, Jim, has discovered a lot of dirty little secrets about one Jenna Rosenthal. Most are insignificant for our needs but one transgression will be of use. I say we invite Miss Rosenthal to dinner. I don't believe a phone call will do."

"What are you going to do?"

"Something not befitting a gentleman—and I want to see her face when I do it."

※

WE WAIT IN THE RESTAURANT AT THE HOTEL WHERE ALL OF THIS SHIT BEGAN —the one where I came to Jack Henry as someone else. Worst idea ever.

I can't believe Jenna agreed to meet us here. It's really sort of stupid on her part since it's her place of employment, at least the hotel is, but the restaurant is inside. I wonder what she does here—and what she did three years ago that drew Jack Henry to her.

He hasn't told me what Jim found on her. Frankly, I don't care as long as it gets her out of our lives. I shudder when I think of how differently this could have gone. What if Jack Henry had been her son's father? What a nightmare that would've been.

"She's late." That irritates him even further.

"Don't worry, that money-hungry bitch is coming. She didn't do all this to not carry through on it."

She arrives ten minutes later. "You're late."

"I couldn't get here sooner because Ashton is sick. He probably caught whatever it is at that medical clinic you made us go to."

Jack Henry is quick to reply. "Maybe you should've tried knowing who fathered your child and we wouldn't have been there in the first place." I think I'm most glad her son wasn't his because I don't think I could have taken the bickering between them.

Our server comes by and Jenna orders a glass of wine. "I'm only staying long enough to discuss what I want from you." She looks at me.

"I must say I'm surprised to see you here, so that can only mean one thing: you once agreed to be his whore just like the rest of us."

I don't respond because I can't deny what she's saying.

"She was never my whore."

"Right." A glass of wine is placed in front of her and I watch as she goes through the process of using her senses to judge it. "Logan Ross, that's who he was to me, taught me a lot of things but appreciating a great glass of Shiraz is something I've kept with me. Which wine has he taught you to enjoy?" She looks down at my water. "What... no wine for the vineyard princess?" Neither of us replies and she begins smiling. "Ah-hah... you're pregnant. I guess congratulations are in order for the perfect couple." Her voice is saturated with venom. "Is that why you stood firmly by his side? Or is it because he's filthy rich?"

Jack Henry is fuming. "Not what we're here to discuss."

She's grinning. "Then let's get down to why we're here. I've done a little research on you since we spoke and I'm glad I did because it turns out you're even wealthier than I first thought."

"Say what you want," he tells her.

"I was going to ask for a million but then I decided I was lowballing myself. I want two million dollars and all of this goes away. I won't go to the press about your nasty little practices and you'll never see me again."

"Two million dollars for your silence seems reasonable until I consider that I can have it for free."

She's clearly confused. "It's not free."

He passes a manila envelope to her. "But I think it is... Aurora Dawn."

She doesn't even open the envelope. "Do you seriously think you're going to convince me to keep my mouth shut over some stupid porn video I starred in for a lousy hundred bucks when I was eighteen?"

"No. I just brought that to humiliate you. The thing that'll keep your mouth shut is the proof I have of you embezzling a shitload of money from this hotel, the very one we're sitting in. So while it might be uncomfortable to know your coworkers can watch you take it up the ass on film, jail is a hell of a lot more uncomfortable. And I'm sure you'd miss your son terribly. Maybe he wouldn't be completely grown by the time you got out."

She appears indignant. "Well, you have me over a barrel and you've fucked me again." She throws back the last of her wine before taking her purse and the manila envelope from the table. "I'd be careful with this one if I were you, Mrs. McLachlan. He always gets his way."

She's right. Jack Henry generally gets his way—whether the means are reasonable or not.

CHAPTER TWENTY-TWO
JACK MCLACHLAN

Our friends and family have known about the baby for weeks but there's something grand about hitting that twelve-week mark. We're finally able to breathe a sigh of relief since that typically means the pregnancy has made it to safety and the miscarriage risk is behind us.

We hear twelve to fourteen weeks is when the morning sickness gets better so we're hoping for sooner rather than later. These past several weeks have been miserable for L, but she never complains. She does what she needs to in the mornings, while listening to the beating and banging of the construction work going on in her studio, and then works writing music as soon as she's able to get up and around. It's not ideal but she somehow manages.

I'm ready for work but I'm sitting next to L on the bed while she trudges through another morning of nausea. Damn, it's been relentless but at least it doesn't usually last beyond the morning hours. I hear some women have it all day. "Do you have anything planned for today?"

"I'm hoping to put the final touches on a song I wrote for Southern Ophelia and then go see Addison for a little while."

"How's she handling the whole bed-rest thing?"

"Not good, I'm afraid. She feels like a caged animal but I keep telling her to be compliant so she doesn't end up back in the hospital. Her doctor warned her that if she had problems at home, he'd admit her for the rest of the pregnancy."

I don't care who you are, that would be a shit-ton-load to handle. "I'm sure she's bored and needs something to do. Maybe a project would take her mind off everything. Why don't you hire an interior designer to decorate the nursery? It can be our gift to her."

"You are amazing. She hasn't been able to get out and buy anything since they found out it was a boy, so she's going to be so excited." She sits up to hug me. "I would kiss you if it wouldn't make me throw up."

"Nice, L. Thanks a lot."

She shrugs. "You know what I mean."

Another reason the morning sickness needs to go away. My wife won't kiss me—or anything else—in the mornings, and I really miss our first-thing romp before I shower for work. Evan warned me a baby would be a cock-blocker—and it is—but only in the mornings so far. L's pregnancy hormones have her primed and ready to go at it all the other times of day. Really. "So I don't get a midday naughty at lunch?"

"Not unless you can talk Mrs. Porcelli into it?"

I could've gone my whole life without her saying that. "Damn, L. You could've just said no."

"But that wouldn't have been near as funny."

⁂

THE ALARM GOES OFF, WAKING ME FROM ONE OF MY MORE EROTIC DREAMS, SO I'm hard. Damn.

I lie in bed thinking about anything except the only thing that'll relieve my raging hard-on, but it's no use. This isn't going away without some kind of action and I know the kind I prefer.

We're at the fourteen-week milestone and L has felt much better this week, so I decide to test the waters. She's lying on her side, her back to me, and I creep my hand around her waist. I rub her lower belly where our baby is growing and recognize the firmness now present. It doesn't seem like that was there last week.

I slide my hand lower and kiss the back of her neck before I cup my hand between her legs, rubbing up and down. "Babe, I'm getting up to shower."

"Why don't I believe you?"

I press my hard-on against her bum. "I'm sorry. I was having a really good dream when the alarm went off and I'm still wound up by it." Wound up is putting it mildly. I want inside L bad. I kiss the back of her neck and down her shoulder. "But it's fine if you don't feel up to it. My palm can become better acquainted with my cock in the shower."

She places her hand around my wrist and pulls it away from her body, deflating my hopes for an early morning fuck, but then shocks me when she slides it down the front of her knickers and begins moving her groin back and forth. "Fuck me from behind."

She doesn't have to ask twice.

I shove my hand further into her knickers and hear threads popping. I've never ripped her undies off but the sound is hot, I give the crotch a hard yank, tearing them to give me access to get inside her. "Oh, fuck." I want to slam my cock into her hard but I can't. I have this phobia about hurting her or the baby, so I use every ounce of self-restraint to ease inside gently.

I'm only a few strokes in when L starts talking. "I know you want it harder than that."

This isn't the way we fuck hard but it's still good. "I do but you know why I hold back." I've told her my fears.

She pulls away from me. "Get on your back." This is how we do it most of the time now, with L on top, and I don't mind a bit. She's in control and I'm able to enjoy sex without the fear of being too rough with her. We both get what we need.

I move my hand to her clit and stroke it as she slides up and down on my cock. I want her to come too. If she doesn't, I feel like a selfish, inadequate lover. "Does that feel good?"

"Yeah, don't stop."

And just like two, perfectly synced bombs, we explode together.

EIGHTEEN WEEKS—ALMOST HALFWAY THROUGH THE PREGNANCY. I CAN'T believe how much L's belly has changed in the last month. It's a small bump you can barely detect beneath her clothes but I'm amazed by the way it feels when she lies flat, like a firm grapefruit protruding from her lower abdomen.

L has a visit with her OB today. I had to skip her last appointment because of work but I wouldn't miss today for anything in the world. She's getting her first four-dimensional ultrasound. I've been looking online at some of the pictures and we should be able to see our baby's face for the first time today.

Dr. Sommersby comes into the room and does all the routine stuff first. I get to hear the heartbeat for the first time and I swear it triggers something in my chest, a sensation I've never felt before, and I have this crazy picture pop into my head of my heart growing like The Grinch's.

"Are you okay?"

"That's my first time to hear the heartbeat. I didn't know it would make me feel like this."

Dr. Sommersby laughs. "Well, Mr. McLachlan, you're going to be feeling a lot of different things when you see your baby on this ultrasound. He or she is going to look a lot different than when we looked at six weeks."

L pushes the waistband of her bottoms down and the good doctor begins the scan. It takes a minute for me to get my bearings but then it becomes clear. "Look, L." I laugh—maybe even sort of giggling. "It's a hand—and I can see all of the fingers." I watch the screen, mesmerized by what I'm looking at because it's so much better when it's your own child you're seeing.

I'm not sure I blink for fear of missing something. It's moving so much—she hasn't mentioned feeling anything. "Do you feel those somersaults?"

"Maybe little flutters here and there—nothing I registered as the baby moving. I thought it was gas bubbles or something." She giggles.

Dr. Sommersby moves the probe and we get a perfect shot of the face so she still-frames it. "This is a nice one."

"Look at that. It has to be a girl because that little face looks just like you."

Laurelyn doesn't take her eyes from the screen for a moment. "I don't think so. That's definitely your nose and chin so I think it's a boy."

"Do you want to find out who's right?"

Neither of us answers because we've been having this discussion for weeks. She's dying to know and wants to have everything purchased gender-specific and ready to go when the baby arrives. It's killing her that Addison already knows she's having a boy. But I want to be surprised. I think nothing would be more special than seeing your baby for the first time and hearing it's a boy or it's a girl.

"I've seen that look before. Can't agree, huh?"

L shakes her head. "Nope, and no one is budging."

"I can always write it down and seal it in an envelope for the one wanting to know."

I'd rather be told now rather than her know and let it slip in casual conversation or me find out when I see a nursery painted pink or blue. So I give in, pushing aside what I want just as I always do with L, because I love her so much and want her to be happy. "It's fine. You can tell us."

"Let's see if this little booger will cooperate and shows us." She moves the probe across L's belly. "I make it a habit to not look until I've been given the go-ahead so I don't let it slip." I hold my breath, waiting to hear the verdict. Do I have a son or a daughter?

"No, don't tell us." L looks at me and squeezes my hand. "I'll know what the baby is when it gets here and I can buy all the clothes I want then. You deserve to have this surprise."

I don't want her to give in—that's my job. "But you're dying to know."

"It's okay. I have the rest of my life to know if it's a boy or girl, so let's enjoy the angst of not knowing."

I lean up to kiss her. "Thank you, love."

"All right, then, we'll move on to measurements." Our fun is over as the diagnostic part of the ultrasound begins—no more cute shots of the baby's features. "Laurelyn, have you been having any contractions?"

"Not that I know of." She laughs but then sees the concerned look on Dr. Sommersby's face. "I'm assuming that's something I would recognize, wouldn't I?"

"You're a first-time mom, so you might not. Any cramping at all?"

"No, nothing. Is something wrong?" I hear the panic in her voice and it sends my heart to racing.

"Your cervix length is shortened and you appear dilated. The membranes are hourglassing through the cervix."

"I don't know what that means."

Dr. Sommersby stops the exam. "When a mother goes into labor, her uterus contracts and over time, this is what causes her cervix to shorten, or thin, and dilate. The contractions start out mild and gradually become more intense, but that's not the case for about one percent of pregnant women. They have weakened cervical tissue, for one reason or another, and the weight of the fetus causes dilation without any contractions at all. It usually isn't diagnosed until the mother has had at least one second-trimester miscarriage. I'm afraid that's what is happening here."

I hear the word miscarriage and I'm confused. I thought we were beyond that risk. "How serious is this?"

"Critical, I'm afraid. You're at least two centimeters."

She's too early. I already know it but I ask anyway. "What about the baby?"

"Viability is considered twenty-four weeks but even then, survival rate at that gestation is around fifty percent and the lifelong deficits can be devastating."

"That's at least five weeks away." Laurelyn looks at me, her face pained. She doesn't have to say the words—I doubt she could if she tried—because we both comprehend what the outcome will be. Our baby won't survive being born now.

"We have two options: let nature take its course and allow the pregnancy to terminate on its own, or do everything possible to maintain it."

We look at one another but don't need time to talk it over. "We want everything possible to be done."

"You should know this will be a very long road. We'll make decisions about your plan of care on a daily basis since your condition can change rapidly." Dr. Sommersby picks up the phone to make a call. "I want you transported to the hospital by ambulance. There will be no going back if those hourglassing membranes rupture."

The shock sets in and Laurelyn begins to cry. "I'm so sorry. I didn't know anything was wrong. I felt completely normal."

This isn't her fault. It's mine. I'm the one ramming my dick into her when I should've been keeping it to myself. "I think I did this—last night. I was too rough with you." I knew I'd end up hurting her and the baby.

Dr. Sommersby ends her call. "I'm admitting you to labor and delivery and your orders will be there when you arrive. The nurses are going to be doing a lot of things to you at once but most importantly, you're on strict bed rest in Trendelenburg position. That means the head of your bed will be in the lowest position and the foot will be elevated so you'll almost be standing on your head. It's going to be an uncomfortable position but if we're lucky, the membranes will go back up into the cervix. If that happens, it's possible I can take you to surgery and place a cerclage where I'd weave a suture through the cervix and then pull it closed and tie it shut."

"How long does the cerclage stay in?"

"I'd clip it around thirty-six weeks."

"So there's a chance I could still carry the baby to full term?"

"We have a shot if I'm able to get the cerclage in, but it's tricky because there's risks associated with placing it. The needle I'd use to place the suture can rupture the bag of waters. That's why I want you lying with your head down—so it can go back inside the cervix—or I won't even make an attempt."

This is scary as hell. I don't recall ever feeling this kind of terror.

"Could I have caused this during sex?" The guilt I feel is killing me and if I did this, I should know I'm the cause.

"No. With incompetent cervix, there's nothing you can do to prevent it. And there's no way of knowing you have it until there's a problem. But the good news is that we know Laurelyn's cervix is weak, so I'd bring her in with her next pregnancy, somewhere around fourteen weeks, and place a cerclage before this happens again."

I hadn't even considered future pregnancies. I've barely had time to wrap my head around this one. "So it's possible for her to become pregnant again and carry the baby to term?"

"As long as the suture is placed in time, she shouldn't have any complications." That's such a relief to hear.

The ambulance service arrives and I can only stand back and watch as they move her over onto the stretcher. "Are you her husband?"

"I am."

"We can't let you ride with her but you can follow us in your vehicle."

I want to argue, tell them they're nuts if they think they're separating me from my wife, but that'll cause an unnecessary delay. "Okay." I kiss her forehead. "I'll be right behind you."

I'm following the ambulance and the harsh reality of our situation hits me—Laurelyn and I could lose our baby. Suddenly, all the problems we encountered along the way to this place seem so insignificant. "Oh God, please take care of Laurelyn and our baby. I beg you to not take our little one before it's had a chance to live."

L is already admitted to her room in labor and delivery by the time I park and find her. Just as Dr. Sommersby promised, she's already been positioned in a bed with the head down and her feet up. Gravity. It's what we used to get her pregnant and now it looks like we're going to use it to keep her that way.

Several nurses are doing different things to L at the same time—one starting an IV, another getting vital signs and placing a monitor on her stomach, a third asking a long list of questions about her medical history. It's a lot to take in at once seeing so many things done to your wife simultaneously. And I have no control over any of it. All I can do is sit back and hope these people know what they're doing.

An hour later, the whirlwind of getting L admitted and the nurses completing the doctor's initial orders is over. She's settled in—best she can be while almost turned upside down—and we're left alone for the first time since this nightmare began. I scoot my chair to the head of her bed so she can see me and I take her hand. I lean over and kiss it. "Can I do anything for you?"

"Wake me up and tell me it's all a bad dream."

"Everything is going to be okay. Our baby has a fighter's heart. She's part of you so she doesn't have a choice."

"You said she. You're so convinced this baby is a girl."

I am. "You're so convinced she's a boy."

"Why a girl? I thought every man wanted a son."

Too much emphasis is placed on men wanting sons. "When I lost you, I had a lot of time on my hands. I spent most of it thinking about what my future would look like if I got you back. You holding a little girl with long brown curls and your same caramel-colored eyes... that's what I always saw and I guess her image stuck with me, but I'd be thrilled with any child you give me."

Tears fill her eyes but they run toward her hairline instead of down her cheeks. I reach over and wipe them away. "I should call my parents to let them know what's happening. I'm sure my mum will be in the car immediately."

"Tell her she doesn't have to come. There's nothing she can do but look at me... like this."

"As if that's going to happen." Margaret McLachlan will be here in less than four hours. I predict it and pity any who gets in her way.

This is going to be miserable for L. Only an hour in and she's already slid toward the headboard so far that her head is pressed against it. "Want me to pull you down in the bed?" Or up? I don't know which you'd call it.

"Yeah, but don't tug on that." She points to a plastic tube hanging on the bed.

"What is it?"

She wrinkles her nose. "A catheter."

Oh God. "Inside you?"

"Yeah. That's generally where they go."

I didn't see them put that in her. "Why?"

"I can't get up to the bathroom and I think you can imagine why a bedpan isn't going to work."

"Oh, L. I'm so sorry you're the one going through all of this." I would do it for her in a second.

"I can do anything I need to for our baby. I'll forget all about this little bit of discomfort when they place him in my arms."

I lean down to kiss her forehead. "Her."

I help L with repositioning before going out into the hallway to phone my parents. I'm not sure I've ever dreaded a call so much in my life. Mum is going to be devastated.

We do our normal greeting but then the part comes where I have to tell her why I'm calling. I start at the beginning, careful to not leave out any details, and I can hear her crying before I even get to the part about the cerclage. "Listen, Mum. The doctor is optimistic that the membranes will go back inside so she can stitch the cervix closed. There's hope."

"How is Laurelyn handling this?"

"She's okay—willing to do whatever it takes to keep this baby inside for as long as possible."

"I'm packing a bag as we speak. I'll be there as soon as I can."

This is going to be a long road per Dr. Sommersby. "You don't have to come now, Mum. There's nothing you'll be able to do except sit in an uncomfortable chair and look at Laurelyn while she slowly slides toward the head of the bed."

"Then that's what my job will be—not staying four hours away."

I hang up and prepare myself for the other call I have to make to Jolie Prescott. I still haven't forgiven her for making Laurelyn cry, telling her she had made a stupid mistake by becoming pregnant. L didn't tell me so but I wonder in the back of my mind if her mum might have encouraged her to have an abortion. If she did, she's smart for not telling me. I don't think I could ever forgive her for such a thing.

"Jolie, it's Jack. Laurelyn asked me to call you because something has happened."

"Is she okay?"

"She is but there's been a complication with the baby and she's in the hospital."

"Is she having a miscarriage?" Her voice sounds a little too hopeful.

"She could lose the baby but the doctor is doing everything possible to prevent it."

"I need to talk to Laurelyn because I have some great news. Jake and I are getting married."

All I see is red. What a bitch. She finds out her daughter is in the hospital fighting to save the life of her grandchild and her response is to tell Laurelyn about her happy news. Un-fucking-believable! Perhaps she's mentally ill on some level. No sane person would be so indifferent to their child.

"She's asleep," I lie. I won't allow her to upset Laurelyn. "I'll have her call when she wakes." Or maybe I won't. I'm not sure speaking to her mum is beneficial right now. I think it could cause a lot more harm than good.

CHAPTER TWENTY-THREE
LAURELYN MCLACHLAN

I DIDN'T SLEEP MUCH LAST NIGHT. EVEN AFTER I WAS GIVEN A SLEEPING PILL, I only dosed in intervals. I don't think Jack Henry nodded off once all night, although I repeatedly asked him to try and get some sleep. The nurse showed him how to turn the chair into a bed but he refuses, and each time I open my eyes or move, he slides to the edge of his seat and asks me if I'm okay. He's like a guard dog watching over me and our baby.

I brush my teeth and Jack Henry helps me wash up. "Did you tell Margaret they're doing an ultrasound this morning?"

He's standing at my bedside wearing his cotton sleep pants and a T-shirt, rubbing his scruff. He has a case of bed head, although he never slept, and he couldn't look more adorable. "Yeah. She wants to stay and watch if it's okay with you."

Of course, it's fine by me. "I don't mind. I'd love for her to see the baby."

"She'll be really happy about that. She never got to be with Em when they did any of hers."

I'm almost afraid to ask about my mom but I need to. "You never mentioned it, but did you talk to my mom?"

"I did."

"What did she say?"

He looks like he's thinking up something to say. "I told her what was happening and that we were going to do everything possible to save the baby."

"What did she say about that?"

"She asked if you were miscarrying and then told me she wanted to talk to you because she had good news. She and your dad are getting married." He looks like he's angry. "I didn't think her timing was appropriate, so I told her you were asleep and would call her later."

Asking about the miscarriage without any concern for me or the baby and then jumping straight into her good news… that hurts. But it's just like my mom. I don't get the disconnect there. I haven't even laid eyes on this baby yet and I already know I'll put his happiness ahead of my own. That's what a real mother does.

She's hoping I'll lose the baby because she thinks I should be pursuing my career instead of a family. This is a problem for me and I'm not sure she'll continue to hold a place in my life if she's going to wish my child away. "She probably won't call to check on us but if she does, tell her the nurse is with me and I can't talk." I can't handle her right now.

Margaret arrives only moments before Dr. Sommersby comes into the room for my scan. "Is it okay if my mother-in-law stays?"

"That's fine with me if it's all right with you."

I look at Margaret and she's wearing a huge grin. That's how a grandmother should be, ecstatic about seeing her grandchild, not wishing it away. "Yes. I would very much like her to be here."

The ultrasound procedure is the same as yesterday—lots of measuring and documenting—but Dr. Sommersby is nice enough to show Margaret some great close-ups of the baby. She agrees with me—that the baby looks like Jack Henry—but in the end there's no change in the membranes, so we'll continue doing what we did yesterday. I'll continue to lie with my head down and we'll check for improvement tomorrow.

Day four. I didn't think I'd become sick of this so quickly but I am. I don't want to stay here any longer. I want to be home at Avalon. I cried like a baby after Jack Henry finally went to sleep last night because I didn't want him to see me. I've been holding it in, putting on a tough exterior, because I don't want him or Margaret to see my weakness and mistake it for selfishness.

I can see how one could lie here and become depressed. Maybe that's what's happening to me now, but I'll keep doing what I have to for this baby and pray the membranes have retreated.

I wait on pins and needles, lying on a bed of nails upside down, as I hold my breath for the verdict. "I don't see hourglassing, Laurelyn. I think we can put you on the surgery schedule and place the cerclage today."

Hallelujah! I want to jump out of bed and turn cartwheels down the hall.

Jack Henry squeezes my hand and leans up to kiss me. "I knew you'd do it. I never doubted you for a second."

Things move rapidly, prepping me for surgery, and I'm nervous. No... more like petrified. There are still risks involved with this procedure, so we aren't out of the woods yet. But the prognosis is much improved from what it was four days ago.

My surgical nurse and anesthetist come into the room to move me to the OR. Jack Henry looks as terrified as I feel. "You're going to do perfect and Dr. Sommersby is going to take good care of you. I'll be right here waiting." He leans down and kisses my mouth. "I love you, L."

"Love you too."

I'm wheeled down the hall backward, the fluorescent lights flashing as we move beneath them. It's disorienting moving in the wrong direction and the flickering doesn't help. It's nauseating. "I don't feel well."

The bed is stopped and a washcloth is placed over my face. "Close your eyes and don't watch the overhead lights." I remember the nurses telling me to notify them immediately if I felt nauseated. Vomiting could cause my membranes to balloon out further or possibly even rupture. "Concentrate on your breathing and take slow, deep breaths. We're almost there." I feel something being placed in my hand. "This is an alcohol pad. Sniff it. It'll help the nausea pass."

I bring it to my nose and inhale deeply. Miraculously, it helps. I sure wish I'd known about that little trick a couple months ago.

The freezing cold air of the operating room hits me the second I'm taken inside and my body involuntarily shakes before it's really even had a chance to cool. My teeth are clenched tightly and a rigor causes me to jerk. "I have some warm blankets for you once we get you moved over."

I'm slid with sheets and a backboard to a table in the middle of the room. Bright lights shine directly on my crotch. Stirrups await, and I'm pretty sure I know what's next. I'll be spread-eagle for everyone in this room to see. How humiliating. I hope they put me to sleep first.

I look up and see the upside down face of the nurse anesthetist placing an oxygen mask over my mouth and nose. "Just a little fresh air for you, Mrs. McLachlan." A moment later the woman standing over me says, "I'm going to give you something through your IV to make you really sleepy."

"Okay."

And everything goes black.

CHAPTER TWENTY-FOUR
JACK MCLACHLAN

I can't sit. I'm restless, pacing L's room from the door to look down the hall and back to the ignored chair.

"The doctor said Laurelyn would be in surgery almost an hour if there were no complications and then she'd go to the recovery room for an hour, so park your ass in that chair before you give me motion sickness." Mum doesn't look up from where she's reading, her glasses low on her nose.

I take the chair next to her. "Sorry. I can't help myself." My heart pounds and bats flutter in my gut.

"You always were a nervous one, watching over Chloe like she was a delicate flower. You could never see that your baby sister was as tough as nails but it was good practice for you. You've transitioned from the sheltering big brother into the protective husband and father."

"I'm still the sheltering big brother." And I don't like Chloe being with that fucker.

"Ben is good for Chloe. He treats her well."

Because he knows I'll kick his ass if he steps out of line. "He's a bastard, Mum. He's using Chloe and he's only going to hurt her in the end. You don't know him the way I do." It's only a matter of time and I'll be there to take him down when he does.

She looks skeptical. "And how well do you know him?"

"Well enough."

"Ben is the brother of Laurelyn's best friend and he pursued her when she came to Australia."

My mum knows Ben went after L? "That's right."

"You were both chasing after her at the same time so he was your opponent in the duel to win Laurelyn's heart."

"But she was mine and he knew that," I argue.

"Listen to me, son. Ben went after his sister's best friend, knowing there would be hell to pay if he screwed it up. He proposed an authentic relationship with her from the beginning, one that might have prospered into something real. Now, think back on what you offered—a fling lasting a few months with no connection afterward. You never even asked her last name while she was living with you and sharing your bed. So, tell me who behaved worse."

Okay. Mum has a point. I was probably more of a bastard than Ben but that doesn't mean I should stop looking out for Chloe. "I'll lighten up a little on him."

"No, son. You'll lighten up a lot. Chloe's in love with Ben and you don't have the right to ruin it because you refuse to let go of a rivalry that ended when you won Laurelyn's heart."

Oh hell. Why'd my sister have to go and fall in love with Ben Donavon, of all fucking people? The earth is populated by billions and she had to choose him. "I can do it but it's going to take some time. I can't cut it off like a switch."

"If it helps, think of it as a favor to your mum."

No. It doesn't help one bit but I don't have time to answer because L's phone is ringing in the cabinet where her things are stored. I'm sure it's her mum. I really don't have the patience or desire to talk to her right now, but she has the right to an update on her daughter and grandchild—if that's the reason behind her call. She could be calling to discuss wedding plans. I wouldn't put that past her. Selfish bitch.

I don't recognize the number and then remember it wasn't her ringtone I heard. "Hello?"

"Good morning, this is Grayson Drake, assistant to the prosecuting attorney in the case against Blake Phillips. I'm trying to locate Miss Laurelyn Prescott."

"It's McLachlan now."

"I'm sorry?"

"She's no longer a Prescott. It's Laurelyn McLachlan. This is her husband, Jack McLachlan," I explain.

"I was unaware you and Miss Prescott had married. May I speak with her?"

"She's not available at the moment and won't be anytime soon."

"Well… I guess I can go ahead and speak with you since you're one of the witnesses to testify in this case. I spoke with Miss Prescott several months ago…"

I interrupt because that's no longer who she is. "It's Mrs. McLachlan."

"Er… yes. I spoke with your wife several months ago when the Blake Phillips case went before a judge for arraignment but I'll catch you up, as you are now her husband and you both live in another country. Are you familiar with the American justice system?"

"Not at all."

"As you know, Mr. Phillips was released on bail months ago since he wasn't considered a flight risk due to his ties in the community, meaning his wife and children." Yeah, I know. The fucker has been walking around free as a bird. "The judge in the preliminary hearing felt there was sufficient evidence to move the case to trial, and the grand jury did as well, so Mr. Phillips was officially indicted. He entered a plea of not guilty to all charges against him and a trial has been set for next week on May seventh. The prosecutor needs to speak with both of you about your testimony prior to that day, preferably in person, but over the phone is acceptable if you can't be present before the trial."

Seriously? We live on a different continent and we're given a week's notice? "Our presence isn't possible at this time. My wife is pregnant and is experiencing some complications so she's been admitted to the hospital for an indefinite period of time."

"We can try to move the date back but not more than a few weeks at most."

That won't work. "Laurelyn won't be traveling for the remainder of her pregnancy." Or soon after. She'll be nursing and there's no way we're dragging a newborn across the globe because of Blake Phillips.

"Well, that certainly poses a problem, Mr. McLachlan. Mr. Phillips is already making a lot of noise about his constitutional right to a speedy trial being violated with the date as it is."

That sends me into orbit. "Who gives a fuck about his rights after the things he did to my wife?"

"The American justice system does."

"Well, that's very unfortunate." This is a technical world we live in. "What about testifying via video?"

"It isn't unheard of for a witness to testify over closed-circuit video but it's a long shot. I wouldn't expect the judge to go for it. Allowing a victim to testify from the other side of the globe is unprecedented in a criminal case where constitutional rights are at stake. Not to mention that cross-examining over webcast would be terribly difficult. Frankly, Mr. McLachlan, I'm surprised this case made it to trial because you and your wife are basically the only evidence we have. It's weak even with your testimony because it's otherwise unsupported. The remaining evidence is circumstantial, at best, and likely inadmissible, so it would be damn near impossible to get a guilty verdict without your testimony. I would expect his defense attorney to make a motion for the charges to be dropped and that will likely happen if you don't testify."

This is incredible. "You have our statements. Can't you use those?"

"They're hearsay, and even if we could use them, they are unpersuasive." He has an answer for everything.

Un-fucking-believable. "So, you're telling me he can attack my wife, attempt to rape her, and get away with it?"

"It's hard to win a case when the defendant has connections and the best defense attorney money can buy," he explains.

"Well, he's not the only one with money and connections. So, I guess that's the American way." But it's not the McLachlan way. There's no way I'm letting that fucker get away with what he did to Laurelyn. "It truly sickens me to see him walk but we can't risk the safety of our unborn child. As such, Laurelyn won't be coming and I can't leave her at this critical time."

"I'm very sorry to hear that, Mr. McLachlan. I wish you and your wife the best."

I end the call with Mr. Drake and I'm beyond furious. "Blake Phillips attacked Laurelyn—left her body bloody with bruises—and attempted to rape her. He would have been successful had I not gotten to her in time and he's going to walk without any repercussions."

I'm sorry my mum had to hear that conversation. "It's not right but at least she's here now and not in Nashville. He can't get to her from where he is."

"I'm not done with him."

"Son, there's nothing you can do. As much as I hate what that man did to our girl, you have to let it go."

I'm set to argue with my mum and throw her words back in her face. "She's one of us now and we protect our own… at any cost." But I'm not able because the door opens with L being brought back into her room.

I'm happy to see the head of her bed in a normal position. I reach for her hand but she's sleeping and doesn't stir when I take it in mine. "I thought she'd be awake when she came back."

"Some people are a little groggier than others after anesthesia. It's just sticking with her a little longer—doesn't mean anything's wrong." The nurse reapplies the monitor on her belly. "I'm putting the contraction monitor back on so we can make sure she isn't having contractions. Sometimes a cerclage will cause the uterus to contract. If that happens, we'll need to give her some medicine to stop them."

So, the cerclage is a step in the right direction but we've yet to hit a safe place. "The procedure went well as far as you know?"

"She did great. Dr. Sommersby should come around and talk to you within the hour."

I breathe a sigh of relief because nothing catastrophic, such as ruptured membranes, happened. This woman is my life and now this baby is as well. I don't know what I'd do if anything happened to either of them.

CHAPTER TWENTY-FIVE
LAURELYN MCLACHLAN

It takes a moment for my eyes to focus but I'm able to make out Jack Henry sitting at my bedside. He's holding my hand, brushing his thumb over the top the way he so often does. "Hey, pretty girl."

"McLachlan," I croak out and realize how sore and scratchy my throat is. I try to cough, to clear what feels like a plug but to no avail. "Can I have something to drink?"

Margaret comes to my bedside with a cup and spoon. "The nurse says you can have a few ice chips and progress to sips of water once you're more alert."

Jack Henry lifts the head of the bed and it dawns on me—I'm no longer lying with my head down. I panic, my hands immediately reaching for my stomach as I fear the worst. "The baby?"

My husband's hand joins mine on my abdomen. "She's fine."

Margaret purses her lips while looking at Jack Henry. "You little shit. It's a girl and you didn't tell me."

He's in trouble now. "No, Mum. We don't know what the baby is. I think it's a girl so I call it a she to aggravate L—she's leaning toward a boy."

"Oh."

Although I just had surgery, I feel more normal than I have in days. "I guess everything went well since they're letting me sit up?"

"Yeah. Dr. Sommersby came in about thirty minutes ago. She's optimistic the cerclage will hold because your cervix felt firm and is thicker than it appeared on the ultrasound. She said the bag of waters ballooning through the cervix probably had it stretched." What a relief.

Margaret comes over to kiss me. "All right, kiddos. I'm going to step out and let the two of you have some time together. Can I get you something?"

I have everything I need right here. "I can't think of anything, but thank you."

Jack Henry waits until Margaret is gone before he hovers over me, his head against mine, and places his hand on my stomach. "I was so scared, L."

I reach for his face because I want to feel it. He's been too preoccupied with me and the baby to trim his facial hair. His scruff is too long to be considered stubble so it's almost a beard. "I know. I was too, but for the first time in days, I finally feel like everything's going to be okay."

"Dr. Sommersby says she wants to observe you today and most of tomorrow. If you don't have pain or contractions, she's going to discharge you late tomorrow evening."

"Omigod, what a relief." I can't wait to get back to Avalon. I can't believe how much I've missed it. "I could've pushed through as long as I needed to but I must admit, I'm ready to get out of here. Four days of lying in this bed staring at these walls is a lot to take."

"Babe, you've been a champ. Even the nurses have bragged on how well you handled standing on your head for days. You never complained once."

Complaining would've only made it harder on Jack Henry and would've accomplished nothing. "There was no reason to. I was prepared to do whatever was needed for this baby and there was no other way of looking at it."

"I know you would and it's only one of the many reasons I love you so much."

I shouldn't but I want to know if my mom has checked on us. "Has anyone called?"

A peculiar look claims Jack Henry's face and I can only interpret it to mean my mom isn't concerned enough to call for an update. "I've updated Addison. She said to tell you she loves you and wishes she could be here. Emma called and wants you to know she loves you and is thinking of you and the baby. Chloe, pretty much the same—loves you, thinking of you."

"But nothing from my family?" I bet she didn't even tell Nanna and Pops. I know they would've called if they knew something was wrong.

"I'm sorry, babe."

"It's fine—she's wrapped up in him. I'm used to it." I guess I was stupid for thinking she might put me before herself, or him, for once, but it's okay. Margaret's been more of a mom to me this year than my own has been my whole life. The McLachlans are my family now and they love me. And I love them.

※

I'M DISCHARGED FROM THE HOSPITAL FOR GOOD BEHAVIOR—NO complications such as pain, bleeding, leaking, or contractions—but I'm given instructions to return immediately should any of these things occur. I'm to be on modified bed rest at home, meaning I can only shower and go to the bathroom. Otherwise I'm to do a lot of nothing while lying around. Dr. Sommersby says I may progress to routine activities after two weeks with one exception. No sex. My vagina is completely off limits so nothing is allowed within the temple. Strict doctor's orders and one of the few things she isn't lax about.

This is going to be a rough five months.

"Couch or bed?" Jack Henry asks as we pass through the kitchen.

"I'm sort of sick of the bed so I think I'd prefer the couch for a little while. Maybe you can sit with me and we can watch TV."

"Absolutely. Mum thought you might need something comfy to wear the next couple of weeks so she brought some to the house this morning. Would you like me to get them for you?"

Margaret is so thoughtful. "Yes, please." Mental note: Call and thank her for that.

Jack Henry returns with a pink T-shirt and a pair of white and pink pinstriped pants. Both are soft cotton and freshly laundered. "I can't believe she washed them too."

"She would do anything for you." He hands the clothes to me. "She loves you dearly."

My eyes fill with tears and my heart aches, but I don't know if it's the hormones or the sadness I feel when I think of how little my own mother cares about me. "I love her too."

"She knows."

I change into my new jammies and stretch out on the couch with a fluffy pillow under my head and my feet in Jack Henry's lap. He's rubbing my feet as we watch television and it's one of the most boring times we've ever spent together. And I love it—just being with him in our home doing nothing. It's absolutely shitastic.

<hr />

I'VE BEEN HOME FROM THE HOSPITAL FOR A WEEK AND EVERY DAY IS PRETTY much the same. I go to bed with Jack Henry every night without sex. We wake up. He showers and goes to work. I shower and go to the couch. I lie there all day and when he comes in after work, we have dinner together on the couch. When's it's late, we go back to bed, again without sex, for another night of sleep.

I'm a very compliant patient but it's killing me.

Poor Addison. I don't know how she maintained her sanity for as long as she did, especially in that small apartment, but her jail sentence ended this week. The placenta previa is gone and she's allowed to return to her normal activities. First on her agenda is coming to see me, and I'm glad because I have questions for her.

I forgo the comfies and put on yoga pants and a T-shirt. It seemed much more fitting for company, although I have no doubt Addison spent her fair share of days in pajamas.

She comes into the living room and looks so adorable in her fitted white top and faded jeans with her belly bump. "Oh, Addie. Look at you." I get up from the couch to hug her and put my hands on her stomach. "He's grown so much since I saw you last. I can't believe it."

"I know. This is happening crazy fast." She puts her hands on her stomach and caresses it. He'll be here in my arms in ten weeks. Can you believe that? I'm going to be a mom and then you will be too a couple of months after me." She reaches out and touches my small bulge. "You'll be this big before you know it and you'll wonder where all the time went."

"Are you and Zac any closer to choosing a name?"

"I want him to be named Donavon but Zac says everyone will call him Donnie and he hates that name."

"So what are his choices?"

She rolls her eyes and huffs. "Gareth. Tell me—if you had to guess—what do you think people would call my son when they shorten his name?"

Ugh! "Gary."

"Exactly." She puts her hands out. "So, how is Gary better than Donnie?"

Poor Addison. "They're both pretty… not great for a little newborn baby."

"Yeah, I agree with you there but Donavon is my maiden name, or it will be after we're married, and I want to use it. It has meaning behind it. Nothing about Gareth is special." I like Gareth, although I tend to agree with Addie on this one.

"But do you like the name?"

She shrugs. "Eh… it's okay."

"Then what about Donavon Gareth or Gareth Donavon?" It's a compromise and they both get to use the name they want.

"I want Donavon Zachary." That also seems fair since each of them will have one of their names used.

"What does Zac think about you wanting to use Zachary after him?"

"Oh, he's fine with using his own name, just not mine. This baby is going to have Kingston as his last name so he gets his way on two of the three names by default. Shouldn't I get to choose the other? I'm the one who's been lying in bed miserable for over three months. Look at my ass. I've already gained fifteen pounds because I couldn't do anything but eat."

Thank God I only have another week to go with the bed rest.

It only seems fair to let her choose at least one of the names. "Have you told him how you feel?"

She looks at me quizzically, or maybe like I'm stupid. I can't be sure which because both look about the same coming from Addie. "Are you kidding me?" I'm assuming that's a yes.

I was once given some marital advice by a very wise woman, and although Addie and Zac aren't married yet, I think Addie could benefit from it. "Margaret shared some secrets with me about getting what you want. I haven't put it to the test yet but she says we, as women, hold the power of the nookie and can use it to our advantage."

"How does that work?"

She isn't going to like this part. "Withhold sex."

She immediately shakes her head. "Nope. I don't want to withhold sex. I just started having it again and frankly, I missed the fuck out of it."

"Zac doesn't have to know that."

"He can kind of tell how much I missed it. I've been making up for lost time." For some reason, I don't doubt that for a moment.

"Do you want to embroider your son's clothes with the name Donavon or Gareth? Your decision."

"I highly doubt Zac will let me embroider any of his clothes."

Talk of withholding sex reminds me… I'm not withholding but I won't be getting any, either. "I've got a question. How did you survive not having sex for three months?" I'm looking at five whole months and then a six-week recovery period. Six and a half months total. That's brutal.

"We had plenty of sex—just not the penetrating kind. Nothing in the vagina—that's what my obstetrician told me—so Zac got plenty of blow jobs and I got lots of oral. And magical fingers. Zac can stroke me off like nobody's business." She shrugs. "I don't have to tell you that the baby's safety always came first, so we did what we had to do to get by." I knew I could depend on her to give me an honest answer.

I've spent very little time considering the alternatives because I've been so scared about everything. But we have other options. And they're good ones so we can still give and receive pleasure. We'll just need to go into it disciplined, knowing Jack Henry can't get inside me.

"I gotta know. What is Ben saying about all of this?"

"He was so pissed off when I told him. He didn't want to accept that his best friend was fucking his baby sister. I think he was pretending Zac was sleeping on the couch all those nights I stayed over at his apartment."

I think my caveman would like to think there isn't anything like that going on between his sister and Ben, but I know differently. "Jack Henry isn't taking it too well about Ben and Chloe, but he'll come around."

"I don't think he has much of a choice. Ben seems to have fallen hard for Miss Chloe." I'm really happy to hear that since she has it pretty bad for him.

"She told me she thought Ben was the one."

Addie puts her hands together and cups them over her mouth. "Oh… that's so sweet."

"And she said he was supremely fucklicious."

"Ugh!" She points her finger at me and laughs. "You are so wrong for telling me that. No one ever needs to hear that her brother is… those words you said." She grimaces and feigns gagging.

I hold up my hands in surrender. "Okay. Moving on, then…"

"What about the case with Blake? Heard anything else about that?"

"Not in a while but it should be coming up soon. I should probably call the prosecuting attorney and let him know about my… condition. I hope they can postpone everything until after the baby is born because I have to testify. I want to."

"As you should. It's your right to stand up and tell people what he did to you. No way he'll walk away from this and when he's found guilty, I hope he gets a horny cellmate with a huge dick." Eww. Leave it to Addison to come up with something like that.

I'd like to call for a case status when Addison leaves, so I look at the clock and calculate the time change in my head. Bummer. It won't work out today. I'll have to wait until morning to catch Mr. Drake during office hours.

Addie and I laugh and catch up for hours. It's good to be with her. I feel like we've spent too much time apart, although we're living in the same town, only fifteen minutes between us.

I like the Addison I'm seeing. Motherhood is good for her. I guess it's true—a baby really can change everything.

CHAPTER TWENTY-SIX
JACK MCLACHLAN

Laurelyn's second week of bed rest has been uneventful and her late-morning appointment with Dr. Sommersby went well. Her cervix is unchanged—no bleeding, leaking, or contractions—and the baby has grown well since her last scan. It finally seems everything is getting back on track with this pregnancy. Except no sex. "Since you're officially released from bed rest, can I take you out to lunch to celebrate?"

"That sounds really good."

Eating anywhere besides our living-room couch will suit me. "Where do you want to go? Sheridan's? Or what about that new hibachi restaurant? I've heard their sushi is amazing."

She's grinning. "I really want a big, fat, juicy cheeseburger and a huge order of fries with a giant chocolate shake from that fifties diner on the square—the one you took me to last year."

Ah, yes. She was my companion then and things were still new. That morning was when I learned her real name and then she danced for me later that evening for the first time. It was a very memorable day and the recollection nudges me in the cock, encouraging him to wake up. But I have to learn how to get that under control. I'm going to have a really long drought ahead of me.

We walk into the diner and nothing has changed—still a black-and-white-checkered floor with fifties décor. The aroma of freshly dropped french fries and frying hamburgers hangs in the air. "Want to sit at the bar again?"

"Probably not a good idea. I don't think they'll be very comfortable for my back so I'd rather sit at a booth."

We choose one directly behind the spot where we sat a year ago. "I want to put some music on. You already know what I want if the waitress comes by." She walks toward the jukebox and I watch her bum sway side to side. Even pregnant, my wife is smokin' hot.

She isn't gone long before she returns and I hear a familiar tune playing overhead, although I can't immediately place it. She's smiling and I know she wants to play name that tune, a game I can't win with her. "I know this song but the name hasn't come to me just yet—hold on a sec."

I listen for a moment and then it hits me. "'I Only Have Eyes For You,' but I don't know who sings it."

"The Flamingos, silly."

"Of course, how could I not remember? Oh yeah, maybe because I've never heard of them." She's a musical genius. "I can't believe I married a musical Wikipedia. Is there anything you don't know about music?"

"Possibly, but I haven't found it yet."

Our food arrives and L doesn't hesitate to jump in. She takes a huge bite of her cheeseburger and ketchup drips down, landing right in the center of her swollen, pregnant cleavage. She was already beautifully endowed but the pregnancy has given her a little extra boost. Her tits look even more spectacular.

She looks down at the ketchup in the cleavage and then back to me. She licks her lips to clean the smear of ketchup from her mouth. "You'd really like to lick that off, wouldn't you?" My cock immediately awakens at the thought of my tongue running down into that cleft.

I put my cheeseburger on my plate and lean across the table to look into her eyes so she understands my seriousness. "I haven't been inside you for three weeks and it doesn't look as though I will be anytime soon, so you can't say things like that to me. It's torturous."

Her chewing slows and she puts her cheeseburger down. "Abstinence isn't going to be all that pleasant for me, either. I enjoy sex too."

I hope she doesn't get mad at me for what I'm about to say. "I sort of have this hysteria that started when we left the doctor's office. It's sinking in that it will be months before I'll have you again."

She uses her napkin to wipe the ketchup from her cleavage. "I'm sorry. I thought I was being cute."

I don't want to sour her mood. "You are terribly cute… and that's the problem. I want you but can't have you."

Her smile returns and I know we're fine. "I'll try to keep the cuteness to a minimum, then."

"That's probably best."

We change the subject of sex back to music and L tells me about every song playing overhead. "I chose this one because I love it so much, but they made a mistake putting it in the jukebox because it wasn't released until the early sixties." I listen and recognize "Can't Help Falling in Love" by Elvis Presley.

"I really like this song too." I get up from our booth and put my hand out to her. "Dance with me."

She looks at me as though I've lost my mind. "This is a diner. People don't dance here."

"Maybe others don't but you and I do."

She giggles and slides out of the booth. I grasp her hand in mine and place my free one on her lower back. "I wouldn't do this if it weren't almost empty in here."

The only other customers are an older couple admiring us from the corner booth. "They see how in love we are and it reminds them of how they were once like this too."

We sway to the tune of the song and I hold her close. "I couldn't help falling in love with you." She smiles and I kiss the top of her head.

I hum the words I don't know and whisper-sing the chorus as we sway. I return to humming when it comes to the next part I should know, but don't. "I've never heard you sing before."

"It's not really my forte."

"No, it's not. Your singing sucks," she laughs.

"Thank you for breaking it to me gently."

"I doubt I'm breaking anything to you."

She's right. I can't sing worth a damn. "I'll bow out gracefully from the job of teaching our swarm to sing."

She stops swaying and looks up at me. "Sure you still want several after all that's happened with this pregnancy? This problem with my cervix isn't going away. I'll need a stitch every time and will be on pelvic rest for the entire pregnancy."

No way we're giving up on our swarm. "Abstaining for months won't be fun, but we'll do what we gotta do for the family we dream of having."

"I love you, McLachlan." I pull her close again and return to humming.

It's true. I couldn't help myself from falling in love with this woman. When she took my hand, I willingly gave her my whole life.

※

L IS NO LONGER ON BED REST BUT THAT DOESN'T MEAN SHE CAN RETURN TO doing anything she likes. She needs to take it easy, so I bring her home after our lunch date and encourage her to rest on the couch. She isn't excited about it but eventually concedes. I can see that she's tired, although she refuses to admit it, and I'd bet money she's napping within fifteen minutes once I'm out of the house to scout on the vineyard.

Harold and I get in a good four hours of scouting over a vast majority of the northwest corner and I'm pleased to find no additional evidence of downy mildew. The vines look quite good for this time of year and that pleases me greatly, but not near as much as returning home to see my wife.

I enter through the kitchen and Mrs. Porcelli appears to be putting the final touches on dinner. "Smells good in here. What are we having?"

"Laurelyn said you had a heavy lunch so she asked for a lighter dinner." I totally agree with her on that. I love cheeseburgers, fries, and shakes but that isn't a meal that should become a habit, especially not when you have a family history like mine. "I hope salmon with rice and asparagus fits the bill."

"Sounds perfect." I open the fridge and take out a beer. "Did Laurelyn rest after I went to work?"

"She's been on the couch most of the afternoon and I'm fairly certain she took a nap." Good. She needs plenty of rest. "She says the doctor gave her a good report. I'm very happy to hear that. I've been quite concerned about her and the baby."

"We're told the danger is behind us and the remainder of the pregnancy should proceed normally with the cerclage in place."

"That's such good news." She opens the oven door to check the fish and the aroma fills the kitchen. "Will you be eating in the living room again?"

L's sentence there is over and I'm guessing she's as sick of eating on the couch as I am. "No. We'll dine at the table tonight."

"Then dinner will be there for you in ten minutes or so."

"Thank you. I'll let Laurelyn know."

L isn't on the couch and I don't find her in our bedroom. There's only one place I assume she'll be. She's out in the music studio checking on its progress. She hasn't seen it in three weeks so she's going to be surprised at all they've accomplished.

Although I'm quite content with her no longer working, she's determined to get back to composing. She argues that it isn't right for her to not work, that she should be bringing in some kind of income, but I disagree. She's my wife and I make more than enough to support us.

I'm not wrong—the studio is where I find her. "What do you think of it?"

She's looking around, a look of awe plastered on her face. "I'm shocked. I can't believe how much they've done in the last few weeks. It's almost finished."

"I spoke with the contractor this afternoon. He said another week and we should be able to get you in here, songbird."

"Songbird," she repeats. "I like that."

"Did you take a tour without me?"

She looks guilty. "I did. I saw the workers leave and I couldn't resist coming out for a peek."

"It's okay. Have you seen all you want to see?"

She takes another glance around the room. "Yeah, I'm good."

"Dinner's ready. I told Mrs. Porcelli we'd dine at the table tonight."
"No argument here. I'm sick of that couch."
"Me too."

⚜

WE SPEND THE EVENING ON THE COUCH WE'VE COME TO DESPISE. LAURELYN'S sitting on one end reading, probably the only thing that's kept her sane these past two weeks, while I'm on the other end catching up on missed work. It's just sales reports, something I could do in my office, but that would mean being away from her. I enjoy this quiet time together, even when we're not talking. Just her nearness is enough sometimes.

I look up and notice L has placed her e-reader on top of her belly and has dozed off. I'm not surprised. She sleeps a lot now, much more than she did before she became pregnant. I'm glad because rest is important for her and the baby.

I place my work on the coffee table and scoot over to her. "Time for bed."

She stirs a little and slowly opens her eyes. "Wow. I was reading a hot sex scene one minute and then bam, I fall into a coma."

"Really? You were reading about hot sex?"

She grins, maybe even blushes a little. "Did I just admit that?"

"Yes, you did." I place her e-reader on the table next to my paperwork and grasp her hands to help her up. "Come on, pervert."

She goes into the bathroom to do her nightly ritual and I'm already in bed when she comes out. She climbs in next to me, wearing a pink and white cotton gown. It's lacy around the neck and innocent looking, not intended to be sexy at all, but my cock rouses simply by seeing her get into bed next to me. I know better. I shouldn't look at her when she leans over to turn off her bedside lamp, but I can't not look because her gown has gathered around her bum. I catch a glimpse of her pink cotton knickers and I'm immediately sorry. Ugh! I'm going to have to downgrade to jerking off—and soon. It's not like I haven't done it before, although it was mostly as an adolescent.

She leans over to kiss me goodnight and reaches for the back of my head to hold me close. I kiss her back, although I shouldn't, and she becomes more aggressive. That's when I realize this is not the same simple goodnight kiss she has given me each night for the past two weeks.

"This is another example like the ketchup incident today. You can't do this to me. It's agony."

"But it doesn't have to be. There's still plenty we can do." She slides across the bed and climbs over to kneel between my legs. She puts her fingers in the waistband of my sleep pants and tugs. "My mouth isn't off limits."

Oh fuck. My girl is going to suck me off.

I lift my hips, beyond excited about what L is going to do to me. I haven't gotten off in weeks so I'm happier than a camel on Wednesday.

I've wanted to jerk off many times over the last few weeks but it felt wrong to experience any kind of pleasure while L was going through so much, especially while she was in the hospital fighting to save our baby. I couldn't even consider it then. I thought about it after she was home and the initial danger was behind us, but it still didn't feel right since she was in such a miserable state.

This, however, doesn't feel wrong, so I grab her pillow and prop it with mine behind my head so I can watch her every move.

She puts her palms on my thighs and glides them upward until her fingertips brush my balls. She teases me for a moment, lightly sweeping her fingers back and forth, and I think I'll implode from the anticipation.

Her hand moves up and holds the base of my cock as she circles her tongue around the head. The stiff tip flicks several times at a supersensitive area just below the crown. She alternates these motions several times before taking me fully into her mouth. "That feels so fucking good." I put my hands in her hair and pull all of it into my fist in a high ponytail because I love watching my cock slide in and out of her mouth. I could almost come just by the sight of it alone.

She takes me out of her mouth and anchors my cock against my stomach. Then she does something new. Her tongue starts at the base of my balls and she licks the pleasure trail running top to bottom along my scrotum, the seam separating my boys. She draws the loose skin of the seam into her mouth and lightly sucks, bringing the blood, and the pleasure receptors, to the surface. "Fuck!" I groan.

She smiles and looks up at me. "You like that, huh?"

"Yeah," I laugh. "I like that a-fucking-lot. Please don't let this be the one and only time you do that."

"I've got plenty more for you, caveman."

She takes my cock back into her mouth and massages my balls for a moment before I feel her finger against the skin under my sac. She presses it more firmly and rotates it in a circular motion. Slow, and then fast. Soft, and then hard. I've never been harder and what's building has never felt more powerful. "Ohh…" I tap her on the head, our signal that I'm about to come, but I can't say the words. I'm speechless aside from the incomprehensible garble leaving my mouth.

She stops and holds my cock so it's pointing toward my stomach as she continues pressing that spot under my balls until I have this crazy, powerful explosion, by far the most intense orgasm I've ever experienced. "Holy shit, L. That was…" I can't even think of a fitting word to describe it.

"Great?" She looks so hopeful, as if she's afraid she hasn't pleased me.

Calling it great would be an insult. "Mind-blowing is a better word, but even that doesn't do it justice. Don't get me wrong. You've given me some fantastic head in the past but that was the best ever. What was that you were doing with your finger?"

I think she's blushing. "It was my knuckle and I was stimulating your prostate."

I look at how much cum is on my stomach. "You stimulated me, all right. I think you milked me dry."

"I've heard there's more semen when you press the prostate so I was afraid to swallow." She shakes her head. "This pregnancy still has my gag reflex working overtime." She slides to the edge of the bed. "I'm gonna grab a towel."

She returns and wipes me clean. She rolls the towel up, tossing it out of the way, and then slides in next to me. I pull her close and kiss her as I slide my hand under her gown, but she grabs my wrist. "No."

"I'm only going to touch on the outside."

She moves my hand away. "I don't think it's a good idea."

"I know anything on the inside is off limits, but I want to make you feel good too."

She shakes her head. "Lying next you after giving you a mind-blowing orgasm makes me feel good."

"I can do much better than that."

"I'm afraid to have an orgasm even if nothing goes inside me. Maybe we can try later when the baby is far enough along to survive, in case it puts me into labor or something."

She's right. It isn't worth the risk just to feel good. "Okay."

She puts her head on my chest and traces an infinity on my stomach around my belly button with her finger. "Don't be mad."

I could never be upset with her over something like this. "Baby, I'm not mad. You're thinking of our child's safety. I could never be upset with you over that."

"Pleasing you pleases me, so I'm fine with getting you off and not having the favor returned. You can make up for it later."

I will definitely make this up to her. "I know you don't mind but I love making you come. It's quite satisfying for me to watch your face when you squeeze your eyes shut and scrunch your cute little nose as you open your mouth and pant."

"That's what I look like when I come?"

"Almost every time."

She turns and props her chin on my chest. "What do I look like the other times?"

"Sometimes you bite your bottom lip. Both of your come faces are really hot. Lets me know I'm doing something right."

"Everything you do is perfect. You always make me feel great." She lifts her face and stretches to kiss me. "Never doubt that, McLachlan."

She lowers her head to my chest and settles in as though she might be ready for sleep. Again.

We lie there for a brief moment when I hear her sharp intake of breath. "What is it? Are you having a pain?"

She lifts her head to look at me and grins. "No. The baby is moving."

I've yet to feel a single movement. Every time I try, the baby either stills or I simply can't detect it. It may seem silly, but I think I'm a little jealous that L's feeling it and I can't. "This little stinker is turning flips tonight so I bet you'll feel it this time. Give me your hand."

L turns to her back and lifts her gown. She takes my hand and places at the top of her small bump. "It's more on the left side." We're silent, waiting, as if the absence of sound will help my sense of feel.

And then it happens. I feel a gentle nudge beneath my hand. "I felt that." And I feel something else as well. Love—the true and real kind.

CHAPTER TWENTY-SEVEN
LAURELYN MCLACHLAN

I GOT INTO MY MUSIC STUDIO A FEW WEEKS AGO AND I'VE BEEN BANGING OUT the tunes like crazy. It's weird—maybe like the break I had from the time I left Southern Ophelia to now was what I really needed to make this transition from performer to composer a successful one. Or maybe I'm just happy with my life and it's finding its way into my music.

I've conferenced with Charlie and the gang a few times and they're really excited about the material I'm working on. Randy wants first pick and that totally works for me. I have no problem selling my songs minus the pain of marketing them.

Kim, my female lead replacement for Southern Ophelia, says she loves my lyrics because they speak to her. She's like me in a lot of ways. She only sings songs that touch her so we've been working on a special single together. The guys don't know about it—and she's asked me to not tell them—and I think I know why. This song is her story and the way she feels about a man. I happen to believe the song is about Charlie. I guess it could be anyone, but the lyrics she's contributed tell me she's in deep.

I'm absorbed into the song in my head when Jack Henry comes into my studio. "L, you're going to be late for your appointment."

I look at the time and he's right. I should've been gone ten minutes ago. "Shit." I get up from my stool at the piano and go over to give him a kiss. "I gotta run."

He grabs my arm to get my full attention before I'm able to get away. "No speeding to make it on time. I mean it. You can't beat the clock so don't try."

That's something I would have once attempted, but not now. "I'll obey all the traffic laws."

He kisses my cheek. "I'm really sorry I can't go with you today."

He feels bad he doesn't make it to the doctor's with me every time. "It's okay. I see her every week so you can't take off from work for every appointment, even if you are the boss."

"Get a picture of her for me so I can see how much my girl's grown this week."

He has to stop doing that, always calling this baby a girl, but I don't have time to scold him. I think that's one reason he's doing it—because I'm on my way out the door and I don't have time. "I always do."

My ultrasound goes well, as does my cervical exam. No change. I'm twenty-six weeks now and everything remains on track, so I decide it's a good time to speak with Dr. Sommersby about my concerns. "My husband and I have a question. We understand that we can't have penetrative sex, but is it okay for me to... orgasm other ways?"

"Oral sex and mutual masturbation are fine as long as nothing goes inside the vagina and you don't experience contractions, leaking, or bleeding afterward. You'd need to come to the hospital immediately if any of those things occur." She never misses a beat as she continues documenting in the computer, a sign this isn't the first time she's answered this question, so I feel minimally better about having asked. She finishes her documentation and closes the laptop. "Have any other questions or concerns?"

"I think that's it."

I use the drive home to think about what Jack Henry and I will do tonight. I want it to be great, not that it isn't always, but I deserve something special seeing as I haven't had an orgasm in eight weeks. Eight. Weeks. That's crazy. He'll probably touch me once and I'll come. Yeah, it's that bad.

I see Jack Henry on the vineyard as I'm coming up the drive so I stop.

He abandons whatever he's in the middle of doing and walks my way. I watch him coming toward me, in his rugged wear and Indiana Jones hat, and my heart still skips a beat. Oh my, he's so damn good-looking. I still can't believe he's all mine.

He takes a couple of brisk steps before jumping the white fence surrounding the vineyard. "Everything go okay?"

"Yeah." I reach into my purse to take out the ultrasound picture. "I even have proof."

He takes it from me and a grin spreads. "My girl is growing."

"Indeed I am. I gained another two pounds since I saw the doctor last week."

He holds up the picture. "I meant this girl."

I knew exactly who he meant. I just wanted to aggravate him the way he does me. "You're going to feel really weird when this baby comes out a boy."

"I don't think so. I feel it deep down in my gut."

I'm the mother and the baby is inside me. You'd think I'd be the one with the gut feeling. "Okay, clairvoyant one. I hope you can also see a name in your crystal ball since we don't have one yet."

"We have plenty of time to come up with the perfect name."

I'm tired of she, her, he, him, and it. "I'd like to choose one for each gender so I don't have to continue thinking of this child as nameless." We look at one another and laugh. "I guess that would be fitting—the nameless companions to have a nameless child."

"I'm ready for my daughter to have a name, so we'll work on it this weekend."

I roll my eyes. "You aren't going to contribute a boy name, are you?"

He shrugs. "Probably not."

Maybe I'll make it a little more appealing for him to think about a boy name. "Then that means I get free rein on the boy name and you can't veto anything I choose."

"Fine. Have at it since it doesn't matter. We won't be using a boy name so it's a waste of time—at least this go-round—but maybe the next one will be a boy. I'd like to have one."

He's killing me. "I hope this baby comes out with a big ol' doodle just so I can wipe that smug look off your face."

"Any son of mine would have a big doodle."

I can't believe he'd say that about a baby. "You're awful."

He shrugs. "You brought it up."

I reach for the ultrasound picture. "Give me that. I'm going to the house." I take it from him and put it in the passenger seat. "What time will you be in?"

He takes his hat off and leans inside my window. The weather is mild today so he's not hot and sweaty, but he still smells like a working man. It's sexy as hell. "What time do you want me in?"

He radiates sex and pheromones, almost like he can sense that I got the all-clear from Dr. Sommersby about having an orgasm, and my insides flip. Umm… I'd really like right now, please and thank you, but I remain disciplined. "I don't have anything special planned so whenever you finish here is fine." Lie. I have something very special planned. I schemed on it all the way home from my doctor's appointment.

"Then text me when dinner is almost ready."

"Will do."

❁

WE CLEAR THE TABLE FROM DINNER AND JACK HENRY TELLS ME HE NEEDS TO go to his office and make a couple of business calls—couldn't be more perfect. That'll give me time to take care of the things I need to do for my special surprise. "No problem. I was planning on reading anyway." Another lie, but one he won't mind.

I go into our bedroom and look through my pole-dancing outfits. I've accumulated quite a few since we've been together but I haven't worn one in months. I'm not really sure I'll find one to fit anymore.

None of my one-piece rompers will work—they won't fit over my belly—so I choose a two-piece skirted cowgirl outfit. I can wear my boots with it so it's the obvious choice. I don't intend on attempting the fuck-me pumps. My balance has been so off the last month, I'd fall for sure.

I get ready in the bathroom and listen for Jack Henry before sneaking down the hall toward the gym. I feel safe once I'm there because it's the last place he'll come looking for me.

I set up the music, "Anemone" by The Brian Jonestown Massacre, and then the lights before I place his chair front and center. I put a pillow under it within my reach—I'm sure he'll wonder what that's for—but a pregnant woman doesn't tolerate being on her knees for long without some cushioning.

When everything is in its place, I text him to see if he's finished making his calls. He confirms he is so I tell him to come to the gym. I'm sure he'll be wondering what I'm up to, but he won't have time to hash it out. That's just the way I want it.

When he enters the gym, the deep, dark bass thumps in the darkened room. The sole illumination is the stage light, directed on me. I give him the come-hither and he crosses the room, passing his chair. He's shaking his head and looks like he wants to drag my ass off the stage and spank it for real. "No, L."

"I'm not going to do any high climbs, drops, or inverts—absolutely nothing that'll hurt me or the baby. I just want to dance for you. My feet won't lift more than two feet off this stage so park your sweet ass in that chair and enjoy the show, caveman." Then it dawns on me. Maybe this isn't at all sexy to him. "Unless seeing me dance with this pregnant belly is a turnoff for you."

"Baby, nothing you do is a turnoff. You breathe and I'm turned on." He backs up and sits in his chair. "This better be good. I only have big bills in my wallet."

His humor has returned, so I know he's okay with this—as long as I keep it tame.

I begin by backing up against the pole so it's in the center of my back. I reach overhead, holding it as I bend at my knees, sliding down slowly. When I'm halfway down, I push my knees apart and glide one of my hands down my thigh and then back up again. I straighten to stand and turn to face the pole. My hand grasps it tightly and I step out, taking a whirl around—it's nothing special and my feet don't leave the ground, so it's more than safe.

I'm wearing boots so I couldn't use my feet to climb if I wanted, but I'm good at using the insides of my thighs for ascending. I squeeze them around the pole and use my upper body strength to lift myself—no more than a couple feet, as promised—and do a two-handed corkscrew. It's probably one of the easiest moves ever in my book, definitely a beginner level, but it probably looks like I'm doing more than I actually am so I return my feet to the floor before he scolds me.

I decide to not do any more climbs, just basic whirling and erotic dance moves so he doesn't freak out. That wouldn't be sexy.

I snake my body around the pole one last time as the song ends and decide I'm done with this. I've waited long enough. He's turned on, I'm turned on, so let's do this thing. I slink toward him to the beat of the next song, "I've Got to See You Again" by Norah Jones. Slow and seductive, just the way I want it.

He grasps my hips and squeezes before gliding his hands down my legs and then up the back of my thighs under the fabric covering my bottom. "That was hot, babe." He leans forward and kisses my exposed belly.

I run my fingers through the back of his hair and notice it's time for him to have a haircut. I put my nose against it and breathe deeply. Sweat and leather—it sounds like a turnoff but it's the complete opposite. It's evidence my man has worked hard today for our family.

"I'm glad you enjoyed the show."

He leans back and I climb onto his lap, straddling him. I grasp his face and kiss him with more passion than I have in weeks. I've been too frightened the past couple of months, afraid I'd become carried away, but not now. I get to have fun tonight, not as much as I'd like, but I'll take what I can get.

He smiles when I release him. "Someone's frisky tonight."

He has no idea.

I pull my top over my head and toss it to the floor. "I want your mouth on me." He's surprised—I can see it on his face but he doesn't question me—as he leans forward to take my breast into his mouth. Omigod, the sensitivity there is at an all-time high. I'm not sure if it's the pregnancy or how long it's been since I've let him touch me, but I don't remember ever feeling this much response in my nipples.

He rakes his teeth over my already hardened nipple and then sucks it into his mouth, swirling the tip of his tongue in a circular motion around my areola. I swear it feels like there's a direct connection to my groin, making me instantly wanting and wet.

I'm panting and trembling as I slide my groin back and forth over his erection. I'm sure I'll come like this if given enough time, but dry humping isn't what I want. "Touch me."

He moves both of his hands to my breasts and begins lightly squeezing and releasing them as he rolls my nipples between his fingers. It feels fantastic but he's misunderstood my meaning so I grasp his wrist and push his hand to my crotch. "Here." He slides it inside the waist of my bottoms and he cups me. I hold his wrist and rub my slick center against his fingers, riding them. "I want you to make me come."

"Baby, you are soaking wet so I can feel how turned on you are, but are you sure?"

"Positive. It's fine for me to orgasm. Dr. Sommersby told me so today." I'm shaking and panting between sentences, so horny my face feels like it's gone numb. "Please. Please. Please." I'm desperate and I'll beg if he wants.

"We can do better than this." He gets up from the chair, me clinging to him for dear life. He moves to his padded weight bench and lowers me. He grabs the waist of my cowgirl bottom, dragging it down my legs, and I'm sprawled completely naked before him, wearing only my boots. He goes down on his knees and pushes my legs back and apart. I arch, staring at the ceiling above me in anticipation of his touch. And then I feel it, the first upward swipe of his soft, wet tongue up my center. I grab the top of his weight bench overhead and hold on, afraid I might buck hard enough to fall onto the floor. "Easy, L."

Easier said than done. It's been two months since I had an orgasm.

He allows me to relax again and then I feel the second flick of his tongue, sending another jolt of pleasure straight to my groin. "Ohh..."

"Mmm," he groans. "I've missed tasting you." He places his tongue flat against me and licks straight up. "You are so fucking sweet."

I'm pretty sure my eyes must be rolling back in my head because I can't see a thing. I'm lost to all my senses but one, the feel of Jack Henry's mouth on me.

After he licks me several more times, he sucks my clit into his mouth and uses the suction to pull on it. Sometimes soft tugs, alternating it with a firmer pull. As much as I'd like this to go on forever, it can't because I'm unable to last any longer. That once very familiar feeling begins to build and it's coming closer until my inner walls and uterus contract—

but this time it feels different. My womb is much fuller. It's occupied by our growing baby so the tightening has a whole new sensation—and it's magnificent. "Ahh… Ahh." I can't form a coherent sentence.

A moment later, it's over and I'm incredibly relaxed, very much like my body is made of jelly. I'm not sure I could stand if I tried. "I really enjoyed that."

"Good because I really enjoyed doing it."

I feel the baby doing what can only be described as acrobatics. "Good grief, that stirred her up. Feel."

He moves up my body and places his large hands around my bump, completely encasing it in his hold. "Wow. That woke her up for sure." He smiles as he feels our child performing beneath his hands. "You said her."

Yeah, I did, but I'm not ready to admit it. "No, I didn't."

"Yes, you did."

He won't convince me to confess. "If I did, it's only because that's all I hear out of you. Her. She. Girl."

"Because she is a girl."

"Jack Henry, you don't know that. It's a fifty-fifty chance it's a boy."

He shakes his head. "I know what I know."

"Okay. I'm giving in and rolling with you on this. You want to call this baby a girl, we will, but just between us. Don't do it in front of other people. It'll confuse them."

He's grinning and I'm sure it's because he thinks he's convinced me. "Whatever you say, love."

CHAPTER TWENTY-EIGHT
JACK MCLACHLAN

What a relief. Laurelyn is finally at a point where I can make her come again. Receiving without giving is a problem for me. I feel beneath inadequate when she doesn't come—that's why I typically get her off first—making her one orgasm ahead of me. That's just how we function, so deterring from our ritual has been unsettling.

My workday is almost complete and I'm ready to go home to my wife. I can't wait to make her come again. Who knows? I might not even wait until we go to bed. I could find her in the kitchen and lift her to the counter and go down on her. I hope she's wearing a dress. That always makes things so much easier.

I look at the time and see that Mrs. Porcelli has left for the day. Good thing. The little fantasy in my head has made me rock hard. I think I'll go home and turn it into a reality.

I come into the kitchen but Laurelyn isn't there. I call out for her.

"In here."

Her voice sounds like it's coming from the living room so my fantasy immediately changes course. I'll pull her up from the couch and bend her over the arm and go down on her from behind. I've never done it like that before.

I walk into the living room, primed and ready to give L a surprise orgasm, and see the look on her face. Something is wrong. "What is it, babe?"

"I spoke with Grayson Drake this morning." Oh shit. "He says Blake was scheduled to go to trial last month but charges were dropped because you told him we weren't coming to testify."

I could be in trouble here. "He called you a couple of months ago while you were in the hospital. You'd just gone back for surgery."

"You didn't tell me."

"You were in a fragile state. Our baby's life was hanging in limbo and I was afraid telling you might tip the scale in the wrong direction. I wasn't keeping it from you—only postponing until our baby was out of danger—but then the right time never presented itself. It was easier to not address it than it was to mess everything up once our lives were back to some semblance of order." She's staring at me, unmoving. "I didn't want to upset you."

"Well, I'm beyond upset about it now." She's looking at me in what I think is disbelief, like maybe she feels I've betrayed her. "He knocked me around and then shoved his fingers inside me before he ripped my panties off." I didn't know the fucker got his hand inside her. She's never told me that before. "He had every intention of raping me and he'd have been successful if you hadn't come in when you did."

It's a sickening feeling in the pit of my stomach.

I didn't give in without trying. "I questioned him about postponing the trial until your condition permitted you to come and he told me that Blake had the right to a speedy trial and it couldn't be postponed longer than a couple of weeks. I suggested closed-circuit video for our testimony and he basically dismissed the idea, saying the judge wouldn't allow it."

"How is it possible for him to get away with doing that to me?"

She needs to know I'm not letting this go. "He's not. I have someone on it."

"What does that mean?"

I knew she'd want details and that's why I haven't told her what I'm doing. "I won't go into particulars because I don't want you involved. I won't allow you to be tainted by anything that might happen."

"Should I be scared about what you're doing?"

"I have to ask something of you. I hope it's a one-time request." I see the confusion on her face. "Sometimes knowing the truth isn't what's best for you—and this is one of those times—so I need a no questions asked from you."

"A what?"

"A no questions asked. It's an understanding between two people when one agrees to go along with the other and not ask for explanations or details."

She's pissed. "This isn't the equivalent of you calling for a change of underwear because you were plastered and pissed yourself at a frat party." She covers her mouth and then removes it. "You're doing this so I can't be implicated in something."

She's reading too much into this. "We're done talking about it."

"What are you planning?"

I laugh because I can see she's going to continue to ask questions. "You clearly don't understand the gist behind no questions asked."

"This isn't funny."

"You're absolutely right. There's not one damn thing that's funny about Blake getting away with what he did to my wife, and that's why I'm going to rectify the situation." I've said more than I meant to so I change the subject because I'm not discussing it further. "What's for dinner?"

She looks at me, as if in disbelief, before finally answering, "Chicken parmigiana over linguine."

"Perfect. I haven't had a good chicken parma in ages."

I go into the cellar to choose a wine for dinner and linger because I need a minute away from her to get my head straight. She probably thinks I'm going to do something terrible. Truth is, I don't have a plan yet. Jim has uncovered some terrible things about Blake and I'm not sure what I plan to do with the information.

I want to kill him. My innate response as L's husband is to protect her and avenge any wrong against her, but the law doesn't see it that way. The American justice system makes it very easy for people like Blake to get away with terrible things so they may go on to do it again, which seems to be a pattern for him. L isn't the first woman he's attacked; she's just the first to come forward.

L has plated our dinner and is sitting at the table, her hands resting in her lap, waiting for me to join her. I open the wine and pour a generous glassful before I sit in my usual place. I take a big drink as she pushes her pasta around on her plate.

She's upset with me, maybe even fearful about what I'm going to do, but I don't want this ruining our evening. I make an attempt at normal conversation—something that might bring a smile to her face. "Will you tell me the names you're thinking about for the baby?"

"Really? You're going to bring up baby names after the conversation we just had?"

We're not discussing Blake Phillips any further. "I like James."

She sighs and doesn't answer but after a moment she takes the bait. I knew she couldn't resist the baby-name talk. "I thought you were convinced it was a girl."

"I am but I really think I like James for my girl. Thoughts?"

"I don't know. I gotta think about that one since it wasn't on my radar at all."

I'm not sure she likes it. "What is on your radar?"

"I've been kicking around Maggie, short for Margaret."

I'm surprised. "You'd want to name our daughter after my mum?"

"Yeah. I love Margaret and it would be an honor for our daughter to be named after such a strong, loving woman."

"What about Maggie James?" Hmm… it sounds like a southern Yank name. I love it.

She looks at me and smiles, a sign she may be forgetting our earlier strife. "Maggie James McLachlan." She says it aloud, testing it on her own tongue. "I think I love it, but I want to use it as a double name. Not just Maggie or just James."

Just like that? We go with the first name we discuss? I thought there would be more debate to it than that. "I'm fine with that."

"You'll call her MJ, won't you?"

"My girls, L and MJ… yeah, I probably will. What about the boy name you've been wasting your time thinking about?"

"I want Henry in it—for obvious reasons—but now you have me thinking James Henry. What do you think?"

"That it doesn't matter because we're having a little girl and her name is Maggie James."

※

L IS TOSSING AND TURNING IN THE BED, ALMOST CONSTANTLY. I DON'T KNOW if it's because of discomfort or if she's thinking of our no questions asked discussion. If it's the latter, I don't want her affected like this because it's not good for her or the baby.

Her back is to me so I scoot close behind her and put my arms around her stomach. "You're restless, love. What's wrong?"

"You know what's wrong."

I was afraid she would say that. "What can I do to put you at ease?"

"Tell me you aren't going to do something crazy."

"I'm not going to do anything crazy."

She rolls over so we're facing one another. "Are you saying that because it's what I want to hear?"

"No." Maybe. I'm not sure yet.

"We have a baby on the way and I can't afford to lose you because you're looking to settle a score with Blake. Yes, he attacked me and deserves to be punished for that, but not at the expense of me losing my husband because you took matters into your own hands."

I don't think it's possible to make her understand the way I feel. "I'm your husband. Your safety falls on my shoulders and I didn't protect you from him, so I have this intense need inside me to make him sorry for what he did to you."

"I want him to be punished too, but I'm the one who will suffer if you break the law and get caught."

That isn't going to happen. "I'm not going to get into any kind of trouble."

"Swear to me."

"I swear." I want to get her mind off this. "Please try to get some rest. Tomorrow is going to be a busy day for you. What time do you have to be at the rehearsal?"

"Six."

I should bring up tomorrow night. "You aren't taking Addison out on the town for her last night as an unattached woman?"

"I think that kid bouncing around in her belly is considered an attachment, but what would two pregnant women do in Wagga? We can't drink, smoke, or have random sex, so what's the point?"

Damn right she can't do any of those things—with one exception. "I can provide you with one of those three things—some form of random sex, here, tomorrow night. The kitchen table, the bathroom counter, maybe the arm of the couch. What do you think?"

"Eh, if nothing else comes up, you can pencil me in." That's my girl.

✺

I CAN HEAR A VOICE BUT CAN'T MAKE OUT WHO IT IS OR WHAT IT'S SAYING AS I struggle to abandon the dream. I feel someone shaking my shoulder and I become more alert to my surroundings. "Wake up."

"Hmm?" I groan.

"I've got to go to the hospital."

My heart takes off like a helicopter as I shoot up in bed. "What's wrong?"

"Nothing's wrong with me. Addison's in labor."

I roll over and look at the clock and see it's two in the morning. "They just got married—like eight hours ago."

"The baby doesn't care how long they've been married because he's coming."

"Ugh!" I groan as I sit up and turn to put my feet on the floor. "I'll get up and drive you."

"I can drive myself. Besides, this could take a while."

No way I'm letting my pregnant wife go out by her herself at two in the morning. "Sorry. Not happening."

She scoots over to put her arms around me and places a kiss between my shoulder blades. "Thank you, my sweet, darling husband."

"You can properly thank me later."

She squeezes me. "Horn dog."

"You've got that right, babe."

CHAPTER TWENTY-NINE
LAURELYN MCLACHLAN

I'M NERVOUS ON THE DRIVE TO THE HOSPITAL AND IT'S NOT EVEN ME IN labor. "I can't believe Addison will be pushing another human being out of her body today."

"I can't believe they were married only eight hours ago and now she's in the hospital having a baby. I guarantee he fucked her into labor." Leave it to Jack Henry to say something like that.

"If he performed anything like you did on our wedding night, then I can believe it."

"I'm telling you, L, it doesn't matter how many times you've been together before your wedding night, having your wife for the first time is different." He squeezes my hand. "And having your pregnant wife for the first time is even better."

I know how it was different for me but I'd like to hear his take. "What was different about it?"

"There's a surge of testosterone when the human male takes a mate and then that combines with a man's intrinsic drive to procreate."

"I'm calling bullshit."

"You're right," he says, laughing. "I totally made that up."

"You were scared as hell the first time we were together after we knew I was pregnant." I had to get on top because he would hardly move.

"True, but doesn't mean I didn't enjoy the hell out of it."

As if. "Name a time you didn't enjoy the hell out of it."

"Right."

We pull into the parking lot and Jack Henry lets me out at the front entrance. "Do you want me to wait for you in the lobby?"

"No, you go on up. I'll be hanging out in the waiting room if you need me." I'm not worried about him finding his way. He's very familiar with this place after our scare a few months back.

I go through the waiting room outside labor and delivery on the way to Addison's room. Her family is here. Even if she's delivering early, the timing couldn't be better since her family is here for the wedding—unless she has complications because the baby is early. I hadn't considered that until now.

All of Addison and Zac's family is here, including Ben. Great. Jack Henry sitting in the waiting room with him won't go over well, but at least Chloe's here to defuse her brother.

"Where's Jack?" Chloe asks. "He better not have stayed at home while you drove yourself here in the middle of the night."

"He's parking the car. He'll be right up." I make small talk until he arrives because I feel like he's been forced to tolerate Ben a lot lately and his patience could be coming to an end.

He walks in and I detect frustration on his face when he sees Ben. I can't tell him what I'd like, so I mouth for him to please be nice before I leave the waiting room. He draws his imaginary halo over his head. "Thank you," I mouth. That's one less thing for me to worry about.

I walk into Addison's room and she's sitting straight up in the bed, her legs frogged out, applying makeup. Good grief. That's not at all what I pictured. I thought she'd be bucking and screaming for sure. "Why are you putting on makeup and not acting a fool?"

She stops and looks up from her mirror. "I want to look good for the pictures."

What the hell? "I thought you were in labor."

"My water broke but I'm not having contractions yet."

This doesn't sound right. "Don't you need to have contractions to birth a baby?"

"Apparently so since I'm not dilated, but they're about to start a drip that will stimulate contractions."

The drip is one of the topics I read about on a childbirth forum I follow and everyone said it makes the contractions much harder. I bet Addison has no idea what's about to happen to her. She's not a researcher like I am. "Maybe you should be practicing how you're going to breathe if you're about to be given a pitocin drip."

"I've got this, Laurie."

Ninety minutes into the pitocin drip and Addison so obviously does not have this. She's writhing in the bed so hard, she has a huge rat's nest in the back of her hair. "Omigod, this is the worst thing I've ever done in my life. I didn't think it was going to hurt this bad. It's awful, Laurie. Terrible."

I don't know what to say except to remind her of the things I'm learning in my birthing class. "Breathe in slow, deep breaths."

Zac is sitting in a chair at the bedside watching the fetal monitor. "Here comes another one."

"Shut the fuck up, Zac!" She beats her hands on the mattress. "You think I don't know when another one's coming? I'm the one feeling this shit!"

I make my best attempt at giving Zac a look of encouragement, although I'm not really sure what that looks like right now. One thing I do know? Your water breaking before you're in labor—turns out that's not what you want to happen. It often takes longer to get into active labor—four centimeters—which means you have to hurt longer before you can get an epidural. Addison was one centimeter on her last exam. This is going to take a while.

I pray this doesn't happen to me.

"I've got to have something for pain. Call my nurse and tell her."

Amy, Addison's nurse, is a sweet, young woman with a high ponytail. She radiates happiness, which is great, but I want to warn her that her smiles aren't flying with her patient right now. Addison's being downright bitchy. "It's time to check you, Mrs. Kingston."

Amy lowers the head of the bed to do her exam and her hand disappears under the bed linens. Addison squirms, I'm sure making it harder on her nurse to see how much she's dilated. "Oh God. Here comes another one."

"You're much thinner this time. Will you try to tolerate me checking you with this contraction so I can stretch your cervix?" Amy looks like she's digging with all her might as Addison writhes. "Hang in there, Addison. Almost… finished."

"Motherfucker!" She grabs Amy's wrist and I can tell that she's squeezing it. "You've got to stop."

Her nurse takes her hand out from under the covers and removes her glove. "Got you to four centimeters. How you feel about getting an epidural?" She returns to the bedside after depositing her bloody glove in the trash and begins lifting the head of the bed.

"Yes!" Addison calls out. "Stat!"

Amy giggles with her childlike grin. "Okay. I'm going to start your IV fluid bolus and I'll get the anesthetist in here."

"Thank you, Amy."

"Oh, you're welcome. Glad we could get you to that point," she says before leaving the room.

That's a lot of change since her last exam. "That's fantastic—from one to four centimeters. They said you'd only dilate a centimeter an hour once you got going, so maybe things are going to pick up."

"Thank God. That exam felt like she was ripping me a new one, but I don't think I'd be getting an epidural if she hadn't stretched my cervix."

"That's good. Means you a have a nurse who knows what she's doing and can get this done." I want Amy to take care of me when I come in.

Zac remains in the designated chair where Addison told him to park his ass. "Baby, I'm not sure I can handle seeing them put that long needle in your back. I'm getting a little woozy just thinking about it."

"Zac Kingston, you are not going to wuss out on me."

"I don't want to but it's not like I can help it. I'm weak when it comes to medical stuff—especially needles. I can't handle them."

"Too bad. You're not going anywhere. You're staying right here."

Addison is being rough on Zac. I hope I'm not this way with Jack Henry when the time comes. "I'll stay in case it becomes too much for you and you have to leave." I want to tell my best friend she's being a total bitch to her new husband and he doesn't deserve it. Zac has been there for her through everything from the moment she told him about the baby, so I'd really like to tell her to cut him some slack. I don't have the chance, though, as the anesthetist and Amy come into the room.

The man with Amy is wearing blue scrubs—and must be at least sixty since his hair is solid gray—so I'm hoping that's a sign of experience. "I hear someone in here is looking for an epidural."

"Yes, honey, bring it on. Where you want me?"

"Sitting—either cross-legged or with your legs dangling. Either is fine. Just make sure both legs are in the same position so your back doesn't twist."

Amy positions Addison so she's holding a pillow around her pregnant abdomen. "Poke your lower back out. The more you curl around the pillow, the more you open those spaces. When you sit up, it closes the space, so try to curl your spine into a C and hold that position until he tells you that you can sit up."

Addison gets situated and I watch from across the room, mesmerized by what they're doing to her.

"I don't feel so good." I look at Zac—he's a sick shade of white.

Amy gives me directions from where she stands. "Can you help him to the couch and get his feet up." Addison is leaning against her nurse for support. "I can't move from this position."

I steer him toward the sofa and I'm instantly worried because Zac's a big guy and I'm a not-so-big girl. "Please don't pass out on me because I can't catch you if you go down." I'm relieved when his ass hits the cushion and he spins to put his legs up on the arm. "What now?"

"Put some pillows under his feet," Amy answers.

"And then take pictures," Addison calls out, still remaining in position. Zac doesn't laugh or argue. He really isn't feeling well but maybe a tiny little bit of pink is returning to his cheeks.

I go into the bathroom and wet a washcloth for him. "Here. Maybe this will help."

He takes it and wipes his face. "Thanks. I think I'm gonna be okay now." He sighs. "I can't fucking stand needles."

I look at the black ink on his biceps. "Both of your upper arms are covered in tats."

"That's different. Those only tap the surface of the skin. Nothing gets shoved into your spine."

"They didn't shove a needle in Addison's spine." But it did sort of look like that's what they were doing.

"I think I can sit up now." He rises to a sitting position and puts his feet on the floor, staring down so he doesn't catch a glimpse of Addie or what they're doing to her. "You all right over there, blondie?"

Addison doesn't answer and we both spin around to see what's going on. Amy smiles and points at Addie. "Already asleep."

Is that normal? "Did the epidural put her to sleep?"

"The epidural didn't do that. She's exhausted because she's been at this for a while, and it's quite early, so the poor thing is worn out." And I'm sure she wasn't in the bed sleeping when all of this got started. I'm guessing Jack Henry almost had the scenario right.

I use Addison's little nappy time to step out and see Jack Henry since it's been hours. I'm surprised, or rather shocked, when I find him in a civil conversation with Ben. I think they're discussing work from the little bit I hear—something about vineyards and the management of them depending upon the location. Chloe sees me before they do and shrugs, giving me a baffled look. I want to eavesdrop, just to see what they're talking about, but Jack Henry looks over and sees me. "Hey. How's it going in there?"

"Better now, but it was really bad for a while. She's four centimeters, got an epidural, and is comfortable. She's napping."

"Are you scared now?"

Hell, yeah. I'm terrified. "I was scared before but what I just saw confirms that there's reason to be and she hasn't even had the baby yet. It's going to be rough, McLachlan."

"You're tough as nails, L. I have faith in you."

It takes the better part of the morning for Addison to get to ten centimeters—thirteen hours from the start—but we're told that's about average. Next comes the fun part: pushing this child out of her body. He's thirty-six weeks' gestation so technically, he's still considered a preterm infant. Surely, he can't be too big if he's almost a month early, right?

"Ten centimeters is my cue to go, Addie."

"You're leaving me because you're a chickenshit and don't want to see what's about to happen."

Probably. "This time belongs to you and Zac."

I lean down to hug her before I leave. "I'm scared, Laurie."

"No fear. You're gonna rock this."

I join Addie's family and Jack Henry in the waiting room and we wait for an excruciating ninety minutes before we're allowed back.

We enter Addie's room and the most beautiful baby boy in the world rests in her arms. He's red and wrinkly, and screaming because he's pissed off—how fitting for Addison's child. Zac is leaning over kissing Addison's face, telling her how much he loves her, and I get a glimpse of the happiness Jack Henry and I are going to feel when James Henry or Maggie James arrives. I can not wait.

Addison turns her son around for us to see and Zac announces, "Donavon Zachary Kingston arrived at eleven forty-one, weighing six pounds, two ounces, measuring nineteen inches."

Yeah. Addison got her way on her son's name, but I never doubted she would.

CHAPTER THIRTY
JACK MCLACHLAN

Mrs. Porcelli has the week off so this morning, I'm eating a lovely country breakfast my wife has cooked for me—bacon, biscuits, and gravy made just the way Nanna taught her. My wife is quite the little cook but then again, she's good at everything she does.

It's funny how she never used to get out of bed before I left for work, but now she's up with me every morning. I think it's the pregnancy playing tricks on her, or maybe preparing her body for less sleep since she's thirty-two weeks now. Only eight more to go—if she reaches her due date. Either way, she still crashes midafternoon, so her body is still getting the rest it needs.

I'm finishing my last bite when L's phone rings—her mom's ringtone. They've spoken very little since Laurelyn was in the hospital, and I don't have a problem with that. Jolie Prescott rarely has anything positive to say.

She looks at the phone and I think she's debating if she'll answer. "I wonder what it will be this time."

"You don't have to answer it. I certainly wouldn't think less of you."

"I always worry something has happened to Nanna or Pops. They're the only reason I answer most of the time." She picks up her phone. "Hi, Mom."

Laurelyn motions for me to leave my dishes as I gather and take them to the sink to rinse before placing them in the dishwasher. I know she doesn't mind doing that for me, and maybe it even makes her feel more domestic when she does. I've often pondered how she feels about having Mrs. Porcelli here taking care of our home—if it's an intrusion into her role as my wife or if she's happy she's freed up from household demands so she may devote her days to composing, rather than laundry.

I close the dishwasher door and see Laurelyn grab the kitchen counter for support. "When?"

I reach for her, afraid her legs will give beneath her, and assume the worst—that something has happened to one of her beloved grandparents. I steer her toward a barstool and she sits, placing her elbow on the counter and propping her head in her palm, pushing her hair away from her face. She leaves it there, her hand holding her head. "That's all the information they're releasing?"

She ends the call with her mum and looks at me, saying nothing. "What's happened?"

"What have you done?"

I'm baffled as to what she's talking about. "What do you mean?"

"Blake Phillips was found dead this morning—a gunshot to the chest."

And she assumes I had something to do with it? "Are you asking me if I had Blake killed?"

"Yes."

I can't believe she thinks I'm capable of something like that. I've had lots of thoughts about it, and maybe even insinuated I'd like to, but I'd never be able to take someone's life. "What kind of person do you take me for?"

"One who loves his wife and would take care of the man who attacked her and got away with it. And one who asked me for a no questions asked."

That's what this is about. "I had some things I was working on where Blake was concerned, but I had no part in his death."

"I want to know what you were doing."

I guess the no questions asked is null and void now. "Jim went to Nashville when I found out the charges against Blake were being dropped. I was going out of my mind because he was going to get away with what he did to you, so I wanted to find another way to make him pay. If he didn't do time for attacking you, I was going to ruin him any way possible."

"What did Jim find?"

She's going to be sick all over again when I tell her what we know. "You weren't the only one Blake attacked. He raped a young woman last fall while you were dating. She was being represented by Blake and suddenly dropped off the grid, leaving the music industry. It seems there's a pattern of that with his female clients so Jim took a closer look. He located a few of the women but none would talk—until Hannah Dody."

She's nodding. "I remember Hannah well. She was really young, something like nineteen, but quite good. Blake told me she left because she couldn't cut it in the music industry, so she went home to Mommy and Daddy, his words verbatim."

"She's the only one who would talk to Jim. She admitted that Blake raped her."

"You haven't gone to Grayson Drake with this?"

No, but I'm wishing I had now. "No. Jim is still investigating the other leads."

"Are they going to look at you for this?"

It's a possibility after the way I acted when I spoke with the prosecutor. "I don't know the circumstances of his death, so I have no idea."

"Please tell me you didn't make any threats when you spoke with Drake."

I was frustrated and outraged when I spoke with the assistant prosecutor. I have very little memory of that conversation, with one exception. "I may have mentioned something about having money and connections."

Laurelyn covers her eyes with her hand. "Oh God, you didn't."

I could've said much worse, and it's a million wonders I didn't. "I'd just been told Blake was going to walk, so I was pissed off. They can't use that against me. I've been right here with you all this time and that's easily proven."

"But they could say you hired someone."

She's assuming the worst. "We have no idea what the circumstances are. They might already have a suspect in custody. Someone could've confessed. We don't know."

"You have to contact Grayson Drake and tell him what you know."

That could be mistake. "I don't know if that's the best thing or not. I had a PI under my employment investigating a man who attacked my wife, and then he turns up dead. That doesn't look great for me."

"Withholding information doesn't look great, either," she argues.

Agreed. "I should contact my lawyer."

"I think that's a good idea."

My attorney, Rhett Clarence, is able to speak with me when I call—one of the privileges of being considered a VIP client. I explain everything from the beginning and he feels we have no choice but to notify the prosecutor's office about the information Jim uncovered. But he insists on making the call himself.

Waiting to hear from Rhett is brutal. Hours pass and I realize for the first time that I could actually be suspected of hiring someone to kill Blake. I certainly had motive and I hired someone to investigate his life. They could say I was studying him and his routines to pull off the perfect crime.

L and I are sitting on the couch. She's leaning against me, her head on my shoulder. "I wanted Blake to go to jail but I didn't want him dead. I know what he was, but there are three little kids without a dad now. At least if he'd gone to jail, they'd still have him. Sort of."

"You didn't wish him dead because your heart is good and you want the best for those three innocent children. You're compassionate, and it's only one of the many things I love about you." I, on the other hand, wished a thousand times over that I'd killed him in that hotel room that night.

My phone rings. I don't hesitate in answering. "Hello."

"Rhett here."

"What did you find out?"

"They're still working out the details of what happened but that young woman you told me about, Hannah Dody, committed suicide two days ago. She left a letter saying she couldn't live with what Blake had done to her. They believe her father was overcome by fury and grief to the point that he was waiting for Blake in the parking garage of the recording studio. He shot him as he was getting into his car."

My heart goes out to Hannah's family. No one should ever have to experience an attack or its aftermath. And now this family has lost not only Hannah but her father as well. That could easily be me. Blake wasn't able to finish his attempted rape of Laurelyn, but what would I have done had I not gotten there in time? I don't have to answer my own question—I already know.

"Thank you, Rhett. You've put my mind at ease."

I end the call and Laurelyn looks at me in anticipation. "What?"

"Hannah Dody killed herself two days ago and left a note naming Blake as the reason. Her father shot Blake because he was so distraught over his daughter's suicide."

"That poor family. I met Mr. Dody. He came to the studio with Hannah several times. He always called her his shining star and she'd get embarrassed and kid that she wasn't going to let him come back. They were a close father and daughter, and I envied her for that."

I pull L close and squeeze her. My girl is strong, but who knows how she would've coped if Blake had finished what he started with her. "I never want to let you out of my sight again." I put my hand on her tummy. "Or Maggie James." I haven't even laid eyes on her yet and I already know I'd kill to protect her. "I hope Hannah's father isn't convicted for what he did."

"I'd be surprised if he can afford a good attorney. I remember Hannah telling me money was tight. I let her borrow clothes more than one time because she didn't have anything that didn't come from a thrift store."

Hannah's father was out of his mind with grief. He deserves proper representation. "I want to help her father. He deserves a decent chance at defending himself." L doesn't say anything so I'm not sure what she thinks about that. "How do you feel about me paying his legal fees?"

"Very proud, McLachlan."

CHAPTER THIRTY-ONE
LAURELYN MCLACHLAN

THIRTY-SIX WEEKS AND I'M SEEING DR. SOMMERSBY TODAY FOR THE REMOVAL of that stitch that's been holding James Henry or Maggie James inside for eighteen weeks. One of two things will happen: I'll either go into labor due to the manipulation of my cervix, which causes contractions, or I could do nothing and be pregnant a month from now. No one knows until it happens.

I'm sent to labor and delivery for the removal of the cerclage so I can be observed for labor afterward. I'm thrilled when Amy, Addison's nurse, comes into my room. She stops once inside the door and looks at my face.

"Wait a minute. I recognize you. Have I taken care of you before?"

"I was admitted for a week several months ago, but you were never my nurse. You're remembering me from when my friend had her baby a couple of months ago. Addison Kingston."

"Yes! I remember Addison well."

She's a hard one to forget. "Probably because she showed her ass so bad."

"She was fun to take care of. Her poor husband is the one who had to lie down on the couch with his legs up."

"What happened to Zac?"

Oh, I forgot to tell Jack Henry about that. "He got a little woozy during the epidural. Said he can't stand needles." I shrug. "He says tattoo needles are different than medical needles so he totally wussed out. I had to take care of him because Amy was busy with Addison."

He's highly amused. "You didn't tell me that."

"The only thing on my mind was Donavon's arrival."

Amy passes me a gown. "Take everything off, ties go in the back, and I'll return in a few to get you hooked up on the monitor."

"That was kind of hot hearing another woman tell you to take everything off."

Good grief. "Oh, give me a break."

"I have—an eighteen-week break." I slip my top over my head and then remove my bra.

He never needs to throw this break in my face after all I've done for him. "Hey, I've compensated in other areas for you. Not every pregnant wife would be so generous."

"I'm so very thankful. You'll never know how much I've enjoyed every single time you wrapped your pretty little mouth around my cock. Your hand jobs are an art form in themselves, especially with that little trick you do, but I've got to tell you that I'm beyond excited about getting inside you again."

What he just said registers in my head. "Omigod. You don't want me to go into labor after the cerclage removal because you want to go home and fuck."

He's all smiles. "No, babe. I want to go home and make love to you."

Does he really think he can show me his dimples and talk about making love to get me on board with staying pregnant so he can get some? "Don't give me that bullshit. Call it what you like but both equate to you getting what you want."

"You don't seem excited about it."

He looks hurt but I don't want him to be. I'm just really excited about getting our baby. "Don't take it personally, but I'm way more excited about having this baby in my arms."

"I'm ready for her too, but I'm not opposed to knowing my wife again, at least once before this little one decides to arrive. It's been a really, really long time."

He's been so good throughout the whole pregnancy, never asking me for anything and cheerfully seeing to my every whim—driving into town in the dead of night for a cheeseburger and fries, massaging my lower back when it ached, shaving my legs for me, and painting my toenails when I was too embarrassed to show my swollen feet at the salon. He's been beyond considerate of my feelings, even when I wasn't on my best behavior because of pregnancy hormones. "Okay. If I don't go into labor, then you can know your wife again tonight."

He whispers, "Yes," and does a fist pump. "No way I'm waiting until tonight and chancing you going into labor. If you don't stay to have this baby, we're going straight home to our bedroom. Do not pass go. Do not collect two hundred dollars."

He's being so silly. "Can you wait until we get home, or should we stop for a hotel room to be safe?"

"That's not a bad idea."

Surely, he realizes I was joking. "I was kidding, horn dog."

Amy returns and places two monitors on my abdomen, one for the baby's heartbeat and the other to pick up contractions. I've heard the baby's heartbeat many times but never for this long at once. I can't stop being mesmerized by it. "What are you having?"

I expect Jack Henry to blurt out that it's a girl but he doesn't. "We don't know. It's a surprise."

"I love when parents don't find out. It's so much fun. What do you think it is?"

"I think it's a boy." I look over at Jack Henry and he winks at me. "He thinks it's a girl."

Amy picks up the printout and looks for a moment. "I'm going girl based on the higher heart rate."

I read that online. "Is that true? A girl has a faster heartbeat?"

"It's an old wives' tale—and obviously isn't a hundred percent—but I can tell you that after working here for thirteen years, I think there's some truth to it."

Jack Henry is grinning, so sure of himself, as he has been since eighteen weeks when he saw the baby's face for the first time. "She said it's an old wives' tale so calm down."

"She also said she's worked here thirteen years and believes there's some truth to it," he argues.

Dr. Sommersby comes into the room and interrupts our debate. "Are we ready to get this stitch out?"

"Ready as I'll ever be."

The bed is converted so my feet are placed in footrests and a speculum is inserted. "This part is just like when you get a Pap." I try to relax, concentrating on my breathing, but I'm nervous. I researched cerclage removal before we came and most people said it hurt.

She's moving the speculum around and it's a lot of pressure. I tense when I shouldn't. "Hang in there, Laurelyn. I know it's uncomfortable but I'll try to keep the discomfort to a minimum."

I hear the sound of the scissors snip and I swear it feels like she nicked my cervix. I involuntarily jerk. "Sorry, Laurelyn. There's a little bit of scar tissue grown over the suture so you're going to feel a little tugging."

A little tugging, my ass! A much more accurate description would be that I'll feel like my cervix is connected to a four-wheel drive and will be yanked out through my vagina. I tense again, squeezing Jack Henry's hand, and cry out because I can't stop myself. "Ohh…" It's not my good kind of ohh that Jack Henry evokes. It's my damn, I'm hurting really bad ohh. Huge difference!

"The stitch is out so I'm going to check your cervix and see how much you're dilated." I feel the pressure of her fingers, which is minimally better than the speculum. "You're between two and three centimeters so we'll let you hang out here for a few hours and see if anything happens. I don't want you to eat because if you go into labor, I'm not stopping you, even though you're technically still considered preterm."

I know all babies aren't the same, but Donavon was a month early and he did great. I'm not worried.

The transformer birthing bed is converted back to normal and I get as comfortable as it will allow me to be. It's not really a bed made for relaxation, though. "Need anything, love?"

"I can't think of a thing."

I'm observed for hours and I'm only having irregular contractions, so we're awaiting the final verdict as Dr. Sommersby does another cervical exam. "Okay, it's been three hours and there's no change, Laurelyn. You're still between two and three centimeters, so I think it's fine for you to go home. But I want you to return for the usual things we've talked about—leaking, bleeding, contractions every five minutes or less for at least an hour."

Jack Henry smirks and wags his brows at me. I might be mad if he wasn't so damn cute doing it.

Dr. Sommersby leaves and I slip out of the patient gown so I can get back into my clothes. "You are loving this, aren't you?"

He's watching me shimmy back into my panties. "The degree to which my happiness has risen is absurd. You'd probably want to smack me if you truly knew."

I put my arms through my bra straps and reach around to fasten it. "I'm pretty sure I want to smack you now."

"You can if you'd like because there's no way to steal my joy—unless you change your mind. You're not, right?"

I consider jacking with him about it but he's desperate. I'm not sure the poor boy could take it. "You can bone me like you own me."

He does another juvenile fist pump in the air. "Fuck, yes! Get your clothes on so we can get to the house—fast—and take them off again."

Well, at least he's romantic about it.

※

WE PULL INTO THE GARAGE AND JACK HENRY, AS USUAL, COMES AROUND TO open my door and help me out of the car. I step out and he pulls me into his arms for a sweet, delicious kiss. It begins slow and rhythmic but quickly turns rushed and heated. His mouth leaves mine and trails down my neck while his hands move beneath my shirt to my pink lace bra. He rubs his thumbs over my nipples and I feel them instantly harden beneath his touch.

I wasn't sure I'd really feel like doing this after being placed in stirrups doing the spread-eagle with a pair of scissors stuck up my vajayjay, but Jack Henry has a way with me. I can never tell him no. Almost. I don't have a problem with turning him down after he's pissed me off.

He decides he's done with kissing in the garage and takes me into the house through the kitchen. Mrs. Porcelli is there putting away dishes when she turns to see us. "Aww… no baby today. I'm sorry, Laurelyn. I know you were hoping it would happen."

"It's okay. The baby will come when he or she is ready."

Jack Henry wastes no time in trying to shove Mrs. Porcelli out the door. "Laurelyn and I had a big lunch in town, so I think it'll be fine if you want to take the rest of the day off. We can have sandwiches tonight or I'll go into town for takeout."

"I don't mind staying to prepare dinner. I was planning to cook beef stroganoff."

I'm afraid he's going to toss her out on her keister, so I step in to persuade her. "We had a big lunch so a sandwich is fine for tonight. You can do the stroganoff tomorrow night."

She looks like she's considering it, but what she doesn't realize is that Jack Henry isn't giving her a choice. "I have a few things I need to take care of in town. I wouldn't mind leaving a little early to save myself from spending Saturday doing them."

"Perfect. I'm glad it'll work out so you can enjoy your Saturday off."

"Okay. I guess I'll see you in the morning." She goes to the cabinet to retrieve her purse. "Enjoy your day together."

I blush at her words but wait until she's gone to say anything. "She knows."

"Knows what?" he asks.

As if he doesn't have a clue what I mean. "What we're up to."

"So?"

"It's a little embarrassing."

"What's there to be embarrassed about? You're my wife and you're pregnant so I'm pretty sure she knows we have sex."

I know he's right but I still feel awkward at times. "I don't know. Sometimes it feels weird having another person in our home privy to our personal lives. It never seems like we have complete privacy." I try not to think of her washing our linens and seeing the evidence of our lovemaking on them.

"Do you want me to let her go?"

"Oh, no. I love having Mrs. Porcelli around. She frees me up to do the work I need to do."

"She's getting older and has a new grandchild she doesn't see as much as she'd like. She might be interested in cutting her hours back. That would give us more time at home, just the two of us." I point at my belly and he laughs as he cradles it with his hands. "Pardon me, Miss Maggie James. I meant to say the three of us." I no longer say anything about him always calling the baby Maggie James. I gave up a while ago.

He takes my hands and pulls me out of the kitchen toward our bedroom. We're almost through the door when he turns and cups my face, giving me another loving kiss. "I love you so very much."

"I love you too."

We move toward the bed, kissing en route, before we stop next to it. He peels my jacket from my shoulders and tosses it to the bench at the foot of our bed before pulling my shirt over my head. I'm wearing a pink lace bra, not what I consider sexy, but my breasts have gotten bigger the last couple of weeks so they're really jacked. "These are fantastic." He caresses each one before pulling my bra down and reaching into the cups to lift them out. He thumbs my nipples again, watching them harden before he takes one into his mouth. I glide my fingers through his hair as he sucks one and then the other.

When he's finished, he bends at the knees and crouches down to remove my socks and boots. I unfasten my bra while he pulls my leggings and panties down my legs. I'm left standing completely naked before him. He steps back, looking me over from head to toe, and I suddenly feel self-conscious about my body like never before. I clasp my hands in front of my large belly because I'm afraid he'll think I'm unattractive.

"Don't cover yourself. I love looking at your pregnant body and the only thing I see is beauty when I look at you." He comes to me and caresses my bump. "I may be one of those guys with a weird pregnancy fetish because this really turns me on."

I unbutton his shirt and push it from his shoulders while he takes care of the cuffs. After he's shirtless, I work on his pants as he kicks out of his shoes. Teamwork. That's why we're a perfect pair.

He pulls me close and my abdomen presses against his. The contact sends chills all over my body. My hair stands on end. I covet the feel of his warm skin against mine. He holds my hips as he lowers his lips to my shoulder and drags a slow kiss up toward my throat. "I want you ninety-nine different ways right now but tell me what's going to be best for you."

I don't really know. My belly wasn't huge the last time he was on top of me. If we had continued having sex throughout my pregnancy, I'm sure we would've adapted our positions as I grew. But we're going from doing it while I had a near flat stomach to… this. "I don't know except I can't tolerate lying flat. It makes me lightheaded." It's been so long and I want this to be good for him. "I can get on my stomach—sort of. I mean, I can get on all fours." I guess I should have just said rear entry—it's the way he loves it best anyway.

He slides his hand down my cheek. "No, I want to see your beautiful face while I make love to you." He pats the bed. "Sit here for me." He reaches up to the head of the bed to grab several pillows and places them behind me. "Lean back on these."

My feet are on the railing of the bed and I'm in a reclined sitting position. He puts his hands under my thighs and pushes my legs back. "Feel okay?"

I'm already rocking my hips in anticipation. "Yeah."

His erection is rubbing against me and I anticipate him sliding inside at any moment, but he doesn't. I wait some more. And he still doesn't. "What's wrong?"

His eyes are squeezed shut as if he's in pain. "I'm psyching myself up so I don't come two strokes in."

"Not gonna happen. But if it does, we'll keep doing it until you get it right." He opens his eyes to look at me and I wink at him. "Go for it, tiger."

He eases into me and groans, "Fuck!" He pulls back and then thrusts slowly again, appearing as though he's savoring the best moment of his life. "I can't believe how tight you are." He shakes with a rigor. "My God, it's sending chills up my spine, it feels so good." He pushes into me a few more times. "Is this good for you, babe?"

"Mmm-hmm."

He moves his hand to where he's moving in and out of me and strokes the sensitive spot above our union. "You like me thumbing your clit?"

Is he kidding me? "Oh, yeah. Don't stop." He circles it fast and hard and then slow and soft. Just at the moment I think he's going to alternate the strength and speed, he changes motions completely and rubs it back and forth, side to side. He's stroking me on the outside with his fingers and the inside with his cock at the same time. He thought he would be the one to come fast, but it's going to be me if he keeps this up. "I'm already getting close."

He's moving faster now. "Do it. I want to feel your body quiver and contract around me because you're coming hard."

I prop on my elbows because I want to watch Jack Henry moving in and out of me. Seeing what he's doing and the look on his face jump-starts the onset of those pre-orgasm sensations that will give life to the quivers low in my groin. I lean back and lift my hips, meeting him stroke for stroke. Then the first wave comes. "Ohh... Here it comes." I clench my legs around him tight but he keeps moving when my insides squeeze around him.

"L... " That's all he manages to get out and I know it's because he's in that place with me. I see it all over his face. Very little sets him off faster than hearing me say that he's made me come. I think it's because he loves knowing he's the only man in this world holding the power to shatter me into a million magnificent pieces.

He gives me a naughty little sideways grin and leans down to kiss one of my bent knees. "That was so fantastic."

I move the pillows behind me and scoot to the middle of the bed. "Come up here with me." Since I can't tolerate lying flat, I turn to my left side and he spoons behind me, wrapping his arm around my waist and rubbing my tummy.

The baby is active, moving all over the place. "I do believe that stirred her up."

When I look down, I can see the waves of movement under my skin like a restless sea. "I'm going to miss this."

He pulls me close and kisses the back of my neck. "You won't because she'll be in your arms instead."

Nothing is holding this baby in now. "He or she could come any day."

"Are you sad you didn't go into labor today?"

Of course, I am. "Yeah, but mostly because it's what I'd come to expect. Clip the stitch—a baby drops out. My cervix is incompetent, so why does it decide to suddenly become capable of holding this baby in?"

"I don't know. You'd need to ask the good doc that question."

"I am a little sad we aren't in the hospital having a baby right now, but I'm happy we're getting this special time together before it comes."

He snuggles behind me and I know where it's leading. "I'm glad you feel that way because I'll be ready to have some more of this special time together in a little while."

Greedy horn dog.

CHAPTER THIRTY-TWO
JACK MCLACHLAN

It's been three weeks since the cerclage was removed, making Laurelyn thirty-nine weeks—seven days from her due date. To say she's disappointed that we haven't had a baby is an understatement. She's beyond miserable, tossing and turning all night because she's so uncomfortable, and last night was no different. She finally dozed off from exhaustion around three. I did as well. But now it's barely five and she's restless again.

"Mmm... ohh..." I hear her moaning as she tosses in bed. That's a new sound.

"You okay, L?"

"Sss..." I hear her sucking air through her teeth. "Ooh..."

I sit up to turn on the lamp and see her lying on her side with her legs pulled into a half-fetal position. "What's happening, love? Are you in pain?"

She's covering her face with her hand. "Mmm-hmm. Bad."

My heart takes off in a sprint to race my stomach up to my throat. "Is it labor pains?"

"I think so."

Shit. I've been preparing myself for this for months but I'm seeing there is no being prepared. "When did they start?"

"About an hour ago."

An hour? How did I sleep through her being in pain for that long? "Why didn't you wake me?"

"I was waiting to see if they went away. I didn't want to get you up if it was false labor."

Laurelyn's selflessness can sometimes get her in trouble. "You have an incompetent cervix. Dr. Sommersby told you to not wait around if you thought you were in labor."

"Well, I don't think it's a good idea to wait any longer because the last couple of contractions were really bad."

I'm out of bed and at her side to help her up. "Will you help me change into my yoga pants and a T-shirt?"

"Yeah. Where are they?"

"Second drawer, right side of the dresser."

I dig through the drawer. "The black or gray ones?"

"Black." I shove the others back in, not caring if they're neat or not.

"Which top?"

"The cream and silver striped V-neck."

I help her dress and then she goes into the bathroom to brush her teeth and fix her hair. When she finishes, she sticks her head out. "I'm going to use the bathroom and then we can go."

I'm sitting on the bed with her bag in my hand when she calls out for me. I open the door and she's sitting on the commode, her legs pressed together. "I felt pressure like I needed to use the bathroom. When I sat down, I felt something pop."

She wrinkles her brow when we hear something dripping. She parts her legs to look. "That's not pee—I guess my water broke. Whatever it is won't stop coming out and I can't control it." Then it's past time to go to the hospital. "Can you get a towel for me to put between my legs? It's probably going to gush when I stand up."

She places it between her legs and stands. "Eew, it feels like I'm peeing on myself. Get some more towels for the car because I have a feeling this is gonna keep coming."

I don't care about the car's seat. "We can have it recovered."

"It's silly to ruin the leather by not protecting it with towels."

I reach into the cabinet and grab a handful. "Fine, let's just go."

We get into the car and I notice her tensing and holding her breath every three or four minutes. "Just how much pain are you having?"

"What? Like on a pain scale?" she asks.

"Sure. One to five."

She grimaces and air hisses through her teeth. "Four and a half."

"What would classify as a five?" I probably don't want to hear her answer.

"My leg being sawed off without anesthesia." Nope. Didn't need to hear that.

Shit. She's going to be dilated a lot when we get to the hospital. That's what Dr. Sommersby warned us about—a precipitous delivery. I looked it up when she used that word and it means the baby comes in under three hours from the onset of labor. She's almost two hours into having painful contractions.

There's no way my family can make it in time, so we're going to be alone when the baby gets here. "I should call my mum and tell her so she can be on her way."

"I'm getting admitted for sure since my water is broken, so I guess we can call people."

I dial my mum and she answers on the second ring. "Is it time?"

"We're on our way to the hospital now. She started hurting a couple hours ago and her water broke."

"I'm on my way." I hear the excitement in her voice. "Tell our girl to not have that baby until I'm there. I've been present every time one of my grandchildren was born and I don't intend on missing this one."

I don't break it to my mum but I'm fairly certain she'll miss this one. "I'll tell her to squeeze her legs together until you're here."

"Tell her I love her, and this baby is worth every bit of pain she's feeling."

"I will. Love you, Mum."

I end the call, knowing there's no need to phone the rest of my family because she'll do it for us. "Do you want me to call Addison… or your parents?"

She looks at the time. "It's really early so I hate to disturb Addie and the baby if they're sleeping. Let's wait until a little later since she'll depend on Zac's mom to watch Donavon when she comes."

It's a sore subject but I have to ask. "And what about your parents?"

"I want Nanna and Pops to know, so I guess you can call them. But tell her I can't talk if she asks for me."

I dial L's mum and it goes straight to voicemail. "Hi, Jolie. This is Jack Henry and I was calling to let you know Laurelyn is in labor and we're on our way to the hospital so please give me a call when you get this message." I hang up and glance at Laurelyn.

"My parents have very little place in my life now, and that's fine. I'm okay with it because the McLachlans are all I need. I reconciled with that reality a while ago."

"You're one of us now and always will be." I reach over and spread my palm over her stomach. "And this one too." Her abdomen becomes rock hard beneath my hand and she grabs the edge of her seat, panting. "Whoa! Is that a contraction?"

She doesn't answer but breathes in and out until her abdomen softens. "Yes."

"Wow, that was really hard."

"You think you're telling me something I don't know?" she asks.

"I guess I'm just surprised. I thought you'd have an epidural by the time it got this bad."

"I wish. It feels like it's in overdrive now."

"We're almost there, babe."

Laurelyn is taken to an observation room where a nurse comes in to check her. It's the same routine as always—glove on, hand disappears under the covers. "I'd call you every bit of six, almost seven centimeters, so we need to get you admitted to a labor room as soon as possible. Are you planning on an epidural?"

She looks at me questioningly. "Don't look at me. I'm not the one hurting."

"It would be different if I was one centimeter and was going to be in this kind of pain for hours, but I'm almost seven. I only have three more centimeters to go. I'm just wondering if I really need an epidural because I think I can do it without one."

"It's up to you, Mrs. McLachlan, but be forewarned that when the baby comes, there's going to be a lot of pressure and burning."

"I wish your mom were here. I don't know what to do." I wish my mum were here too.

"We can't get an epidural placed until you're moved and have an IV anyway, so think about it while we work on those things."

That sounds reasonable. "Okay."

The nurse promises to return shortly to move Laurelyn to her room. When she's gone, I see how torn she is. "You are tough and I know you can do it without the epidural, but I hate seeing you hurt when you don't have to."

"It's childbirth—a natural process women have been doing for a bazillion years without anesthesia." I know, but those other women aren't my wife and it kills me to see her in pain. "It's a good kind of pain—one I think I can tolerate."

I'm afraid it'll come to a point where she'll change her mind and want an epidural but there's no going back. "Pain is pain."

"I can do this."

She seems so confident. "It's your body and you're the one who's hurting—it's your decision."

Amy, the nurse we saw when the cerclage was removed, returns and L is moved to a room like the one we occupied for a week when we were in danger of losing Maggie James. She does her admission work while a second nurse starts an IV and a third sets up the room. Amy comes to the part about L's birth plan, and L announces her decision.

"I've decided I'm gonna do this natural."

I groan inwardly because I don't want to watch my girl hurt. I hope I don't freak out if she starts screaming. I look at the time and see that my mum is probably still three hours away. I wish I'd called her as soon as L told me she was having pain. I really need her to be here to calm me. "I'm going to step out and call my mum. She'll want an update."

"Okay."

I stop at the nurses' desk and catch Amy's attention. "I wanted to let you know I'm stepping to the waiting room to make a call in case you need me."

"No problem. I'll come out and get you if anything happens."

I phone my mum and she's quick to answer. "What's going on?"

"Laurelyn's almost seven centimeters."

"Oh, dear. I won't make it in time for delivery."

I'm certain the incompetent cervix is why she's progressing so quickly. "Her doctor warned us this could happen, but I'm worried because she's decided to go natural."

"Why are you worried about that?" she asks.

"I don't want her in pain."

I can hear my mum laughing at me. "Newsflash, Jack Henry. Childbirth hurts. I'm sure Laurelyn knew that when she made the decision to not get an epidural. She knows her body and what she can handle. She'll be fine, son." I won't be convinced of that until I see a baby in her arms. "I'm sure you snuck away to make this call, so get your arse back in there with your wife since she shouldn't be alone. I expect to be there around ten, but do call if anything happens before then."

When I hang up with Mum, I don't have the feeling of relief I was hoping for. I have no one I can talk to… except maybe my brother. He's been in my shoes and done this three times, so I dial his number. It's early but he should be awake.

It takes several rings before he answers. "What!"

What an impolite dick my brother can be. "What the fuck, Evan? Why you being so damn rude?"

"Because you just interrupted my morning lay." Okay. I'll let him off the hook this time. "Em made me stop to answer the phone because she wants to know if you're calling to tell us Laurelyn's in labor."

"She is, but I need to talk to you about something."

I hear him growl. "What's going on?"

"She's not getting an epidural and I'm sort of freaking out about seeing her in pain."

"For fuck's sake, she's giving birth. It's going to hurt. Em didn't have epidurals with the last two and she was fine, so quit your whining, puss, and get back in the room with your wife. She shouldn't be by herself, dipshit. Don't you know anything?"

Apparently not, but he's right. I've left my wife alone while I'm out here making phone calls to get myself some assurance when she's the one in need of comforting. "You're right."

L is breathing harder when I return to the room. "They checked me and said I was almost nine centimeters so this baby is coming super fast. They said I'll probably be ready to push soon."

"Then maybe we should consider naming her Maggie Swift instead."

"The moment is almost here. We're about to meet our son or daughter. I'm so glad we didn't find out. Thank you for being persistent about that." She reaches for my hand and squeezes, her teeth clenched. I watch the monitor as the line representing the contraction rises. "Ohh… this one hurts really bad, McLachlan! I can feel it all the way down… in my butt!"

That doesn't sound good. "What does that mean?"

"Baby's moving down." She rolls to hold the railing so I can't see her face. "Oh, shit! Call Amy. Feels like I… need to push."

She grunts as I reach over to hit the call button. "May I help you?"

"Laurelyn says she feels like she needs to push."

Amy comes into the room and gloves up for her exam. "I bet you're ready if you're feeling the urge." Her hand slips under the covers and Laurelyn squeezes her eyes tightly. "Boy, that was fast. She's ten, so it's time to start pushing. I'll let Dr. Sommersby know because the head is low. I don't think it'll take long at all so she won't want to be far away, especially since you're going natural. Once you crown the baby's head, it's nearly impossible to stop."

Oh fuck. The heaviness of the reality hits me—I'm about to become a father. I bring her hand to my lips for a kiss. "You're about to do this." Naturally.

Amy gets L in position. "Okay, Laurelyn. You remember all this from Addison's delivery?"

"Sort of…"

"You're going to push three times with each contraction. You'll get a deep breath and blow it out, then a second one you'll hold as you bear down in your bottom. Put your hands behind your thighs and pull back and apart as far as you can."

L moves into position, her legs bent and apart, hands wrapped around the backs of her thighs. "Pressure's building. Oh God, I've got to push."

"This can be our practice run. Deep breath in and blow it out. A second deep breath in, hold it, pull back on your legs, and bear down in your bottom." L does as she's instructed. "Push, two and three and four and five…" Amy counts to ten while Laurelyn pushes and then they do it again—three times total with each contraction. "That was really good for your first time. You're a good pusher, so I can already tell you won't do this long before you're ready."

L is great at everything she does. I'm not surprised she's doing well at this.

"Oh God! Another one's coming."

Amy repeats the process, counting to ten three times with each contraction, and then motions for me to look down there.

I've seen L's vagina countless times so I'm not timid about looking at it, but there's something different going on right now and I'm not sure it's a good idea I watch it. "I don't know if I want to look or not." I'm a little afraid I'll never feel the same about it again.

"Up to you, but this is the only chance you'll ever get to see this. It's pretty special."

I can shut my eyes and back off if it's too much. "Okay." I walk from the bedside to the foot of the bed. "You're starting another contraction so let's show him the top of this baby's head."

Laurelyn begins pushing and I watch our baby's head come down until I can see the entire crown and I feel something so very surreal happening. "Oh, wow, L. She has a headful of dark hair." I've never seen anything like that in my life.

L pushes three times and then falls back, breathing heavily. This is a tough workout for her. "Good thing she's taking after you because I was bald."

Amy gets up from the bed and walks toward the door. Where is she going? "We're ready so I'm calling Dr. Sommersby to come."

I lean down and kiss L while we're waiting for her doctor to arrive. "I love you so much."

"I love you too." She strokes my face with her hand. "You're going to be okay if she turns out to be a he?"

"I've told you I'll be thrilled with a son. I've only been persistent about it being a girl because it's what my gut says, not because I don't want a boy."

"I know."

Dr. Sommersby comes into the room and gowns up as the nurses prepare to care for our baby. "This little one got in a hurry about arriving." She settles on a stool between L's legs and looks at me. "So, you're still convinced it's a girl?"

Totally. "One hundred percent."

"And you, Laurelyn?"

"It's either a boy or a girl. That's the only thing I'm sure about."

The doc laughs. "I'm going with you on that one. You're starting a contraction so push hard and we'll find out."

L takes a deep breath and blows it out before taking another and holding it. Amy and I help her pull her legs back and her face turns beet red as she pushes with all her might. She stops midpush and releases her legs as she bows from the bed. "Omigod, there's so much pressure… and I'm burning. I'm on fire."

She looks up at me and there's nothing I can do to help her. This is what I was afraid of. "I'm so sorry, L."

Her legs are shaking and she reaches up to grab me. She pulls me down and squeezes me around the back of my neck. "Help me. Help me. Help me."

"Do something to help her!" I yell.

Amy pulls back on her leg but L has it locked, like unmoving stone. "You've got to push the baby out, Laurelyn. That's the only way we can help you."

"I can't. It hurts too bad."

"Look at me." L lets go of my neck and tears are rolling down her face. She drops her head against the pillow and looks at Amy. "You can do this. You're the only one who can, so pull your legs back and push your baby out. The sooner you do it, the sooner you get relief." I grab her forehead and hold it. "Do it. Push hard."

"Oh God. Here it comes. I've gotta push." Laurelyn rears up and pulls her legs back.

Amy is feeling L's abdomen. "Push as hard as you can and get this over with."

L's eyes are squeezed shut, her brow wrinkled. Tears escape her eyes and it breaks my heart that she's suffering in silence. "You can do it."

"Look down here, Mr. McLachlan, and you'll get to see your baby come into the world." I lean over L's leg and watch our baby's head come out of L's body. The baby came out face down but then Dr. Sommersby turns her so she can suction her mouth and nose.

I see her face for the first time.

"The head's out, Laurelyn."

I've never seen anything more amazing. "L, she's beautiful."

"Let's get the rest of this baby out and see what we've got." Amy pushes against L's leg and motions for me to do the same. "Push, Laurelyn, push!"

I see the determination on her face and know her next push will be the last. And it is.

I hear a gush of fluid and then a piercing cry—our baby's first sound. "You did it, L." I kiss the top of my wife's head. "I love you so much."

Dr. Sommersby is holding our child, wiping away the fluid and cheesy matter. "Want me to tell you or show you what you have?"

L and I look at one another and simultaneously say, "Show us."

Dr. Sommersby lifts our baby up for us to see. No doodle. "I got my Maggie James and she's beautiful, just like her mum." I can only remember a handful of times I've cried since I've been an adult, and it was always about Laurelyn, but now I'm doing it again over my daughter. "I've never seen a more beautiful baby. Thank you for giving me a daughter."

Maggie James is placed on her mother's chest and Amy tucks her inside L's gown so they're skin to skin before she puts a pink beanie on her head. I reach out and stroke my finger down her cheek and I can't remember ever feeling anything so soft. "I already love her so much, L. I didn't know it was possible."

"I know. Isn't she amazing?"

She's lying face down against L, wiggling and scooting, and Amy comes over to assess her. "This is a pretty amazing process that'll happen over the next hour. As she's lying here against you, she'll begin to scoot on her own so she can latch onto your breast. Some babies do it quickly while others take a while. She's already started to make her way down so I bet she'll be a fast one."

"If her delivery is any kind of indicator, then she will be."

L is cleaned up and put into a more comfortable position while

Maggie James remains on her chest, exploring and searching out L's breast. It's an amazing process to watch—this newborn infant slowly migrating in search of her first meal.

Amy's right. It takes about an hour but Maggie James eventually scoots low enough to find L's breast. It's something to see her latch onto her mother for the first time. "Look at that."

L is beaming. "She's incredible."

"This is it—the life I saw when I dreamed of our future. It was always you, me, and her, but this is just the beginning. There's so much more to come. More life together. More happiness. More babies."

L helps MJ latch on with a better suck. "You were once my beauty from pain, before you became my beauty from surrender. Now you've adapted into something different once again."

"And what is that?"

"My beauty from love—both of you. Forever."

EPILOGUE
JACK MCLACHLAN

The tub filled with water for a long time. Red currant fragrances the air, so I know L won't be leaving her refuge anytime soon. Too bad the scented candles don't disguise the odor I'm encountering.

Damn, L. What did you feed this kid today?

Luke's lying on the changing table, his blue eyes watching me as he waits for his nappy to be removed, and I'd swear he's grinning and giggling because he's amused by the deposit he's left for me. I put my finger under his chin and tickle his neck, making him burst into laughter. "Your mother knew you were going to do this. She fed all of you the same thing today and that's why she asked me to change and bathe you." I look over at Luke's clone crawling on the floor and wonder if he's already done the same thing. My guess would be yes. "Hudson, have you blown up your nappy like your brother?"

He crawls toward me and uses my pant leg to pull up. "Da."

I reach down and muss his dark hair. "You're next, little buddy."

I survive the toxic waste left for me by my two sons and wonder how in the world nine-month-old babies can do what they just did. It shouldn't be physically possible but then I decide the universe must be against me when I find that MJ has done the same thing, but on a larger scale.

L plotted this. It's retaliation for me telling her I was ready to try for another baby, I know it.

I guess it's too soon for a fourth. Our hands are pretty full with a two-year-old and nine-month-old twins. The boys are rambunctious, beginning to get into everything, and I'm certain it's only going to get worse. However, MJ is the sweetest child ever born. She's daddy's little girl and has been since I saw her tiny little face when she was still inside L and we thought we'd lose her.

It's true. A little girl can wrap her daddy around her finger. That's what Maggie James has done to me, but what else would you expect from a little angel with warm chestnut hair, the ends kissed with curls? My heart melts every time her caramel eyes look my way but the doozy is hearing her call out for me, her daddy. There's never been a more precious sound.

The trio is bathed and ready for bed when Laurelyn comes into the twin's room. She sits in the rocker for me to hand them off for their last feeding. This is our nightly ritual, so I already know Luke will nurse for ten minutes before he's out with Hudson following five minutes later, and then L will lie with MJ in her bed until she falls asleep.

I can't believe L ever feared that she might be a shitty mother. No one could do a better job with our kids.

But she needs a break.

When the threesome is down for the night, we go into the living room and fall onto the couch, L on one end, me on the other. I bring her feet to my lap for a good rub. "Did you enjoy your alone time?"

L's head rests on the arm of the couch, her eyes closed. She looks as though she could fall asleep any second. "Very much so. That tub of bubbles was much needed. Am I still pruny?" She examines her fingertips. "Thank you for taking over with the kiddos tonight."

She seems more tired than usual. "Is something going on, love?"

She doesn't open her eyes. "I'm just exhausted because one of the boys was into something all day long. I almost wish they were immobile again. Things were so much easier then."

She needs a break before she breaks. "Let's take the kids to my parents and go away for a few days."

Her eyes pop open and she lifts her head to look at me. "You know we can't do that."

"Why not?"

"Because I'm still nursing the twins."

"They can take bottles for a few days. It won't hurt them." I don't give her the chance to argue before I continue with more reasons we should get away. "Our kids need you to be well rested so you can be the best mum possible. You have to take care of you so you can take care of them. As your husband, it falls on me to recognize when you need a break, and it's time."

⚜

Leaving the kids at my parents was a mess. All three were crying and L was too. I practically had to drag her out the door so we wouldn't miss our flight, but all is good now that we're on the plane.

"I'm glad we're doing this." Her tune has changed.

"You didn't look so happy about it an hour ago."

"I'm sorry I lost it, but we've never left them for more than a few hours. I just started thinking about their confusion when we don't come back for them. They could think we've left them forever."

She's going to start again. "Stop, L. They're fine. My parents will spoil them rotten. And don't forget that Evan and Emma are bringing the kids over tomorrow so they can play together."

She's so emotional, convincing me further that this trip is exactly what she needs, so I'm going to do everything I can to take her mind off the kids while we're away. "Our lives revolve around our children twenty-four seven, so I don't want to talk kids while we're away. This getaway is about you and me." I wish I'd booked a private plane. I'd take her to the back and give her something to make her forget it all.

"Okay—not a word about MJ, Luke Henry, or Hudson until we return to Sydney on Sunday afternoon."

"That's my girl."

⚜

We spend our first afternoon on the beach and then go into town for dinner at our favorite restaurant before returning to the house. Since making the decision to get away with L, I've been counting the hours, the minutes, the seconds until I could have her without distractions or interruptions by the kids.

We're barely through the front door when I pull her into my arms to kiss her. It begins slow and romantic but quickly escalates to heated and urgent. For once, the urgency isn't because one of the kids could start crying and interrupt us at any minute. "Tell me what you want, L."

She pulls back and touches my bottom lip with her finger. "To slow down. We're always in a rush and I'd like to take our time so we can enjoy one another."

She's right. Since the kids came along, I usually only operate in jackrabbit speed, but with good reason. Eight out of ten times, we're going to be interrupted by one of the three. It's like they were all born with some kind of sensor enabling them to cock-block me. "You're right. I'm sorry. Trust me. I want to enjoy having you all to myself."

"It's okay. I get it." She splays her hands on my chest and watches them as they move down. "I bought something new to wear for you."

Fuck, yeah. I was hoping she would. It's been far too long since I've seen her in something hot and sexy. She may want to take this slow but it doesn't mean we can't get started as soon as possible. I lean down and pick her up, throwing her over my shoulder to carry her into the bedroom. "Jack Henry, I can't believe you."

I set her feet on the floor once we're in the bedroom and grab her bum to pull her against me. I hover my mouth over her ear. "I'm ready to be inside you so don't keep me waiting too long while you change."

"Will you light the bedroom candles while I change?"

"I will do anything you tell me to."

She grabs my face and pulls me in for a quick kiss. "I won't be long, caveman."

I watch her disappear into the bathroom and then begin my task of lighting the bedroom candles. There are three, giving the room the perfect amount of illumination while setting the perfect romantic ambience. Even I feel lovey-dovey looking at the candlelit canopy bed, flowing sheers kissing the floor. It's a reminder for me to make love to L

BEAUTY FROM LOVE

because it's what she wants, not to fuck her hard and fast... unless it's what she wants later and I'll be very willing to oblige.

I'm undressing when L comes out of the bathroom. She's wearing a red lace slip—not one of her usual colors but it should be because she looks hot as hell in it. Her tits look fantastic, even after nursing our three kids. She's wearing a mischievous grin and I know why when she turns to show me the ruffles over her bum. She shimmies a little before she asks, "Like it much?"

Fuck, she looks amazing. My cock immediately rises to tent the only thing I'm still wearing—my boxer briefs. "You look so fucking hot, babe. Come 'ere."

"Wait. I want the mood to be perfect for what I have in mind." She walks over to the nightstand and picks up her phone. My girl loves to set the pace with music so I'm certain she'll choose something slow—and it's a good idea. Otherwise I might forget I shouldn't rush this.

The song begins and I recognize it as one I've heard her singing. It's a slow, romantic song she composed for Southern Ophelia—inspired by our love—but it's my first time hearing them perform it.

"It's beautiful." I hold my arms out to her. "Come to me."

I watch her slink ever so slowly in my direction. Her movement, each step she takes, seduces my mind and body. I must remind myself of what I'm to do—take my time and enjoy Laurelyn. My wife. My lover. My American girl and partner in life. The mother of my children.

I place one hand at her lower back and cradle her face with my other. She leans into it and covers the top with her own, closing her eyes and appearing as though she's completely savoring the feel of my skin against hers. "The simple touch of your hand against my face is still enough to melt my panties right off my body."

"All you have to do is breathe and I want to slide your knickers off." I reach beneath her red lace slip to feel what kind she's wearing and I get two handfuls of cheek with a tiny strip of fabric up the middle. "Mmm... I love your sweet cheeks in a G." I hoist her up. "Wrap your legs around me."

She does and I move to the bed, depositing her in the middle. I begin at her ankles and kiss my way up her body as I crawl over her. Her body still looks amazing after three babies. She occasionally voices a concern about the stretch marks she got with the twins but they're low on her abdomen and minimal. I don't see them when I look at her. She's perfect to me.

I push her slip up when I get to her hips and look at the tiny scrap of knickers covering her in the front. I put the heel of my palm against her pubic bone and lower it. The lace at her crotch is warm and already wet, so it takes every bit of strength I have to not shove it over and bury myself deep inside her.

I glide my fingers under the elastic waistband and tug. She lifts her bum and I bite the red lace triangle with my teeth, dragging it down her legs. "Oh God."

I toss her knickers and migrate up her body slowly. When we're face to face, I cradle her cheeks with both of my hands. "I love you, pretty girl."

"And I love you, caveman."

She brings her legs up around my waist and wiggles beneath me until I'm positioned at her drenched opening. "I was planning to go down on you."

She shakes her head. "Later. Right now, I want you inside me."

She squeezes her legs to coax me closer and I glide in slowly. I push her legs back, bending them out and she tilts her hips. I thrust in and out several times and she meets each one, bringing me deeper inside her. "Oh, L. This is where I love to be—buried so deep we become one with no beginning and no end."

I move my hand to where we're joined and briefly enjoy feeling myself sliding in and out of her before I seek out her clit. We may be making love instead of fucking hard, but I'm still making sure my girl comes.

She moans when I find the spot and I circle it with my fingers. "Does that feel good?"

"Oh yeah," she moans. "Right there. Don't stop." She still says that after four years, although she knows I never stop until she comes.

She tenses and squeezes her legs tightly, signaling the onset of her climax, and then I feel that magnificent way her body squeezes my cock. That, combined with the knowledge of knowing I've brought her to orgasm, ignites the onset of my undoing. I thrust a few more times and then drive deep inside her, emptying all of myself. I love coming inside her even when we're not trying for a baby.

I'm blanketing her with my body while I remain inside. I kiss her forehead and lift my head so I can see her face. "Hi."

She smiles and giggles. "Hi." She releases her legs from around my waist and they go limp beneath me but I'm not ready to pull out.

I lower my face to hers and gently scrape her with my whiskers. "You're going to take my first layer of skin off with that, caveman."

"I've been thinking of shaving it."

"No way! It's sexy as hell and I love the way it feels when you go down."

"Then I'll keep it for you because I want my girl happy." I plant a quick kiss against her mouth before pulling out and rolling to my back. I reach to take her hand in mine, lacing our fingers.

We lie motionless and I decide it's a good time to bring up the making-a-baby talk, although we agreed we wouldn't talk about kids. Technically, this child I want to talk about doesn't exist so it doesn't fall under the forbidden-discussion category.

"I understand if you're not ready for another baby." She doesn't say anything and I wonder what's up with her—why she isn't agreeing.

She moves her hand to my chest and circles the endless infinity symbol, signaling that she's thinking hard about what I'm saying. "Your hands are full with the three we have so we can wait. Maybe we can think about trying when the twins are two. That would make them three when the new baby is born—that would be a good space between them, right? I'd be thirty-five—much younger than I expected to be by the time we had our fourth."

She brings her hand to her forehead. "Can we have a confessional session? We haven't had one in a while and I think it's time."

I'm surprised. That's not at all what I was expecting to hear. "Sure. Same rules as always?"

"Yes. No discussions. No explanations. No grudges."

"Okay. Three minutes?"

"No timer for this one."

Oh hell. I always depend on the timer to stop the train before it runs out of control. "If you're sure."

"I am, but I want you to go first."

"Okay." I briefly think and say the first thing that pops into my head. "I love our kids but sometimes I feel like our marriage takes a back seat to them." I'm grimacing on the inside because that was a rough way to start.

"By the time I get the kids bathed and ready for bed, a lot of times I'm so exhausted, I don't feel like having sex." That's not a confession, that's a fact—but I'm glad she's at least willing to admit it.

"We came here to get a break and take things slow since we don't often get that luxury, but once you've had enough of that, I'm going to fuck you ninety-nine different ways." I'm thinking about turning over to start with way number one.

"You should probably enjoy fucking me ninety-nine different ways while you can since you'll only get to do it for about seven or eight more weeks before I'm put on pelvic rest again."

"What?" There's only one reason she'd be placed on pelvic rest.

"I know I just killed our confessional time but... surprise."

I rise from the bed so I can see her face. "You're pregnant again?"

She nods. "I am."

I put my hand on her belly and don't detect any change in it. "How far along?"

"I'm guessing around six or seven weeks."

"Oh, L... I'm so happy." And I am but then I remember her telling me she wanted to wait a little while longer when we discussed having another one. "How do you feel about it?"

"Well, I was shocked at first, maybe a wee bit upset, but I've had time to get used to it and now I'm really happy. I'm not exactly sure how I'm going to handle a newborn with a three-year-old and a set of twenty-month-old twins, but I'll figure it out."

"What about Healing Melodies?" I'm so proud of L—her work to create a foundation using music as therapy and expression for children of addicts is nothing short of miraculous. But she has so much on her plate since she refuses to stop composing. I don't know how she'll juggle all of it. Perhaps we'll revisit the discussion of hiring a part-time nanny or maybe Nanna and Pops will take her up on the offer of coming for an indefinite stay. They seem to be warming up to the idea since Jolie is gone on the road with Jake most of the time.

"I'm not sure. Maybe I can talk Addison into helping. She's expressed some interest but there's plenty of time to figure that out."

"I haven't told you yet, but I've decided to sell some of the vineyards so I can spend more time at home with you and the kids. I haven't decided which ones or how many, but I've been discussing it with Ben. I figure giving my brother-in-law first pick is the right thing to do. I'd rather help him get established here so he doesn't relocate my sister to California. I don't think Mum could take that, especially before their baby arrives. And I'm thinking of making a proposition with Zac after I know what Ben wants to buy."

She rises from the bed and throws her leg over to straddle me. "I can't tell you how happy that makes me. The kids and I need you at home with us."

"And that's the only place I want to be—with you and our swarm of kids."

The End

ABOUT THE AUTHOR
GEORGIA CATES

Georgia resides in rural Mississippi with her wonderful husband, Jeff, and their two beautiful daughters. She spent fourteen years as a labor and delivery nurse before she decided to pursue her dream of becoming an author and hasn't looked back yet.

Sign-up for Georgia's newsletter at www.georgiacates.com. Get the latest news, first look at teasers, and giveaways just for subscribers.

Stay connected with Georgia at:
Twitter, Facebook, Tumblr, Instagram,
Goodreads and Pinterest.

THE Beauty SERIES

MEN OF LOVIBOND

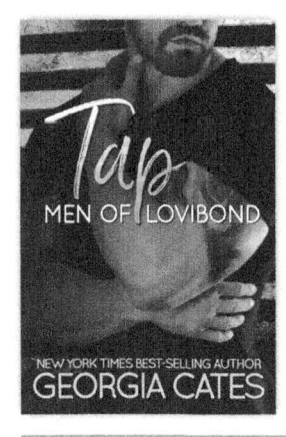

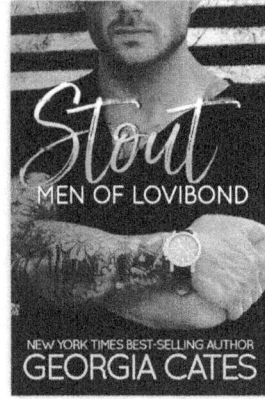

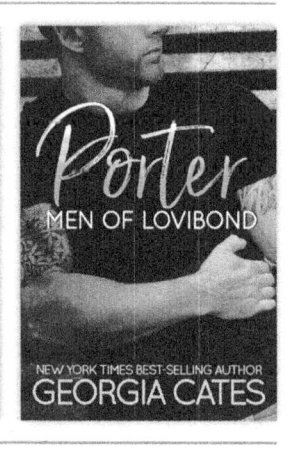

Dear Agony
A NOVEL

Sweet TORMENT

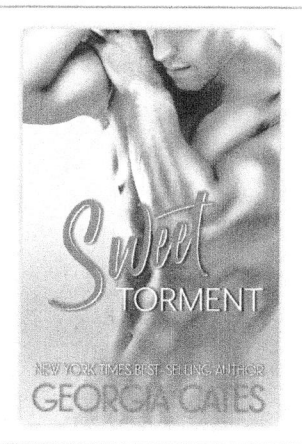

THE SIN TRILOGY

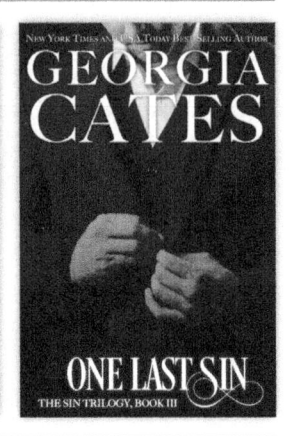

ENDURANCE
A SIN SERIES STANDALONE NOVEL

INDULGE

Going UNDER

VAMPIRE AGAPE SERIES

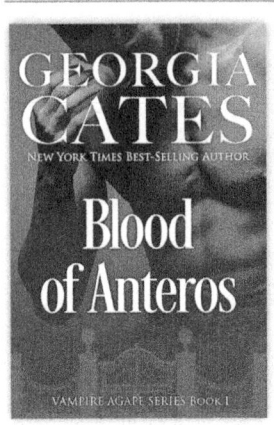

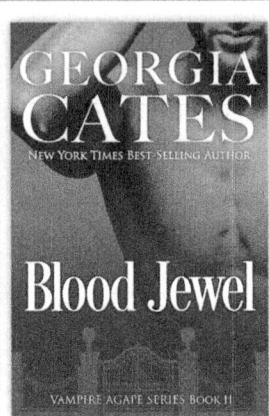

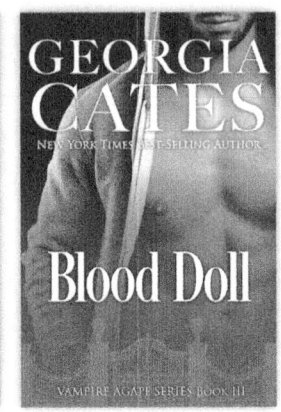